GENEVIEVE

LT. KATE GAZZARA NOVELS BOOK 6

BLAIR HOWARD

GENEVIEVE

A Lt. Kate Gazzara Novel Book 6
By
Blair Howard

ALSO BY BLAIR HOWARD

GENEVIEVE

The sound of the dogs' toenails on the concrete walkway made a pleasant click-click-click-click as Cole Meredith walked his five "clients" on their favorite stroll along the Tennessee Riverwalk.

"I was barely able to get out of bed this morning, man," Cole grumbled into his Bluetooth. "That was, like, a blast last night. Did you get that girl's number? The one with the nose ring? She was hot."

The sun was rising into a cloudless sky as the dogs hauled Cole along the winding path. They were quite a diverse gang: two Chihuahuas, a Dalmatian, a boxer, and a pug, and they barked at any and every other person, dog, bird, or itinerant plastic bag that might flutter into their path.

"You didn't? Oh wow, man. Why not? She was hot. You missed out, bro. She, like, acted like she was interested, for sure," Cole said.

The group was approaching a sharp bend in the path flanked by a stand of trees and bushes, just west of the C.B.

Robinson Bridge. Cole struggled to keep the alpha dog, the Dalmatian, in check as they rounded the bend.

"*No way*," Cole said incredulously, dramatizing the nugget of information he'd just been given. "She had a boyfriend? No way, man. Did he see you? I mean, she wasn't acting shy when I saw you guys at the bar."

The previous evening, Cole had gone to a local hangout called Sid's, a staple in the neighborhood where local talent plays music every Friday night. And, even better, it was within walking distance from his place. The neighborhood, North Chattanooga, was popular among the young and twenty-somethings just out from under mom and dad's thumb. They could act wild, let it all hang out, connect, get drunk, get high, step outside the box, man, and have an adventure for a few hours.

That was what Cole had been looking for, to connect... with a girl—he didn't do drugs. And there was never a shortage of single girls to flirt with at Sid's. He liked the Sorbonne better, but that was too far to walk, and he liked to drink. And driving drunk wasn't cool.

Sometimes he'd bring a girl home, sometimes wake up at her place. But last night had been a bust. He'd been unlucky, arrived home around midnight, half wasted, fell into bed, and slept like one of his charges until the alarm shattered his dreamless slumber at five AM. He'd had just enough time to do the necessary, shower, and shave before picking up Lance, the pug, the first pooch on his route.

Cole had picked up the last of his charges, Rupert, the Dalmatian, at a little before six that morning and had then driven west along Amnicola to the Robinson Bridge entrance to the Riverpark. There, he'd parked in one of the designated lots just east of the great bridge, gathered together his gang of five—with no little difficulty—and had set off on his six-mile walk—three miles each way.

Life was good: the weather gorgeous, he worked only three hours a day, and all was right with the world. Why wouldn't it be? At fifteen bucks per hour per dog, the three-hour daily walk provided him with all the necessities of his simple, uncomplicated life: a roof over his head, nice clothes, a nice Jeep Wrangler, plenty to eat, and the where-withal to show the ladies a good time, whenever the opportunity arose.

As he walked that morning early in May, he talked on the phone with his friend about the events of the previous evening, of which there were none... well, except for the girl with a ring in her nose. He stretched his neck and shoulders, then slipped his sunglasses over his nose while holding all the leashes in his right hand.

"Are you going to the gym today, bro?" he asked, as the Dalmatian hit the end of his leash and almost jerked all five leashes out of his hand.

"Yeah? Good. Me too. What time? Sure man, I'll meet you there," he said as he watched an attractive female jogger in tight black yoga pants and a bright yellow top trot past.

The girl's hair was in a ponytail that swung with her hips as she ran. He glanced back over his shoulder at her and caught her looking back, smiling at him. That was one of the best things about Cole's job. There was never a shortage of pretty girls to flirt with, and any girls who were out at that hour were totally into keeping in shape. He liked that.

The dogs began to tug harder at their leashes. All five of them were acting as if they suddenly had to go to the bath-room. As Cole listened to his friend talk, he clicked his tongue and pulled on the leashes to keep the little beasts under control.

Frickin' little monsters!

Of course it was Rupert, egged on by Lance who was the most aggressive, tugging and pulling on his leash, dragging them all into the dark shadows under the trees and the bushes, down the grassy bank that stretched all the way to the river.

"Yeah, okay, bro. I'll see you there. Hey, do you have any more of that protein powder you gave me? That stuff really made a difference, man. Yeah, I added it to my smoothies and I'm telling you, I had raw energy the whole day. I had—"

Cole stopped talking; something not quite right, something out of place, caught his eye. He froze. The dogs strained at their leashes, but Cole remained still. His friend on the other end of the phone continued talking, but Cole didn't hear a thing he was saying. How many times had he traveled the route under the great bridge and beyond? Too many to count. It was embedded deep in his psyche. He could walk it blindfolded, both ways. But this time there was something different, something that didn't belong, and although he was sure he was seeing what he was seeing, his mind wouldn't accept it.

"Hey... bro, shut the hell up for a minute, okay? Oh wow, man! You... you're not going to believe this," Cole stuttered into the phone. "I think... I'm looking at a dead body. No. Uh-huh! For, for real."

Cole swallowed hard, crept closer, straining to hold the dogs in check, to keep them back from...

Holy crap!

The boxer started to whine. Lance sniffed the air, his flat mug trembling with tiny growls. The two Chihuahuas and Rupert the Dalmatian danced and barked and ran this way and that, braiding their leashes together.

As Cole crept even closer, he saw a woman's foot sticking out from among the bushes. She was lying on her side, crumpled up like she'd collapsed... *right there, on the frickin' spot.*

Nah, it can't be... but...

For a split-second Cole thought he might be wrong, hoped he was wrong, that she wasn't dead, just passed out, wasted. He could see she was a pretty girl with long black hair, expensive clothes, and a body that was made for better things than sleeping one off in the park. She sure as hell wasn't supposed to be found dead lying in the grass.

No.

"I don't know, man," Cole said into the phone. "This is *too* messed up."

But even as Cole's own mind tried to convince him the beauty wasn't dead, the cool flat hue of her skin told him otherwise. Her hair covered most of her face... all but for one milky eye that stared up at Cole, sending shivers down his spine.

Even the dogs had gone silent.

"Bro, I gotta call the cops," Cole stuttered. "This is so bad, man. She's just lying there in the bushes. Knock it off, Lance! Dude, I gotta go. Yeah, I'll call you back."

Cole tapped his ear to disconnect his Bluetooth and quickly pulled out his phone and tapped in 911.

He described the scene to the police dispatcher along with the location as the dogs nervously paced and yipped and snapped and tugged at their leashes, anxious to get on with their walk, but sensing, as dogs do, that something bad had happened.

While he waited, Cole got down on one knee and

gently petted and scratched the dogs, trying to keep them calm.

A crowd was beginning to gather on the walkway, and with every passing minute another person joined him, stretching to see what he was looking at.

A man with long hair who looked like he had yet to sleep off the effects of the previous night joined the small group of gawkers. When he saw what everyone was looking at, he pulled out his phone.

"Yo, dude. Don't do that, man. That's frickin' disrespectful. You some kind of ghoul or what?" Cole heard himself say but hadn't even been aware he thought it.

"Screw you, pal," the long-haired man said, tugging clumsily at his T-shirt and stuffing his phone back in his pants.

"What did you say?" Cole took a step closer to the man.

"You heard me."

"Erase that photo, screw-head. That girl is dead. Don't you have any respect?"

"You gonna make me? Or maybe you ain't even as tough as those little bitches you're walking."

The man swayed with the breeze that had kicked up from the river. Had it blown just a little harder he might have tipped over and joined the dead woman on the grass, face down and motionless.

But before Cole could do anything, the wail of distant sirens that had been wavering in and out above the early morning sounds was now coming through loud and clear.

Cole wasn't alone when he told the drunk to leave. The small crowd of people also urged him along. By the time the police arrived, pulling their cruisers up onto the grass just feet from the concrete walkway, the drunken gawker had disappeared through the crowd only to collapse on a park bench a few yards from the crime scene.

2

"**G**azzara," I snapped into my phone, angry at being disturbed on my precious day off.

It was six-thirty on Saturday morning and I'd planned on having a lazy day, but things never do work out the way you plan, do they? Mine certainly didn't, not that day.

"Captain," the dispatcher said, "we have a report of a female body on the Riverpark Walkway east of the CB Robinson bridge. Officers are on the scene. They have the area roped off, but the morning foot traffic is making things difficult. You're up, Captain," the dispatcher said, sounding more than a little gleeful.

Oh geez, I knew it was too good to last.

"Okay. I'll be there ASAP," I said, tipping my fresh cup of coffee into the sink. "Has the ME been called?"

"Yes, ma'am. Doc Sheddon has been notified. Officers on the scene contacted him immediately upon arrival."

"Good. Tell them I'm on my way." I clicked off the phone without saying goodbye.

I sat for a minute, staring out of the kitchen window,

trying to gather my thoughts. I'd been about to leave my apartment for my morning run, so it was way too early to even begin to think about work.

I sat breathing deeply for several more minutes, then shook myself awake and headed for the shower.

Twenty minutes and a good scalding later, I was dressed in my work clothes, jeans, white top, and a tan leather jacket; I was ready for whatever the body on the riverbank had to say to me.

~

"**G**ood morning, Captain." The Officer on the scene was a pleasant guy I'd dealt with many times before, Randy Tadwell. "Sorry to get you up so early."

"Yeah, who do I file a complaint with about that? What have we got, Randy?"

"We have a problem, Kate."

Randy's lips hadn't moved; he was smiling, nodding. I turned quickly, startled by the voice behind me. It was Doc Sheddon. He was covered from head to toe in white Tyvek coveralls and booties, his eyes looking up at me over his half-spectacles.

Doctor Richard Sheddon, a small man in his late fifties, at five-eight was a good five inches shorter than me, a little overweight, almost totally bald with a round face that usually sported a jovial expression, but not that day. And when he said we had a problem, I knew he was serious.

"What did you do, Doc? Beam over here?" I said as I held out my hand.

"No," he muttered as he handed me his large cup of

Dunkin Donuts coffee. "Don't drink it all. Save some for me."

Gratefully, I took a sip, closed my eyes and thanked the coffee gods for DD. Doc held the yellow tape up for me to duck under.

"Come and take a look," he said. "Tell me what you see."

He led me to the body. It was lying close to the river-bank, half-hidden among the trees and bushes. The first thing I noticed was her shoes: high heels, little more than a series of metallic gold straps crisscrossing her feet and up her ankles. *Expensive!* I thought.

She was wearing skinny jeans, also expensive, and so tight they could have been a second skin, leaving little to the imagination. The silver lamé top had ridden up showing her midriff, but not so much that it indicated sexual assault, not to me anyway.

I took another thoughtful sip then handed Doc his coffee, pulled a pair of purple latex gloves from my purse, and snapped them on. Then, being careful where I stepped, I leaned over her and tried to study her face.

I looked up at the CSI photographer. "You done here?" I asked.

He nodded. I reached out and moved her hair a little.

"What a pretty girl," I muttered and knelt down beside her.

"Such a shame," I said, then turned my head to look up at Doc and said, "Did you see this?" I pointed to the woman's neck. A pair of purple and blue marks circled her throat.

He nodded.

Carefully, I lifted one of her eyelids and observed the

telltale red spots and broken blood vessels—petechial hemorrhage—that indicated asphyxiation.

"I'm going to guess no sexual assault," I said. "No one could get her back into those jeans... and her bra seems to be undisturbed."

I twisted my head sideways and looked up at Officer Tadwell. "Did we get a statement from the witness who found her?"

"We did, but I asked him to hang around in case you needed to talk to him," Tadwell said.

He pointed to a nearby bench where a young man was seated hanging onto the leashes of the weirdest assortment of dogs I'd ever seen; five of them, and they were all sitting too. I nodded and thanked him, asked him to tell the witness I'd be with him shortly, and then turned my attention back to Doc and the body.

"So, we have us a ligature strangulation," I said. "From the looks of it, she must have been on her way home from a night out. I'm guessing, from the position of the body and the mud on her heels, that she was dragged over here and dumped."

I looked up at Doc. He was shaking his head, his arms folded across his chest.

"No? What did I miss?" I asked as I looked back down at the body. Then I saw it. "Aha. Looks like her jewelry was taken. At least her rings were. Tan lines."

I pointed to the lighter stripes of skin on her fingers.

"So where's her purse? She must have had one. She couldn't have gotten even a comb into the pockets of those jeans."

I looked around and found it. "There it is, underneath her left hip. You get this, Jimmy?" I asked the photographer.

He said he did but took several more shots of it anyway.

I took a deep breath and then gently eased the purse out from under her, hoping I wasn't disturbing any key evidence.

As I pulled, the silver lamé top rode up a little higher at the back, thus allowing me to see the top of a white thong and a tramp stamp tattoo... along with the initials EEC4. I had no ideas what that meant, but before I pointed it out to Doc, I looked at the purse, a black snake-skin envelope.

"Holy shit," I exclaimed. "It's a frickin' Gucci, cost at least eighteen hundred." Oh yeah, I know my purses. This one would have cost me a couple of weeks' pay, maybe more.

I looked up at Doc; he smirked, his arms folded across his chest. He looked like a snowman; only the top hat and pipe were missing.

I shook my head, opened the purse and looked inside. She was obviously careful about her sexual activity because there were four condoms tucked inside the small side pocket. There was also a tube of lip gloss, a tube of crimson Clé de Peau Beauté lipstick, a tin of Altoids and a wallet, another slim snakeskin envelope. There was no cash in the wallet, but there was a driver's license and three credit cards, one of them an American Express Black. *What the hell?* I shook my head in awe, then dragged myself back to reality and the job at hand.

"Okay, Doc," I said. "She was strangled. Other than that, and the fact that she must have been worth a dollar or two, I don't see anything unusual. So what's the problem?"

"She's worth a dollar or two all right. Don't you know who she is, Kate?" Doc asked, smirking down at me.

"Uh, yeah. It's Genevieve Chesterton. See?" I held up her driver's license so that he could see the picture.

"I know that, but I'll ask you again: Don't you know who Genevieve Chesterton is?"

"What? Yes... Okay, no, Doc. I don't know who she is. Who is she?" I stood up, took my phone from my pants pocket and photographed the driver's license.

"Genevieve Chesterton," he said dramatically, "is the grand-daughter-in-law to Edward Eaton Chesterton the Second."

He lifted his chin as if that should settle matters. I had to be driving him crazy because when I shrugged, he raised his hands in disgust and shook his head.

"She married into the third wealthiest family in Tennessee," he said, frustrated at my lack of knowledge. "A real Cinderella story, it was. The wedding was plastered all over the news last year. You don't remember?"

I shook my head, grimaced as if I might get a crack aside the head from Doc for not following.

"Do you live under a rock, or something, Kate?"

"I wish," I replied. "Then no one would bother me. Come on, Doc. Just give me the condensed version, okay?"

"Don't you remember? Of course you don't. It was about this time last year that the media was covering the upcoming wedding of Edward Easton Chesterton the Fourth. He was considered Tennessee's most eligible bachelor."

"The fact you know so much about this wedding just shows me how much I really don't know about you, Doc. I think I'm a little frightened."

"Oh, tosh. Seriously, Kate, this is a real problem. It's going to be all over the news before lunchtime." Doc pointed to the crime scene photographer and ordered him to hurry. "The press covered everything about the wedding from her dress to how many bridesmaids she was going to have, to her china pattern and of course, the dream honeymoon to Australia and New Zealand. The paparazzi documented every movement the couple made, every store they shopped, every restaurant... They were an obsession."

"Well, if she married the hottest commodity in Tennessee, it shouldn't be too hard to find that missing wedding ring." I pointed to the line on her ring finger.

And that should be all I need to wrap it up, I thought.

At that moment I really did think it was going to be an open-and-shut case. We had a high-profile victim, out on the town, obviously screwing around on her marriage. All I needed was the jealous husband with means and opportunity—motive, he already had—and I knew I'd be meeting that husband very soon.

Okay, so I didn't really think the rich guy actually strangled her himself, but I did think—because of the missing cash and jewelry—that he probably hired somebody to do it for him. I also figured that "somebody" would probably want to grab a few extra bucks for her rings. That being so, a swift check around the local pawnshops would produce the killer, and a little pressure thereon would give me all I needed to hang said husband... Not literally, of course.

"What did you say her husband's name was?"

"Edward Eaton Chesterton the Fourth," Doc replied.

"Make sure you get close-ups," he said to the photographer as he pointed to the hands and toes of the victim.

"And those, please," I said, pointing out some drag marks in the dirt.

"EEC4," I said to Doc. "Well, in my book that's true love if she gets the man's initials tattooed on her lower back."

Doc was not amused, which was okay because I wasn't trying to be funny. But it is true that in some parts of the country, a woman can express no deeper love than to brand herself with some dude's name. It might not be how I would do it... *And thank the Lord I didn't!* But in some circles it's an acceptable expression of devotion... but then again, not exactly what you'd expect to find on the wife of a member of one of the wealthiest families in Tennessee.

Ah, who knows? Stranger things have happened.

I watched closely as the paramedics loaded the body onto the gurney. I wanted to get a better look at the girl's face.

Oh yes, now I remember, I think... She does look kind of familiar.

But that wasn't important. At that moment I wanted to focus on the marks around her neck. I placed a hand gently on her forehead and tried to move it to the left. It wasn't easy. She was stiffening quickly as rigor advanced.

"Looks like she was attacked from behind. What do you think made these, Doc?" I asked as I pointed to the two thin, deep bloody lines around her throat.

"I have no idea, nor will I have until I examine her."

I nodded, thoughtfully, then said, "So how long has she been dead, do you think?" I smiled innocently at him, knowing full well how he hated that question, and stuck out my hand for more coffee.

He looked at me, pursed his lips, shook his head, handed me the cup, and said, "You know better than to ask... Oh, what the hell. The liver temperature is ninety-one point two degrees. Normal body temperature is ninety-eight point six, so roughly five hours, say between two and three this morning, but I'll know for sure when I get her back to the lab. Meet me there, but for God's sake bring some coffee of your own."

He took the Styrofoam cup from me, sipped and gazed

wide-eyed at me over the rim.

I thought for a minute, then said, "Can't, not for a few hours anyway. I have to inform the husband and go into the office and get the ball rolling first. I have responsibilities now." I looked at my watch. "Oh crap, look at the time. It's almost eight already. Maybe I can get to you at noon... twelve-thirty?" I asked, squinting quizzically at him. "Can you wait for me? Can I give you a call when I'm on my way?"

I just knew I was being more than a little optimistic; I was heading up a new division Chief Johnston, in his infinite wisdom, decided to call Special Projects, so I now had a team of officers and detectives—three—plus my partner Janet, to coordinate. With this being a high-profile case, there'd be a lot to get in motion before I could visit the husband or attend an autopsy. I had a lot to cram into one day, and I still had to talk to the witness who discovered the body.

"Sure can. All right boys load her up," Doc told the paramedics.

They loaded the gurney into the ambulance for transportation to Doc's little shop of horrors.

I thanked him and turned my attention to the guy with the five dogs. The puppies all sat up, paid attention, tails wagging as I approached. I just had to smile.

"I'm Captain Gazzara," I said as I flashed my badge and then realized I hadn't taken off my latex gloves.

"I'm Cole Meredith." He replied. "I—"

"Wait," I said, interrupting him. "Give me a minute, please." I peeled off the gloves and opened the recording app on my iPhone.

"Now, Mr. Meredith, would you please tell me how it was that you discovered the body?"

3

Doggy Meredith was a good witness. He had his facts in order and told his story without much thought. I questioned him as to what he'd observed, and he told me that he'd driven off some drunken fool that had been snapping photos of the dead Mrs. Chesterton.

That raised alarm bells in my mind. Every cop is taught that sometimes a murderer will loiter at the scene and mingle with the gawkers. And taking pictures of his victim was also something a killer might do. That's what I had in mind when I approached the picture-taking man, who was sleeping it off on a bench, but I soon got that out of my head. This guy was totally wasted and no more capable of strangling the girl than was one of Meredith's Chihuahuas. I was pretty confident that this particular drunk was nothing more than that, a drunk.

He insisted on acting like an ass, waving his arms around in the air, rolling around on the bench, talking about his girlfriend—his ex-girlfriend—yacking on about what a bitch she was, and...

I got angry and... Hell, I stepped over the line. I did something that could have gotten me fired, but this guy had really pissed me off. He'd taken photos of the dead girl, not couth, not in my book.

So, I grabbed his phone from his coat pocket, deleted the photo—there was only one—and returned it to his pocket. He was so out of it he didn't even notice.

I shook my head, and beckoned Officer Tadwell.

"I'm sorry, Randy. I need you to take this... thing to Amnicola and make a deposit at the drunk tank for me. I'd do it myself, but I don't have the time to book him. D'you mind?"

"Not a problem, Captain. I'm heading that way anyhow."

I started to back away as I said, "I'm sorry, Randy. I really do have to run."

"See you around the playground, Captain." Randy waved and got behind the wheel of the cruiser and drove away, the drunk making menacing faces at me through the rear window.

I ran to my unmarked cruiser, and two minutes later I was driving back through the Riverpark toward Amnicola Highway. I used my phone's Bluetooth and called my partner, Detective Janet Toliver.

"Morning, Cap," she chirped into the phone.

"Hi, Janet. I'm just leaving a crime scene. Where are you? What are you doing?"

"I'm at home. It's Saturday. Remember? I, that is we, have the weekend off... Oh, I see, now we don't. Okay, what do you want me to do?"

Her voice was cheery, upbeat—just what I needed—and it matched her personality perfectly. She was a bubbly little thing. A rookie detective, only twenty-four years old, she looked like a schoolgirl: red hair, green eyes, upturned nose, freckles, you get the idea. When my partner, Lonnie, retired last year, I was on my own for a while, but Chief Johnston decided I needed a partner and—would you believe—he assigned his own PA to me.

Now, don't get me wrong, Janet and me, we hit it off right from the start. The kid's a natural and soon proved herself to be one hell of a good detective. I was glad to have her.

"Right, the weekend off," I said, dryly. "When did that ever happen? Come on in to the office. I'll meet you there. I was called out early this morning..." And I proceeded to give her a quick run-down of the events.

She arrived in my office thirty minutes later loaded with a tray of two cups of Starbuck's coffee. *Sometimes I could just squeeze that girl.*

I had a new office... Henry Finkle's old office. It was kind of strange to sit on the other side of his desk and see the room from his angle. I had a large, shiny wood desk instead of my old steel one, a really nice leather chair, a matching credenza, and a huge whiteboard on the east wall. I'd also had eight chairs brought into the room. They did little for the ambiance, but I was there to work, not enjoy the good life.

"Thanks, Janet," I said as I grabbed a cup of coffee and sat down. "Sit yourself down and listen up."

I took a sip of coffee, which gave her the opportunity to jump in.

"What about the rest of the team? You want me to have them come in?"

"No, not today. We'll let them have their weekend and bring them up to speed on Monday."

She nodded.

"Okay," I said, "take notes—"

"You want me to record?" she asked, interrupting my train of thought.

I scowled at her. "Whatever."

"Okay, I'll record." She smiled sweetly at me.

Inwardly I shook my head and grinned. *Geez, am I ever going to get used to this kid?*

"So," I continued, trying to look stern, but failing miserably, "we know Genevieve was out on the town last night, dressed to kill and with a pocketbook full of condoms. I want to know where she went and who she was with. The prime suspect is the husband, so I want you to dig up everything you can on the Chesterton family. Now look, you can bet the entire family is steeped in Tennessee folklore, so you'll probably have your hands full," I said.

"I've heard of these guys," Janet said. "We're talking *beaucoup* bucks," Janet replied.

"Right!" I said. "Dig up everything you can on the victim, her husband, her parents, his parents, the whole damn schmeer. I'm thinking the woman was a free spirit, in every sense of the word, and that would *not* go down too well with that family so, as I said, I'm liking the husband for it. Nine times out of ten it's the spouse, right? Clean off the incident board and make a start on it."

We both looked up at the images, notes, theories left over from the last case, then she looked at me and nodded.

"Okay, so that's where we begin. I have the feeling this will be an easy one. So let's get on with it and close it out."

I should have known nothing that appears easy ever is. You'd think after fifteen years on the force, I would have known that simple principle.

"Any questions?" I asked.

"Not right now, but I'm sure—"

"Good," I said, cutting her off.

"I have to go and notify the husband, so don't call him, or any other members of the family until I give you the all-clear, okay?"

"You haven't done that yet?" Janet asked.

"No. I haven't had time, damn it. I haven't even eaten yet."

I stood and walked around the desk. "Make a start, okay? I'll call you when I'm on my way back to the office."

I had the husband's address from Genevieve's driver's license. Surprisingly, it wasn't on Lookout Mountain where I thought all the elite of Chattanooga lived. Nope. Edward Eaton Chesterton IV and his wife lived in a luxury apartment in the heart of downtown. It would have been an easy jaunt to get there from the crime scene, but I had to take care of my responsibilities at the office first. I made it to the Edward Eaton Chesterton IV residence by eleven.

4

The Chesterton apartment was on the top floor of a luxury, downtown complex. To reach it, I had to walk through a lobby full of shops and boutique cafés: the heady aroma of dark coffee wafted over me like an intoxicating tsunami. I hesitated, almost caved, but I didn't dare waste any more time and neither did I dare turn up at a high-value residence with a Café Grande in my hand.

And I had something else to worry about: leaks. I hadn't had time to check the news outlets, and I hadn't heard any gossip around the department, but if there had been even a whisper across the media of the high-profile death, I might well find myself telling EEC4 what he already knew. *That...* wouldn't look good for me, a newly appointed senior police officer.

So I forewent my fix and took the elevator to the top floor, stepped out into the lobby, took a moment to compose myself, then knocked on the door and braced myself for the inevitable hysterical ranting of a distraught husband. Boy, was I ever in for a surprise.

"Yes, what is it?" A groggy, red-eyed Edward Eaton

Chesterton the Fourth asked as he peeked at me over the security chain.

"My name is Captain Catherine Gazzara. I'm with the Chattanooga Police Department," I said, formally introducing myself.

I held up my badge for him to see and inwardly let out a sigh of relief. If the news had reached the press, my man hadn't gotten word of it yet.

"Mr. Chesterton, I need to speak to you about your wife," I said. "May I come in?"

He didn't answer. He shut the door, and I heard the chain slip out of the groove. The door opened, and he stood aside for me to enter. And I did.

I entered an apartment awash in sunlight. The entire east side was a wall of glass, a giant window affording a spectacular view of Lookout Mountain. The place smelled clean, looked spotless, everything in its place and, as far as I could tell, almost unlived in.

"Please, sit down," he said, waving a hand in the general direction of a gorgeous white sofa. "Can I get you a drink, or something?"

I remained standing. "No, thank you, Mr. Chesterton." I looked at my watch and raised my eyebrows; it was a little after eleven.

"Call me Eddie. My father is Mr. Chesterton."

"Eddie," I said, not at all comfortable speaking the name, "I think you had better sit down."

He was a tall, slender man, made even more so by the plush, voluminous white robe the was wearing. His feet were bare, his dark red hair was sticking up at odd angles, and he had a five o'clock shadow that I was sure was not intentional... *Not like... Oh, come on Kate. Stop it.*

He turned around to face me, blinked, rubbed his eyes

with closed fists, then sat down on one of a pair of pale gray Chesterfields. He looked up at me, then leaned forward, his elbows on his knees, hands linked together in a single fist. I remained standing.

"So? You look very serious," he said. "Why are you here? What has Genevieve been up to this time?"

I looked down at him. He gazed up at me, a tight smile on his lips.

"Eddie, I'm sorry, but I have to tell you that your wife is... well, she's dead."

Sheesh, it never gets any easier.

I watched for his reaction, or lack thereof; there was no visible reaction other than a slight tightening of the already tight smile, so I continued, "Her body was discovered by a dog-walker on the Riverwalk near the CB Robinson Bridge at around six-thirty this morning."

His Adam's apple bounced as he swallowed. I waited for the outburst, but it never came. Instead, his lips parted and the smile became bitter, angry. He looked away from me, stared down at the floor between his feet for a moment, slowly shaking his head.

"So, he finally did it," Eddie said, so softly to the carpet beneath his feet that I could barely hear him. He looked up at me and said, "I didn't think he'd actually go through with it, but I guess the old bastard proved me wrong."

"What old... Who are you talking about?" I asked. "Do you mean your father?"

"Ha! My father wouldn't wipe his own ass without first asking permission from the old man. No. I'm talking about good old granddad, Edward Eaton Chesterton the Second, the man with all the money, the man who when he says jump, you ask how high."

Eddie, his face now devoid of color, stared at me, frowning, his eyes blue chips of ice, the knuckles of his double fist had turned white from the pressure he was applying. It wasn't what I was expecting, but it was a reaction.

"You're saying your grandfather killed your wife?" I asked, unable to keep the incredulity out of my voice. "Why would you think that? Wait, just a minute before you answer that, please."

I took my iPad from my purse and turned on the video recording app and held it so that the camera was pointing at his face.

"Edward Chesterton the Fourth, my name is Captain Catherine Gazzara and I must inform you that, for the record, and for your protection, I will now be recording the rest of this interview. Do you have any objections?"

He shook his head. "No! Do whatever the hell you want. I don't care."

"A moment ago, you mentioned that your grandfather, Edward Chesterton the Second, killed your wife. Would you please explain that for me?"

He nodded, somber, his hands still locked together in front of him, and said, "He hated Genevieve, hated that I married her. She wasn't good enough for me. No, scratch that, she wasn't good enough for him, not... cultured enough... Oh hell, let's just say it: he thinks... thought that she's a lowlife, trailer trash. Stupid old bastard."

He paused, looked at his hands, then up at me and chuckled.

"The truth is that, even in his wildest fantasies, he could never have dreamed up a woman like her and it was killing him."

"You think he was jealous of your marriage?" I asked.

Again, he chuckled, but it wasn't a nice sound, then he said, "He would have screwed her if he could... not sure he didn't, now I come to think about it. Would you believe that he tried to bribe her just after we became engaged?"

Eddie cleared his throat and continued, "He offered her half a million dollars to leave me." He shrugged, looked down at the floor, and whispered, "But she was smarter than that. She didn't take the bait."

"That must have made you feel good about her... proud," I said.

"Well yes, it did, at first, until it dawned on me after we were married that she stood to receive a lot more in a divorce settlement and alimony. But now that doesn't matter, does it? She's dead."

He sucked at his teeth as if his wife's death was no more than a minor detail in a much bigger story.

"So... you and Genevieve were talking about getting a divorce?" I asked.

"No. Not talking about it." He let out a deep breath.

As I studied his face, I saw tears fill his already red eyes.

"You see, she didn't think she was good enough for me either. I thought if I married her, she'd come to understand that she was, that she was just as good as the rest of our... so-called bluebloods. Hell, she was better than them. But you know what they say. You can take the girl out of the trailer park but you can't take the trailer park out of the girl."

"So you married a girl from the wrong side of the tracks, knowing it would upset your family?"

I watched for his reaction, hoping to see something that indicated deception, that it was all an act, but I didn't see it. He was distant, as if he was talking about someone he didn't know. My hunch that he killed his wife hadn't changed. What he was saying about his grandfather was typical of a guilty spouse trying to pass the blame. I wasn't impressed.

I did figure, however, that much of what he was telling

me about his grandfather's feelings toward his wife was probably true. And so the point of the spear of doubt inserted itself into my theory. I had just been handed a possible second suspect and I began to feel that my open-and-shut case was slipping away from me. The more players involved, the hairier everything becomes.

"Dear old granddad runs this family like a corporation," Eddie mumbled. "He decides what everyone does. No one argues with him. No one dares to say boo to him." He growled, clenching his fist. "Not even me."

"And that's because?" I asked, probing for more information.

"Because he holds the purse strings, of course. Duh." Eddie smirked up at me. "You obviously don't come from money, do you? If you did, you wouldn't be a cop, that's for sure."

"That's probably true," I said, "but you obviously didn't take much notice of him, did you? You married someone below your station, someone your grandfather didn't approve of. That was a pretty bold move. You weren't worried he'd cut you out of his will... or something?"

"Ha! That'll be the day. You see, I am the only boy in my generation. He has twelve more grandchildren—I guess I'm unlucky number thirteen—and all of them girls. Can you believe it? Edward Eaton Chesterton II isn't going to let his legacy be snuffed out. I'm the golden boy, no matter what I do. I have to carry the Chesterton family flag into the future."

He stood up, stepped over to a small wet bar, poured himself three fingers of some sort of amber liquid from a crystal decanter, and tossed it back in one huge gulp.

"But the silly old fool doesn't realize what he's done," he continued. "Genevieve would have provided him with great-grandsons, plenty of them. Not like my mother who just had me and then swore she'd never go through child-birth again."

He poured himself another drink and returned to his chair.

"What's your mother's name?" I asked.

"Regina Mae... Cottonwell-Chesterton," Eddie replied with a sloppy grin. "Oh, you'll just love her. You both have *so* much in common," he finished, sarcastically.

"What about your father? Edward Eaton Chesterton the Third?" I replied, ignoring his comments.

These damn names are getting to be a mouthful.

"His name should be Absentee Chesterton." Eddie laughed bitterly. "He's been in Europe for the past three weeks 'working.'" He made quotes with his fingers as he said it. Apparently, according to Eddie, his father was too busy jet-setting around the world to worry about the goings-on in his only son's life.

Eddie muttered something under his breath I couldn't hear then looked at me bleary-eyed. It was obvious to me that he'd been drinking heavily all morning. Whether his binge was the result of guilt—that he'd murdered his wife—prior knowledge of his loss—I didn't think so—or a general lack of purpose in his life, I couldn't say. But he was slowly checking out right in front of me.

"I'll need you to identify the body," I said.

"There's no need for that. You'll find my initials tattooed on her lower back." Eddie smiled. "She did that for me right before we got engaged. She could really be sweet when she wanted to."

I shook my head and said, "I'm sorry, Mr. Chesterton, I'll need you to formally identify the body."

He shrugged and said, "Whatever."

"Eddie, you never said where your wife was or who she was with last night. Do you know?" I watched him gulp down the rest of his drink and shake his head.

"No I don't. She was a... free spirit." He thought for a minute then continued, "Like I said, Detective. You can take the girl out of the trailer park..." He wiped his lips with the sleeve of his robe.

I decided to let him ramble a bit longer but to not ask any more questions. His answers at this point were less than helpful, and I could always interview him again later.

His face tightened up as he continued, "I will tell you this, though. My granddaddy is no dummy. He'll have an airtight alibi; he knows people. People in our family who would do just about anything for a buck. Just remember that when you go poking around among the skeletons. Rich people don't go to jail, Detective. Justice is... to my people, quite different than it is to the masses."

I wasn't sure if he was telling me that as a fact or as a slap in the face. Sure, justice could sometimes be slow when coming around to certain people, but it eventually came around. I had to believe that. Otherwise, my whole career was based on nothing.

"Why don't you ask him about the Frenchman?" he said.

"The Frenchman? Who's he?"

"Ask the old man; see if he'll tell you."

"No, Eddie. You tell me."

"The hell I will. Now please, go away."

I stared at him, then nodded and said, "One last thing, Eddie, before I go. Where were you last night?"

He smiled and shook his head, then said, "I was with a friend. We went to eat, then to several bars. We ended up at the Sorbonne and then someone, I have no idea who, brought me home. I think Alex and George must have. They were both here until a couple of hours ago."

Now that's a break, I thought. *If he was at the Sorbonne, it will be easy to check.*

"What time would that have been? And Genevieve wasn't home. Didn't that bother you?"

"Oh, come on. She was never home. Why d'you think I get wasted every night? She was a... she..." He looked up at me like a lost child, tears in his eyes, and said, "I loved her; I really loved her."

"What time did you get home?" I repeated the question, quietly.

"Late, after two, maybe, I don't know."

"How about your friends, would they know?"

He shrugged. "You'll have to ask them."

"Thank you, I will," I said. "Alex and George, I think you said. D'you mind telling me their last names?"

He didn't, and he did, and I stood up, closed out my recording app, put away my iPad, thanked him, and handed him my card.

"If you can think of anything, anything at all that might be helpful, please call me."

He took it, stared at it, looked up at me and told me he would.

"I'll also need you to come down to the Forensic Center and formally identify your wife. I'll have Carol Oats call you to make an appointment. Is that okay?"

He nodded. He was done talking. I had the feeling his binge was about to continue, and that once I was gone he was going to forget all about me. A couple more shots and a long nap would just about do it.

"Will you be all right?" I asked. "Can I call someone for you, someone to come and stay with you for a while."

"Oh, you needn't worry about that. As soon as she finds out, my mother will be all over me."

And so I left him to it. As I closed the door behind me, he was already back at the bar pouring himself another drink.

I took the elevator down to the main lobby, grabbed a cup of coffee, and called Janet to let her know I was on my way back.

"Chief Johnston wants to see you," she said quietly.

"I figured he would," I muttered. "Let him know I'm on my way and will come by his office as soon as I get there."

_____

5

"Hey, Cap!"

I'd no sooner sat down at my desk when Janet opened my door and stuck her head inside.

"Come on in and sit down," I said.

"Did you see the chief?"

"Not yet. Why?"

"He was looking for you. I told him you were on your way, but all he did was nod and walk away."

She sat down on the edge of the seat in front of my desk and dumped her usual stack of notes topped by her iPad on my desk.

"I tried," I said, "but Cathy said he was out. He knows where I am. So," I said and looked up at the big board, "why don't you tell me what you've got?" I glanced at the stack on my desk and said, "From the looks of that, you have a lot."

I leaned back in my fancy chair and took a sip of the fancy coffee I'd gotten from the café in Eddie Chesterton's apartment building. At that moment, life was good. I closed my eyes and wondered how long it would last.

"The Chesterton family is like an octopus," she said,

spreading the files and notes across the desk in front of her. "Just when you think you've seen it all, another tentacle emerges." She shook her head, making her red hair fall across her face. She brushed it aside quickly and began her lesson on the Chesterton lineage.

"According to the marriage license database, Genevieve Chesterton was Genevieve Bluford—"

"Hold on Janet," I said, leaning forward and placing my fancy cup on my fancy desk. "I'm not sure this is the best time for you to disseminate what looks to be an enormous amount of information. We'll need to do it all again on Monday for the rest of the team."

"That's so-oo true," she said. "So what now?"

I looked at the pile she'd placed on my desk and shook my head.

"You can go home. There's nothing more we can do today, it being Saturday. I'd better go find the chief and tell him what we're up to. Then I have to attend the autopsy. Doc's waiting for me. He's patient, but not that much, so... I'll see you here in my office with the others, bright and early on Monday, well, at eight o'clock. If by chance you should make it in earlier," I said, knowing full well that she would, "you can make a start on the board."

I glanced at the great white space knowing it would be filled to capacity by close of day on Monday.

"Go on, get out of here. You can leave all that where it is," I said, as she stood and moved to pick up the pile on my desk.

"See you Monday, then," she said, then turned and left me to it.

I sat for a moment luxuriating in my heavenly chair, then I got up and walked out into the corridor, closing the door behind me.

"Ah, there you are," Chief Johnston said as I bumped into him when I turned away from my office door.

"Chief, I am sorry. I was just on my way to find you to let you know—"

"Not here, Captain. My office, if you please." And he turned and walked the twenty yards or so to his own suite of offices, and I followed him, nodding at Cathy, his secretary as we passed through her office.

"Sit, please, Kate," he said as he rounded his desk and sat down.

I sat down in front of his desk and crossed my legs, placed my hands together in my lap, and waited.

Police Chief Wesley Johnston was an imposing figure of a man. Not over tall, but broad. He was, as always, impeccably dressed, his uniform pressed to perfection, his head shaved—it always seemed to me that he polished it too because it shined brightly in the sunlight streaming in through the window. He also wore an unusual mustache, one that Hulk Hogan himself would have been proud of, and it was just as white, which was, I'm sure, the reason for the shaved head. I couldn't imagine him with white hair. But he also had an air about him, more of confidence than of arrogance. If he had a sense of humor, I'd never seen it; hell, I don't think I'd ever seen him even smile.

"I've had a call from Edward Eaton Chesterton the Second," he began.

My heart sank. "Yes, Chief, I know. I got the call out this morning—"

He held up his hand, so I stopped talking, and he continued, "I received a call from Chesterton less than an hour ago. Apparently you've been to see his grandson, the husband of the deceased, is that right?"

"Yes, I—"

Again, he held up a hand.

"He is somewhat unhappy in the fact that no one bothered to inform him directly, that he had to find out from... let's say his slightly impaired grandson."

"Impaired?" I asked, outraged. "The man was wasted when I left him and still working on it. I'm surprised he was able to talk at all."

The chief nodded. "I assumed as much. However, Chesterton is an influential member of this community and—"

"Which one, Chief? There are three of them for Pete's sake." I was already regretting interrupting him, but he seemed to think nothing of it, much to my relief.

"All of them," he said, staring across the great expanse of walnut at me, unblinking.

"Tell me what you have, Kate, and we'll go from there."

And that's what I did. I also told him that my prime suspect was EEC4 with EEC2 as my second. As to EEC3, I'd not yet met him, but he was likely going to be on my list somewhere.

He listened carefully to all I had to say, nodding occasionally, asking the odd question for clarification, until I was done.

"I have to attend the autopsy in..." I said and looked at my watch, it was twelve-twenty-five, "five minutes. I'll familiarize my team first thing Monday morning. In the meantime, Detective Toliver has gathered a great deal of information, and I'll continue to familiarize myself with that, the victim, family, and friends over what's left of the weekend."

"You didn't think it might be prudent to bring your team in and begin your investigation today?"

"I did think about it, sir," I said, without hesitation, "but

I didn't think you'd okay the overtime," and there it was, just the hint of a smile. "I did bring Toliver in and, of course, myself—"

I was interrupted by my phone buzzing in my pocket.

"If you'll excuse me, Chief," I said, taking the phone from my pocket.

He nodded. I checked the screen and answered it.

"Five minutes, Doc," I said, looking quizzically at Johnston who nodded his assent. "Yes, five minutes." I disconnected and stood up.

"I don't have to tell you how high profile this case is, Kate. Handle it with care. Handle the family with care. Don't hesitate to call on me for help. That's all, Captain. Tell Dr. Sheddon hello for me."

6

I left the great man's office, said 'bye to Cathy, and called Doc back. Oh, was he ever PO'd? He was beside himself.

"Kate, don't ever do that to me again."

"Do what?" I asked, confused.

"Hang up on me."

"I couldn't talk, Doc. I was with the chief. What on earth is wrong?"

"I need you to get over here immediately, and I mean right now."

"Oh-kay. Is it to do with Genevieve Chesterton?" I asked somewhat tentatively.

"Yes, it is. Why the hell didn't you tell me she was black?"

My breath caught in my throat. "What?"

The PD is only three blocks from Doc's forensic center, but to save him from having an aneurysm, I turned on my emergency lights and peeled out of the PD parking lot like the devil was chasing me.

I arrived at the Forensic Center just a couple of minutes later to find Doc pacing back and forth outside the rear doors.

"What took you so long?" he snapped. "Oh never mind, let's get to it. You did bring your own coffee, I hope?" and with that he turned his back on me and pushed through the doors.

"Actually, Doc, I've only had two cups of coffee all day. You have any in the pot?" I asked, hopefully.

He swiped his ID over the small pad on the wall. There was the flash of green, a loud click, and he turned the knob and held the door open for me.

"No. My intern, Mallory, forgot to get some, and she doesn't come in during the weekend."

My heart dropped. I let out a defeated sigh as I followed Doc into the anteroom where we suited up and then moved on into the autopsy room.

Genevieve Chesterton was lying on her back on the first of three stainless steel tables. She looked like a marble statue; the overhead lights made everything look sharp, surreal.

I'd never met Genevieve, of course, but as I looked down at her, I experienced a whole range of feelings, the first of which was that she was no longer a person but just a slab of meat. Cold, I know, but if you've ever been there... well, you'd know what I mean.

My second thought was to wonder what the future, the world, had missed by her sudden and untimely demise.

I looked up at Doc, wrinkled my nose, and squinted at him through my safety glasses. "What makes you think she's black?"

"Before I begin work on a body, I draw blood, so does Carol... Where the heck is she?"

"I'm here," Carol said as she stepped into the room. "I don't want to be here on Saturday afternoon any more than you do, Richard, so ease up, please. I've cleaned and vacuumed the body. She's ready for you. What else do you need?" she said impatiently. "Hi, Kate."

"Umm, hi, Carol," I said.

"Carol ran her blood," he said, totally ignoring her attitude. "Thank you, Carol. Would you like to enlighten the good captain for me?"

She nodded and said, "I actually ran it three times, just to be sure. She has U-negative blood."

I frowned, wrinkled my nose again—*I need to stop doing that.* "I've never heard of that blood type," I replied.

"I doubt many people have," she said. "Only six percent of the black population across the globe have the U-negative blood type, and it's found only in black people. It has never been found in Whites, Asians, or any other race. Never."

"She is, legally, and in fact, a black woman," Doc said.

"But she looks... absolutely white," I said. "I mean, even her hair looks Caucasian. Are you sure?" I leaned over Genevieve's face and studied her features. There was nothing about her that would make me think she was black. And if there was nothing obvious to me, I wondered if her husband knew.

"Yes, of course I'm sure," Doc snapped. "And that isn't all; she was pregnant." He pinched the bridge of his nose beneath his glasses.

My heart sank. There are certain things cops never get

used to, and one of the primary things is when a child dies, especially an unborn child.

"How far along was she?" I asked

"About seven weeks," Doc said.

"Eddie Chesterton didn't mention it," I said thoughtfully, "so I assume he doesn't know, unless he's one cold, calculating SOB."

I sat down on the metal stool at the head of the examining table, folded my arms and stared at the body.

"She'd obviously been out for a night on the town," I said. "How much had she had to drink, Doc?"

"Some. Not a lot. She may not have known she was pregnant, but I doubt it," Doc replied. "Young women are pretty savvy about such things these days."

"Drugs?" I asked.

"We won't know that until we get the tox screen back," Carol said.

I knew that, I thought. *Stupid question.*

I nodded.

"Do you have any more surprises for me?" I asked.

"Do you want some more?"

"Whew. Not really. I really don't think I can take anymore, Doc. But if you have anything, now's the time to lay it on me. If not, let's get on with it. We've been up since six o'clock, and it feels like I've crammed sixteen hours' worth of work and worry into eight hours."

Doc nodded and began his examination of the exterior of the body. I didn't bother to record it. It was already being done: voice and video, every word, every move, every nook and cranny.

Genevieve had a total of seven tattoos, including the tramp stamp: a bird, a swallow on her ankle; an infinity symbol on her left wrist; a heart on her upper right shoulder; the word Sexy on her right hip bone; a rose on her right buttock, and the word Forever with a date beneath it on her mons pubis, or mound of Venus.

Probably her wedding date, I thought. *Something I need to check. If it's not, what else could it be?* I made a mental note to check it out.

"Time of death?" I asked.

"I can now confirm that she did indeed die somewhere between two and three in the morning," Doc said. "Just after closing time for most clubs, I think."

"Cause of death, Doc?"

He sighed and shook his head, then said, "I can't tell you that yet, Catherine, not for sure. At first glance, though, I'd have to say ligature strangulation, but there's a long way yet to go."

I clicked my tongue, stood up, and stepped across the room to the table where Genevieve's clothing was laid out. Carol had had to cut the skinny jeans off her. Beside the silver lamé top and matching shoes lay a white lace bandeau bralette and a matching thong.

All were neatly folded and ready to be bagged. Everything had been vacuumed and treated with four-by-four clear lifting sheets to gather hairs and fibers. Small sections of cloth had been removed to be tested for fluids.

I had no doubt that the testing and documenting of what had been gathered from the clothing and the body would take days.

The woman had been partying—meeting people, dancing, hugging—and, whenever two objects meet—in this case Genevieve, multiple human beings, and her killer—something is always exchanged: hair, fiber, bodily fluids. And they could be exchanged by a simple kiss or even peck on the cheek. This young lady would, no doubt, yield a plethora of useful—and useless—information.

I touched nothing, sighed deeply, and returned to my stool.

"I don't believe she was sexually assaulted," Doc said. "I'll have Carol complete a rape kit." He glanced at her, then continued, "But I don't see signs of force," he said as he continued to examine her skin for anomalous markings, punctures, wounds or bruising.

By the time he reached her head, we were almost an hour into the examination, and I was beginning to see things that weren't there.

He began his scrutiny of the area around her throat. "Now this is very interesting," he said. "You see this?"

He pointed to the two deep, almost threadlike ligature marks that partially encircled her throat, one above the other, separated from each other by about a half an inch.

"I haven't seen this type of ligature mark for many years. It's consistent with people in jail who have hung themselves using their shoelaces."

"Is that so?" I mused and studied the markings even closer.

"It is, and that's why inmates are forced to wear flip-flops. Back in the day, though, I examined more than one inmate suicide all with very similar marks. These, however, are somewhat different. A typical hanging produces similar indentations—usually deeper, but certainly similar. Here's the difference, though. Look at these small bruises."

He pulled her hair aside and, at the nape of her neck, as I leaned in closer, I could see that the ligature marks did indeed end in a cluster of smaller bruises."

"Those were made by the killer's knuckles!" I stated, leaning back again.

"They were indeed," he said. "There's a similar pattern of bruises on the other side of her neck. Obviously, the ligature was quite short, forcing the attacker's fists into contact with her neck. Nasty, very nasty. I would say our perpetrator snuck up behind her, wrapped the shoelaces around her neck, and then twisted them tight using her own neck as a fulcrum, like this..." he held up his two hands clenched into tight fists and twisted them in opposite directions.

He stood back a little, contemplating his scenario, then stepped forward again, took a small penlight from his pocket and snapped it on.

"And see here: You can see the gouges in her skin where she clawed at the laces but couldn't get a finger beneath them because they were so tight."

I'd noticed the gouges earlier, at the crime scene, but under the harsh lights, and against the almost porcelain-white skin, they looked raw, red, turning the ligature wound into a gruesome necklace.

I sat back, hearing but not listening to Doc's words, staring unseeing at the wounds, lost in thought as I absorbed these new developments and wondered at the brutality, the viciousness of the attack.

Someone really hated this poor girl, I thought. *It's... so violent, up close, personal, full of hate, anger. What the hell did she do to piss off someone that much?*

My phone buzzed in my pocket, snapping me out of my trance. I glanced at the screen, expecting to see Janet's number or maybe even Chief Johnston's. But it was neither of them. It was a number I didn't know.

I stood, walked to the door, and accepted the call. "Gazzara."

"Is this Detective Catherine Gazzara?" The voice sounded sweet, feminine, but distressed.

"Yes, it is."

"Detective, my name is Regina Mae Cottonwell-Chesterton. I just received the most distressing call from my son. Is it true? Is my daughter-in-law dead?" The words sounded like they tumbled out of her mouth.

"Yes, ma'am. I'm afraid it is."

I heard the woman begin to sob. I listened for a few seconds, waiting for her to speak, but she didn't, so I took the initiative and dove right in, thinking that this was the perfect opportunity to start the investigation rolling.

"If I may, Mrs. Cottonwell-Chesterton"—*Geez, what a mouthful*—"I'd like to drop by and talk to you. Shall we say in thirty minutes?"

I would have preferred to talk to Granddad first, but since I had Regina Mae on the line...

"Of course, Detective. I'll see you then." Regina Mae sniffled and hung up the phone.

I looked at Doc. He and Carol were hovering over the body like a couple of great green vultures. Doc had a scalpel in his hand and was about to make his first cut.

"Are you done with me, Doc? I have an appointment," I said as I pulled off my latex gloves.

"Yes. I think so. I don't expect there will be any more surprises. I'll call you if I discover anything else. My report should be done by tomorrow if no one bothers me, that is," he said, looking up at me.

I got the message.

"I'll be sure to stay out of your hair, but if you could send it to me..." I replied, smiling sweetly at him as I tossed the gloves in the trash. "And you might want to have a talk with that intern about the importance of coffee."

"I think she drinks tea," Doc muttered with a frown.

"Ugh, and you hired her? Doc, I'm shocked," I teased.

"Well, I don't care if you discover tentacles and an alien implant, I won't be back until there is coffee in the pot. No coffee? No Kate." I jerked my thumb at my chest.

"You can be sure I'll get right on that," Doc said without emotion as he stroked the scalpel through the flesh from shoulder to pubic bone. Then he looked up at me and winked.

Five minutes later, sans the Tyvek suit, cap, booties, mask and safety glasses, I closed the car door, pushed the starter button and glanced at the display and literally gasped; it was almost four-thirty. Where had the day gone? And I wasn't done yet. I'd talked myself into what could turn out to be another lengthy interview.

7

R egina Mae Cottonwood-Chesterton lived in a swanky penthouse at the other end of town, where I had to show a doorman my driver's license as well as my creds in order to pass through the lobby. I flashed my badge and was allowed to retain my license. The lobby was decorated with beautiful pieces of art in gold frames, but there was no café churning out steaming hot coffee. I liked her son's place better.

The doorman walked me to the private elevator and inserted a key to open the doors. There were only four buttons on the panel: one down to the garage, one to the lobby, a third to the second floor, and the fourth going directly to the penthouse. That one also required a key, and again the doorman obliged then stepped out as the doors closed.

My stomach jumped a little when the fast-moving elevator came to a sudden stop. The doors slid open, giving access to another, much smaller, lobby and a beautiful pair of walnut double doors. I exited the elevator and looked around, noting the black glass dome that housed the security cameras, a red emergency phone on the wall, and a door leading to a stairwell.

I raised my hand to knock, but before I could one of the heavy doors opened.

"Detective Gazzara?" the woman asked.

She couldn't have been much more than five feet tall. Her hair was cut very short and was unnaturally white. She was wearing a pale blue, off-one-shoulder sweater complemented by a slim gold chain with a pendant of an eagle claw grasping a tiger's eye gemstone that complemented her light brown eyes. I could easily see that she'd had some work done on her crow's feet and at the corners of her mouth. But she was still a strikingly beautiful woman with a lovely figure, highlighted by her skinny jeans and leopard-print shoes.

"Yes, ma'am. Are you Mrs. Cottonwell-Chesterton?"

"Oh, please, call me Regina Mae and come on in." The accent was pure Southern belle.

She extended her hand, palm down, as if she expected me to kiss it. I couldn't help but note the perfectly red manicured nails and several large rings. I glanced down at her left hand; the wedding set on her ring finger was big enough to choke a pig.

"Jonathan the doorman told me you'd arrived. Won't you come in?"

I gripped her fingers gently, then turned them loose—it was the weirdest handshake ever—and followed her inside to be greeted by the sweet smell of peaches.

Nah, she can't be baking, not dressed like that.

I quickly dismissed the thought when I saw the scented candle burning on the marble island in the kitchen. *Geez*, I thought, as I gazed around the massive open-plan complex. *So this, I guess, is how the one-percenters live.*

It wasn't a critical thought, more one of... not even envy; perhaps it was wishful thinking. I don't know.

The ceilings were high, the crown molding at least a foot deep. Everything was pristine... pure white: white leather couch and matching easy chairs, throw rugs... Unbelievable.

"My son called me just after you left. He's absolutely torn apart," she said as she walked ahead of me, her voice echoing off the hardwood floors in the foyer.

"I'm so sorry for your loss. The Chattanooga PD wants to do everything possible to find the person responsible," I said, remembering the chief said to be extra careful how I handled the family.

She led me into a sitting room area where the afternoon sun was peeking in through vintage lace curtains.

"Please, sit down, Detective. Can I get you something to drink? Sweet tea or a glass of water, perhaps?"

"No, thank you, ma'am," I said as I sat down on one of the easy chairs. "I'd like to ask you a few questions if you don't mind, and I like to record my interviews if that's acceptable."

I watched Regina Mae's expression as she watched me set my iPad on the coffee table in front of me.

"By all means," she said and quickly sat down on the matching chair opposite me. She sat demurely, knees together, feet crossed at the ankles and positioned slightly to the left, her hands clasped together in her lap.

Her well-manicured fingers played with her rings. "I'm sorry. You'll have to forgive me. I'm just a basket of nerves. I cannot believe this has happened. Poor, poor, Genevieve. Can you tell me what happened?"

"I'm afraid I can't discuss the ongoing investigation, Mrs. Cot... Regina Mae. If you don't mind my asking, what was your relationship with your daughter-in-law like?" I watched as she twisted the large diamond around and around her ring finger.

"What did Eddie tell you?" she asked.

"I'd rather hear it from you, if you don't mind," I replied, smiling benignly at her.

"We weren't very close, I must admit. I always thought that Eddie made poor choices, especially when it came to women. Oh please, don't take that the wrong way. I want nothing but the best for my son, just as any mother would. You see, he's my *only* son and someday he will have big responsibilities; he has big shoes to fill, I'm afraid." She looked off to the side for a moment, before turning back to me.

"I do think he could have done better. There were plenty of girls from reputable families that..." She let the thought trail off. She blushed slightly, obviously embarrassed by what she'd said.

"Why didn't you think Genevieve was right for him?" I asked.

"Are you serious?" Regina Mae's voice was losing that Southern softness. "She had quite a reputation. She... Uh! When she began working for Grandfather at the company, it was common knowledge that she was looking for a free ride."

Geez, this is one cold... piece of work. Her daughter-in-law was murdered only hours ago and she talks about her as if...

"Other than your son," I said, "was she seeing anyone else that worked at the office?" I leaned a little closer.

"Was she having an affair, you mean? Not that I'm aware of, but you know how it is when you are part of the family that owns the business. You're the last to know anything. The rank and file... well, they stick together, don't they? Why do you ask?"

I decided it was time to bring the hammer down and said, "Did you know that Genevieve was pregnant?"

"*What?*" Regina Mae asked, stunned.

"The medical examiner took a sample of her blood. He said she was around seven weeks along. So, you didn't know?"

"I had no idea, but it doesn't surprise me. Her Hail Mary, I should think." She turned her head away, lifted her chin, sat up a little straighter in the chair, and continued. "That really does just take the cake, doesn't it? I mean, it is really too bad. It's too bad about Genevieve, I know... and now another innocent life has been taken." She paused for a moment, stared down at her hands.

"Genevieve was no angel, Detective," she continued. "Yes, I know, it's not right to speak ill of the dead, but it's true, and I do believe that Eddie was beginning to realize it."

"Do you believe that Eddie was the baby's father?" I asked.

She heaved a huge sigh, lowered her eyes, shook her head and said, "That, of course, is the question, isn't it, Detective?" She turned her head toward me and locked eyes with me. "I would hope so, but I'm a pragmatist. She was a maverick in every sense of the word. She carried on... If you'd seen how she dressed or how she... Well, we just can't be sure, can we? Let's just say I wouldn't be surprised if my son was not the father."

"Has Eddie ever confided in you that they were having problems? Did he ever mention them having arguments, physical altercations?"

I watched Regina Mae's eyes. She had a strange look on her face. Perhaps she was disappointed that I'd interrupted her rant about what a slut she thought her daughter-in-law was.

"No?" she said. It was more a question than a denial. She looked puzzled.

"You're not sure?"

"Eddie has never said anything to me, and... No!" she said suddenly very confident.

"Did Genevieve?"

"No... Well, yes, she did ask for my advice on occasion, but I tried to stay out of it. If she couldn't cope with Eddie, it was probably because she was out of her league. The Chesterton's are... not like other... Oh dear, how shall I put it? Ordinary people? No, that's not quite right, but I'm sure you understand, Detective. I, on the other hand, knew exactly the type of man I was marrying, and I knew what to expect and how to handle it. Edward and I moved in the same circles. I didn't have to pretend I was something I wasn't."

I watched as Regina Mae nodded her head while looking at me. *Who the hell is she trying to persuade?* I thought.

"Well, you know how it can be," she continued. "It isn't easy having a lot of money." She cleared her throat after realizing what she'd just said. "Please, I hope I don't sound snobbish."

I didn't answer. I waited for her to continue.

She looked down at her polished fingernails, adjusted all of her rings, then said defiantly, "I am *not* going to apologize for being wealthy."

"I'm not asking you to do that, Regina Mae," I replied. It was almost like I was talking to a small child.

"I'll tell you this," she said, the anger rising in her voice.

"I did *not* care for my daughter-in-law. Genevieve did *not* belong in this family."

Wow, why don't you tell me what you really think?

Regina Mae stood up, walked around to the back of her chair, kneaded the soft leather of the back as if she was giving it a massage.

"And now you tell me there's a baby."

I swear she had tears in her eyes, and *that* I wasn't expecting.

"There was a baby," I clarified. "They are both dead."

"Well, maybe that's for the best," she said, in a whisper. "The child has been spared. Perhaps that's the silver lining in all of this." Regina Mae looked at me, shook her head, and then shrugged. "God does indeed work in mysterious ways."

I stared up at her. Wow! I was disgusted, and I'd had just about enough of her crap.

Time for the hammer again, I think.

"Mrs. Chesterton, did you know Genevieve was black?"

She looked down at me, her eyes wide, her mouth open.

"What did you say?"

"I said, did you know your daughter-in-law was black?"

Regina Mae chuckled. "You're joking?"

Hmm, either she's one hell of an actress or she really didn't know.

Slowly, I shook my head, maintained eye contact with her.

"No... You're wrong. She is as lily-white as I am. I don't believe it."

It took me only a few seconds to relay Doc's findings to her, and then I watched her as she stared at me. It was as if I'd suddenly grown antlers.

"Then I can say with all certainty," she replied, "that it *is* for the best that, that this *tragedy* occurred. What kind of life, do you think, would the poor child would have had? It's unthinkable!" Regina Mae shrugged and rolled her eyes.

Wow, I thought. *What kind of person is she? Who talks like this?*

There wasn't a shred of compassion or concern in her voice, not for Genevieve or the baby... her grandchild. Even the concern she'd expressed for her son was absent.

"Regina Mae, where were you between two and three o'clock this morning?" I asked, trying to put my personal feelings for the woman aside.

She glared at me, seemingly stunned by the question, then said, "You can't be serious. You don't think for one moment that I had anything to do with it... *do you?*" She held up her hands, fingers spread, palms inward, as if her bright red nails were still wet. "Since when is it a crime to not like someone?"

"It's not a crime, ma'am. But I have to establish the whereabouts of everyone concerned, including you. Would you please tell me where you were and who you were with?" I bit my lower lip and raised my eyebrows.

"Where do you think I was, for goodness' sake?" she snapped. "I was here, at home, in bed."

"Can anyone verify that?" I asked, knowing that her husband was out of town.

"Yes," she said nastily, folding her arms defiantly. "Yes." The sweet Southern drawl had disappeared, along with her ladylike composure.

"And?" I asked.

"Tyrone and Baker Security Systems." She smirked. "This entire apartment is wired for sound and video... cameras. The feed goes directly to T&B's servers where they are archived. If you want to check *my alibi,* you can. I'll call them and give my permission for you to view the recordings."

"Thank you," I replied. "I'll need the address, please. I'll verify your *alibi* and eliminate you as a person of interest." I'm ashamed to admit I allowed a little sarcasm of my own to slip in.

"Oh, you will, will you? Fine."

She turned and stalked over to an antique desk set against the far wall, snatched open one of the drawers, sorted through the contents, slammed the drawer shut, and then walked stiffly back to me and handed me T&B's business card. I glanced at it, nodded, thanked her, and slipped it into my purse.

"You do understand, Mrs. Chesterton, that none of this is personal. I have a job to do, a murderer to catch."

She stepped away, turned again to face me, folded her arms, and glared down at me, but didn't answer.

"I appreciate your being so honest and forthcoming with me," I said, rising to my feet, thinking I'd just about had enough of the woman, and her attitude, and that she'd certainly had enough of me.

I would have loved to have given her a piece of my mind, but that would have been inappropriate. My job was to investigate, not judge. But what kind of woman—a so-called lady—talks about the murder of a mother and her unborn child that way, intimating that God had a hand in it? It was unsettling, to say the least, but it didn't mean she'd had anything to do with it.

No, it shows her up as the bitch she really is.

"I think I've answered enough of your questions, Detective," she said pompously. "So, if you'll excuse me, I have to go and meet with Grandfather Chesterton. I'm afraid we'll have much to discuss, sad things, so sad..."

And then, slap me if she didn't sniffle. I almost wanted to burst out laughing, but I didn't.

I picked up my iPad, looked unseeingly at the screen, lost in thought, and then I had an idea.

"You're going to see Edward Eaton Chesterton the Second?" I asked. "That reminds me of something your son said to me. Do you have any idea why Eddie would say that his grandfather had killed Genevieve?"

Regina Mae froze.

"I'm sure I don't know the answer to that," she hissed.

"Well, if you're going to visit him, I might as well tag along with you, if you don't mind. I need to talk to him, too." I had a hunch what her answer would be, and I was right.

"Yes, I do mind. I mind very much," she snapped.

"Well then," I said casually. "Perhaps you're right. Maybe it would be better if I had him brought to the police department."

Then, as if it was an afterthought, I said quietly, "You'd be surprised at how quickly the media gets to know of this sort of thing... who we're questioning, and why. They monitor us, you know. If they were to find out that Edward Eaton Chesterton the Second's grandson had accused him of murder... well, that's news. Especially when the accused is as... let's say as well-known as he is. That sells advertising."

Sure, it was petty to add that last tidbit, but it was true. The media vultures were always more interested in the wealthy than the lush in the drunk tank, unless it was a wealthy lush, of course. They'd be all over EEC2 in a second.

"If you think you can make a name for yourself by humiliating one of this country's most respected statesmen, you're greatly mistaken."

Regina Mae lifted her chin defiantly. "He's much too smart for the likes of you. He'll be three steps ahead of you all the way. I will tell you this, though. Eddie doesn't care for his grandfather. I had so hoped that it was just a phase he was going through, but my son is almost twenty-eight years old and nothing has changed."

"But to blame his grandfather for murder right off the bat," I said. "Why would he do that?"

"Look, Detective, I'm not the only one who didn't like Genevieve. Grandfather, Eddie's uncles, his cousins, everyone for heaven's sake. I don't think even the gardener liked the woman. Remember what that Palin woman said? If you put lipstick on a pig... Yes, well it's true. Grandfather may have been the most vocal in his distaste, but only in closed circles. It's no wonder then that Eddie is upset with him."

"Did you ever see Mr. Chesterton senior and Genevieve exchange words? Were there ever any arguments, or threats of violence uttered by either one of them?"

I watched as Regina Mae became noticeably more agitated. I had the notion that Grandfather didn't just rub Eddie the wrong way, but Genevieve too. It was obvious the old man wielded a lot of power, even when he wasn't around. Hell, even I could feel his presence.

"No. Not to my knowledge. I myself have never seen a cross word pass between them." She smoothed her sweater and smiled sweetly. "Grandfather was very discreet. Now, I do believe I have been more than cordial, Detective. I am afraid I must ask you to leave. There are errands I must run."

"Just one last question," I said. "Do you think Edward Eaton Chesterton the Second murdered Genevieve?"

She stared daggers at me.

"I always knew it!" she snapped. "I knew that girl would poison my son against his own family! That a grandfather would murder his own granddaughter-in-law is the most ridiculous thing I've ever heard. He might be a lot of things but a murderer? No, absolutely not. You obviously don't know much about our family, Detective, or you wouldn't have displayed such blatant ignorance!

"My son is heartbroken and not thinking clearly. He'll accuse anyone and everyone who ever expressed any concern for him. Today it's his grandfather, tomorrow it will be his own father, or Uncle Sam Wheaton, or even me. Unfortunately, we spared the rod, and now we are reaping the consequences. Good day, Detective. Please show yourself out," she said, her voice trembling with emotion.

"Uncle Sam Wheaton?" I asked. "Who's he?"

"I said good day, Detective. Now please leave." Then she turned away and disappeared into the nether regions of the apartment.

And so I did as I was told. I left. I went home, exhausted, my mind in a whirl. *Open-and-shut case? Right, and if you'll believe that...*

8

"How did it go?" Janet asked.

I'd called her to touch base and had her on Bluetooth as I drove home; her voice echoed from the car's speakers. It had been one heck of a long day, and all I wanted was a hot shower, a couple glasses of wine and some mindless television.

"It was interesting to say the least," I replied. "You got your pad in front of you?"

"I do. I'm ready when you are."

I first brought her up to date with Doc's findings: Genevieve's ethnic background and her pregnancy. Her reaction was similar to mine.

"Oh dear," she said. "If that doesn't beat all. How sad."

I could see her shaking her head of red hair over the phone.

"Yes... sad isn't the word for it," I said. "But that's not all. I also interviewed Genevieve's mother-in-law, Regina Mae Cottonwell-Chesterton. Try saying that three times quickly. Anyway, she's a real piece of... well, this is not the time or place. I don't want to have to repeat everything for the rest of the team. You did get everybody organized for Monday morning, right?"

"The rest of the new team? Yes, they'll all be there."

"Good. I recorded her interview, and Eddie's. We'll have them transcribed on Monday. We should have the autopsy report by then, too. Okay, so look, it's been a tough day and I'm on my way home, but if you have time, I'd like for you to call Lenny Miller and have him dig into Genevieve's background; give us a bit of a head start for Monday. Ask him to put out a few feelers to the more unorthodox information outlets, if you catch my drift," I said.

"Got it."

"And while he's at it, I'd also like for him to check into a guy named Sam Wheaton. I need an address and the basics: criminal background, credit check, et cetera. You know the drill."

"On it."

Lenny Miller is one of the three members of my new team. He knows computers, so he's my go-to guy for in-depth research: background checks and the like. He's good, but he's no Tim Clarke.

"Good," I said. "It's been a heck of a day and I intend to take it easy the rest of the weekend, so don't call me unless it's urgent, okay?"

"Yes, ma'am. Take it easy. See you Monday," and she disconnected.

Me? I couldn't get home fast enough. Normally when I got home, I'd be greeted by Sadie Mae my chocolate Dachshund, her tail wagging happily. I'd adopted her from a couple I'd put away for murder some months ago. They don't allow lifers to have pets, so I took the little scamp.

I soon realized, however, that I was serving a life

sentence of my own to the Chattanooga PD and that it wasn't fair to leave the little lovebug home alone all day, sometimes at night too, so I boarded her out with my ex-partner, Lonnie. I missed that little brown face and those big black eyes that seemed so full of love and affection... the dog, I mean, not Lonnie.

I dumped my Glock and badge on the kitchen counter, went to the fridge, grabbed an already opened bottle of Cabernet, poured myself a large glass and, with the bottle still in my hand, I closed my eyes and sipped: *oh, how heavenly!*

I took the bottle with me into the living room, flopped down on the couch, snapped on the television and flipped through the channels until I found a romantic comedy about a woman who was in love with two guys. It wasn't what I wanted, but I found myself watching it anyway. It was all stuff that never happens in real life, not to me anyway.

I'm young, right? I told myself. *Well, thirty-seven isn't old... is it? And I'm attractive, funny too, when I want to be, and feel like it. So why doesn't it ever happen to me? I can't find one dude let alone juggle two.*

The truth was, I couldn't find anyone who could live with what I do for a living: my hours, my bosses, my visits to the seedier parts of town, my need to keep my gun with me at all times, even on my nightstand.

Let's see some brainiac in Hollywood make a romantic comedy about that. I won't hold my breath.

I needed a shower, but I just couldn't be bothered, so I finished off my bottle of wine, made a start on another, and sat through the rest of the rom-com, not really seeing or listening to it; it was way above my paygrade, a fantasy but, crazy as it may seem, I was in a state of contentment. Maybe it was the wine.

And then I found myself thinking about Regina Mae Cottonwell-Chesterton. *That name is too much.*

I figured she must have high-tailed it over to Grandpappy's place and told him everything I'd said, and then some. She struck me as a woman on a mission, someone who would say and do just about anything to secure her share of the old man's estate. *C'est la vie.* At that moment, with the wine running through my head and the soft cushions on my couch, she could keep it. *I wouldn't trade places with any of those bluebloods, not for all the money in the world...* and at that point I must have fallen asleep, because I remember nothing more.

I woke early that Sunday morning, and I felt like... Well, you know what I felt like. I staggered to the window, opened the drapes, and looked out on to what was about to turn into a lovely day. It was the perfect morning for a run.

I went to the bathroom, stripped off my clothes from the day before, swilled cold water over my face, donned a pair of running shorts, sports bra and top, and headed out into the cool, early morning air.

I t was just seven o'clock that following Monday morning when I parked my car in my assigned space at the rear of the PD; my batteries were fully charged and I was eager to get to work.

Five minutes later I was at my desk with my office door closed. I tackled my emails first, made a couple of quick phone calls, emailed the interview recordings to the department secretary for transcription, grabbed my first file and, just as I was about to open it, there was a knock on the door. It was Janet.

"Don't you ever go home?" I asked her.

She was carrying her usual stack of notebooks and files, and she smiled at me.

"I do. But I love this stuff so I don't like to be away for too long," she said, smiling. "The others are all here, by the way. They're in the incident room. You want me to have them come on in?"

"Yep, might as well get started," I said, looking at the expanse of shiny white that was the storyboard. "You didn't do much with it on Saturday, did you?"

"No, I didn't. Sorry, Captain." She shrugged. "I was going to but... I had to go to Home Depot."

"Don't worry about it," I said. "I took Sunday off too, remember."

Home Depot? I thought. *What on earth?*

She nodded, smiling sheepishly, and I knew that she knew what I was thinking, but she didn't explain. Instead, she picked up my desk phone and called Detective Hawkins and asked him and the rest of the team to join us.

They arrived together a few minutes later, laden with laptops, iPads, files, notebooks, coffee... and speaking of coffee.

"I'll go get you some," Janet said, reading my mind.

How does she do that?

While I was waiting for her to return, they, my three new team members, exchanged small talk about their goings-on over the weekend. I dug through my files and extracted several 8x10 photographs: Genevieve, EEC2, 3 and 4 and Regina Mae. I taped the photo of Genevieve to the big board at the top dead center—no pun intended—and the other three in a row, in order directly below. Then I wrote the names beneath each photo.

"Here you go, Cap," Janet said, setting the cup down on my desk. "Black, no sugar."

I grabbed the cup and sniffed the contents. *Not bad... not great, but not bad.*

"Where did you get this?" I asked. "It's not that crap from the incident room, is it?"

"No. I made it myself in Cathy's office."

I sipped. "Hmm... Okay, let's get on with it." I grabbed a twelve-inch plastic ruler from my desk drawer, tapped the topmost photo and began.

"Genevieve Chesterton was found strangled to death on

the Riverwalk at six-thirty on Saturday morning. Time of death: between two and three o'clock that same morning. She was attacked from behind. This was not, I repeat, not, a sexual assault. Whoever did this had only one thing on his mind... to kill her. She is ethnically black, although to look at her you'd never know it, but I believe she's been passing herself off as white. She was also pregnant."

I paused, looked at each of the four faces one by one. Three of them, including Janet were taking notes. Hawkins, the oldest and most experienced of them was not.

Arthur "Hawk" Hawkins was sixty-four years old. He'd been a detective for twenty-nine years and had one year left to go before retirement. I think he'd been transferred to me so that he could work out the rest of his term in relative peace. He was a handsome man, five-ten, a little overweight at two hundred ten pounds, clean-shaven, with white hair, blue eyes, a sharp nose, sunburned face and arms, and was wearing suspenders with his shirt sleeves rolled up. He was seated at the back of the room with his arms folded, watching every move I made. To anyone else that might have been unnerving, but I'd known Hawk a long time. He was a tough old man with a big soft heart.

"Genevieve was married to this man." I tapped the photograph of EEC4. "Edward Eaton Chesterton the Fourth, the only grandson of one of the wealthiest men in Tennessee; this man, Edward Eaton Chesterton the Second... Yes, Anne," I said in answer to Anne Robar's raised hand.

"Did he... Edward Eaton Chesterton... Oh hell, we can't keep calling them all by that long, convoluted name—"

"Which one, Anne?"

"The young one, the husband."

I nodded. "Yes, you're right. From now on, the husband

is Eddie, his father is Daddy, and the old man is... the old man," I said, adding the nicknames to the photographs. "So what's your question, Anne?"

I'd also known Anne Robar a long time. At forty-three, she was five years older than me with more than twenty years on the job. True she was no great beauty, but she was quite a striking woman: prematurely graying hair cropped very short, a round face, hazel eyes surrounded by crow's feet—the woman had spent far too long in the sun without protection and now her skin was suffering for it. She wasn't quite as tall as me, but she carried herself with more than a little attitude. In other words, she didn't take crap from anyone. She was also married with two teenage boys, both of them still in high school. She was a senior detective and a good one. Why she wasn't at least a sergeant was beyond me.

"Eddie," she said. "Did he know she was black?"

"Good question," I said. "Eddie, the husband, has to be our prime suspect, so the answer goes to motive. I don't know. I interviewed him yesterday morning—I'll have transcripts for you all later today—but I didn't know she was black myself, not then, or that she was pregnant, so I didn't ask him, which means a follow-up interview. I'll do that myself, later." I paused, turned to the board and picked up a marker.

"One more thing before I move on," I said, drawing a blank square on the board, "Eddie said I should ask the old man about the Frenchman. He wouldn't tell me more than that. We need to find out what, or who, he was talking about." I drew a large question mark beside the blank box. "Regina Mae mentioned a Sam Wheaton, more about that later," I said, and I drew a second empty box and question mark.

"Okay," I said, setting the marker down, "so moving right along, I also interviewed Regina Mae Cottonwell-Chesterton."

"Whew, what a fricking mouthful," Anne said. "What are we going to call her?"

"Regina, I think will do well enough," I said. "She's something else, this one, a real piece of high society, nose in the air, self-centered... Okay, she's a snob, and she didn't approve of Genevieve *at all!* Right at the end of the interview, she threw me a name—not sure if she intended to, but she did—someone named Sam Wheaton. I asked about him, but she ignored the question and ended the interview."

I looked at Lenny Miller.

"Come on, Lenny," I said, impatiently. "Don't keep me on tenterhooks. What did you find out?" I grabbed my own pad of paper and a pen.

He looked at me, puzzled, then said, "I'm afraid the verdict is still out on Genevieve Chesterton. I'm still working on it."

I nodded. "How about Sam Wheaton?

It was Janet who answered.

"Umm, I think I can shed a little light on him." She looked up at me, wide-eyed.

I said nothing. I waited for her to speak.

"Well, I wasn't able to get hold of Lenny until Sunday morning." She glanced at him, then continued, "and... well, I had nothing much to do, so I called my boyfriend. He's a corporate finance major at UTK and a bit of a computer whiz, so I thought he might have heard of him, Wheaton..."

Again she glanced sideways at Lenny. Lenny grinned at her, seemingly not the least bit bothered that Janet was encroaching into his domain.

"Anyway, Josh—that's my boyfriend—was at work at the

Home Depot, and it was late on Saturday. I go there often. At that hour nothing is usually happening so I can learn how to use the power tools. They offer classes and dating one of the employees has its perks." She scooted in her seat.

I heaved a sigh, rolled my eyes and said, "I guess so. Okay, so you went to see your boyfriend at Home Depot, and..."

"I asked him if he could check into Uncle Sam Wheaton." She looked up at me and then to the side at Anne, then again at me and said, "I'm really not sure where to begin."

"Just jump right in," I said. I sat down and waited as Janet began to read through her notes.

"Janet?" I said, after a couple of minutes of her not saying anything.

"Yes, I just wanted to..." She extracted a photograph, jumped to her feet, and slapped it up on the board over the blank square that I'd just drawn on the board.

"This is Samuel Tiegh Wheaton." She stood with her back to the board, iPad in hand, and began.

"Josh took his lunch break and..." She caught the look I was giving her and quickly got back on track. "Wheaton is the founder of a business consulting firm that works primarily for smaller companies, usually start-ups, and he's very good at what he does. However, his main bread-and-butter comes from CDE International Finance Company, the flagship of the Chesterton group of companies where he's affectionately known by the staff as Uncle Sam."

She paused and flipped through a couple of screens on her iPad.

"I came into the office yesterday morning, after I'd talked to Lenny, and did a search of criminal records. Sam Wheaton does not have a record per se, but Josh found that back in 2008 he'd settled a couple of sexual harassment claims by members of his own staff. He was never married, but he did father two children, a girl aged twelve and a boy aged thirteen, by different mothers. Both were adopted at birth," Janet said.

"So, he likes the ladies," I said smirking.

"Younger ladies," Janet said.

"How young?"

"Legal age, barely. But as far as I could tell, he's never crossed the line. We should probably do a thorough background check on him," she said, looking at Lenny.

"So what's his connection to Regina Mae?" I asked.

"Samuel Wheaten is a close friend of old man Chesterton; a very close friend. It was him that bailed him out of his sexual harassment problems. In fact, Edward Chesterton the Second is quoted as saying that 'Uncle Sam is a good man and a trusted confidant.' Apparently, he's run every major financial decision past Uncle Sam for the past two decades and has yet to regret a single one." Janet pinched her lips together like a fish as she continued to look over her notes.

"Oh," she said, almost as an afterthought, "and Genevieve worked for CDE prior to her marriage to Eddie, so Uncle Sam must have known her even back then."

"So," I mused aloud. "Here we have a guy, not related to the Chesterton's, but who has intimate knowledge of all their financial dealings and probably most of the family secrets as well. He's a man with a penchant for young women. He's introduced to Eddie's lovely new bride and likes what he sees. He makes a pass at her, and she rejects him. Or maybe she didn't. Maybe she had an affair with him and then broke it off—for somebody else maybe—or maybe she was about to expose him... Who knows? He's been on his best behavior for a decade. Hmmm." I was liking the sound of this.

"Hmmm indeed," Janet replied. "Here is his contact info." She placed a sheet of paper on the desk in front of me. "He rarely goes into the office," she continued. "Spends most of his time at the golf course or at the gym."

"Well," I said, brightly. "What do you say, Janet? You want to question Uncle Sam?"

Although I wasn't at all disappointed in my own looks, if I wanted to extract information from a pervy guy who was into young girls, I knew younger was better.

"Absolutely," she bubbled.

I thought she was going to start clapping she was so excited.

I checked my watch. It was almost nine.

"Hawk," I said, "I want you and Anne to go check out the crime scene. See if you can figure out what she was doing down there by herself at that ungodly hour of the morning. I figure she must have been coming from a club or bar or... party, whatever. Ask around, see what you can find out; who she was with... you know the drill. Go talk to people."

I turned to Lenny and said, "I want to know everything about everybody, but start with Genevieve Chesterton, then the close members of the family and... okay, I don't have to tell you."

He nodded. "I'm on it, boss. I'll have something for you when you get back."

I stood, grabbed my iPad, my purse, phone and weapon, and walked to the door.

"We'll meet back here this afternoon at two-thirty and compare notes. Maybe between us... well, we'll see."

10

Samuel Tiegh Wheaton's home was all you'd expect it to be for a man of his status: a beautiful, three-story house in an exclusive, high-status subdivision with what the realtors sell as "curb appeal." To me? It looked like one hell of a lot of expensive landscaping.

I parked my unmarked cruiser in the driveway and together, Janet and I walked to the front porch and up the steps to the front door.

"I shouldn't ask you to do this, Janet," I said as I rang the doorbell, "but you said that this guy has a penchant for young girls, so I need you to..." I took a deep breath and continued, "I need you to do me a favor. I need you to act like you're impressed by him, that you're attracted to him. Yes, I know. It's not professional and—"

"I can do that," she said, interrupting me. "Don't worry, I love it; it'll be fun. You'll see." I could almost hear the wheels turning in her head. "I know just how to handle a guy like him."

I was about to ring again when I heard hard-soled shoes on hardwood floor within. The door finally opened.

"Can I help you?"

"Mr. Wheaton?" I asked.

"Yes, can I help you?"

"I'm Captain Gazzara, Chattanooga Police," I said, showing him my badge and ID. "This is Sergeant Toliver." Janet did the same, smiling sweetly. "We need to talk to you for a minute. May we come in?"

"Yes, of course."

I let Janet enter first. He shook her hand, holding it tightly, quickly scanning her face. He did the same to me, holding my hand firmly as he gently tugged me through the opening into the house.

When he let go of my hand, shut the door, and squeezed past me, his smiling face was a little too close for comfort.

I had to admit it, he was a handsome man. In his late fifties or early sixties, he was tall with broad shoulders, a full head of salt-and-pepper hair, a slim waist. I don't think there was an ounce of extra fat on his body. He was wearing a white button-down shirt with cuff links and a pale blue tie. We'd obviously caught him as he was about to leave.

"Please, won't you come on through and sit down. What's this all about?" he asked, leading the way down a long narrow hallway to what was obviously a sitting room where he stopped, turned and waved us on through into the room, leaning a little closer to Janet as she passed. It was as if he was trying to sniff her hair.

The room was quite small compared to those in the grand penthouses belonging to the Chestertons. It was also more homey, more comfortable. The dark leather furniture was soft and complemented the antique feel of the home. To the left, a window overlooked the street; to the right a wall covered with framed photographs of Sam with various politicians, sports stars, the Dallas Cowboy cheerleaders, and even one with a Miss America contestant. It was, in fact, a bachelor pad.

"I'm afraid I have bad news," I said, taking a seat opposite Wheaton as he sat down on the large leather couch — Janet remained standing. "I'm afraid your employer's granddaughter-in-law is... I'm afraid she's dead."

The news didn't seem to shake him very much.

He frowned. "You mean Genevieve?"

"Yes," Janet replied. "Genevieve. She was found on the Riverwalk early on Saturday morning. She was strangled to death."

I watched my sergeant look at Uncle Sam a little longer than necessary when she replied and then walk over to admire the wall of photos.

"I see," he replied, quietly, his face now a mask. "How can I help?"

I nodded, turned on the recording app on my iPad and said, "Mr. Wheaton, if you don't mind, I'd like to record our conversation. It's so much easier than taking notes."

"Yes, whatever you like. Go ahead."

"How well do you know the Chestertons?" I asked.

Wheaton was silent for a moment, staring down at his hands, then he looked up and described his lifelong friendship with the senior Chesterton. He described the family as tight-knit. He talked about what a great man Chesterton was, how he'd provided for his family, all of them, and how he expected them all to wear the Chesterton name with pride. If they didn't, they could kiss their inheritance goodbye and go off on their own; no one ever did.

"But you're not a Chesterton, are you, sir?" I asked. "How does he treat you?"

He smiled, somewhat modestly, I thought, then said,

"Well, I must admit that I'm more than a little blessed. He treats me like family; they all do. They call me Uncle Sam. Kind of corny, I know, but it stuck. I attend all the family functions, the get-togethers and all of the company board meetings. I handle most of Edward's financial affairs."

"When you say Edward, you mean the senior Mr. Chesterton, correct?"

"Yes, that's right. Why don't we call him Grandfather? It's much easier."

I nodded, then said, "How well did you know Genevieve?"

"Everyone in the family knows Genevieve," he said. "By the way, can I get you anything, some coffee, perhaps?"

I declined for both of us.

He tilted his head to one side, closed his eyes, smiled, opened them again and said, "The girl was a breath of fresh air. I wouldn't say this to anyone else, but I thought she was the best thing to ever happen to Eddie."

"How so?" Janet asked, still staring at the photographs on the wall. She was standing with her back to him, arms folded, legs slightly apart.

He glanced round at her, his eyes lingering on her backside a little longer than perhaps they should have.

Is she doing that on purpose? I wondered.

"He was a playboy," Wheaton replied. "But I guess it would be hard not to be when you're getting an allowance of almost twenty-five thousand dollars a month... He's no great catch, you know, besides the money, that is. He's not a handsome man, not like his father, or grandfather; he's something of a throwback, I think. I don't think, even in his wildest dreams, would he have seen himself marrying a beauty like her. Hell," he said and looked sideways at Janet, who was now facing him, "I'd have sacrificed my inheritance for that, too."

"You don't really mean that, Mr. Wheaton... do you?" Janet asked, looking back over her shoulder at him.

Oh, that's a little over the top, Janet, I thought, but he didn't seem to notice, though I did see the look of interest he gave her.

"For that?" I asked. "What do you mean, *that?*" Of course, I knew exactly what he meant, but I wanted to hear him explain it. Could there have been anything between them? Had he given it the good old college try... had she? His answers, so I hoped, might give him away.

"Look," he said, leaning forward, his elbows on his knees, hands clasped together in front of him, "Genevieve was all woman, a real woman in every sense of the word, and that didn't go down well with the belles in the Chesterton family, or the rest of their upper-class, snobby friends. She was unconventional. Traditions and routines weren't her style, meant nothing to her. She was a free spirit. I liked her."

A free spirit? How many times have I heard that today?

"Did you have any dealings with her that were... let's say, more than just familial?" I asked.

He turned and looked at Janet then back at me and chuckled.

"No. I didn't, but if the opportunity had arisen, I wouldn't have said no."

He chuckled again, glanced again at Janet; she smiled sheepishly at him.

"Look, Genevieve was a player, a manipulator. She knew exactly what she was doing. Every time she walked into a room, she was the center of attention, and she loved it.

It didn't matter if they hated her or loved her, she played it like a pro."

He paused, looked hard at me, then said, "Genevieve was no angel, Detective. Let's face it. Most women who come from her side of the tracks aren't. She could smell money a mile away and everyone knew it. I'm not saying she deserved to die; she didn't, but you can only tease a dog for so long before it bites."

"What on earth is that supposed to mean?" I asked. "Are you saying you believe she was murdered by a member of the family?"

He shrugged, smiled enigmatically, and said, "I'm afraid that's your job, Captain.

"Did you know she was black?" I asked quietly.

The man looked at me like I'd just slapped him.

"What? Are you kidding me?"

"Absolutely not. The medical examiner has confirmed her ethnicity."

"Lordy, Lordy, I had no idea." He chuckled. "I bet Regina Mae loved to hear that."

"Why do you say that?" I asked.

"Uhm, you *are* familiar with our Southern heritage, are you not? Very little has changed among the great Southern families. The old traditions, the old antebellum ways are as deeply rooted in this part of the country and, of course, the Chestertons. I never heard any mention of her being of African American ancestry, and if anyone would have known, it would have been me."

"So," I said, "being all-knowing, as you seem to imply, do you know of anyone in the family that might have wanted to do her harm... or made unwanted advances?"

"Since no one knew she was black, I'd say you can take your pick from anyone that had a penis." He chortled. "I'd even say there might be a few ladies in the mix who had unrequited feelings for her. The Chesterton family is big and not nearly as prim and proper as they'd have you believe."

"You saw her flirting with other men besides her husband?" I asked.

"Let's just say I saw her using the gifts God gave her to get what she wanted. Whether it was the last slice of peach pie or the keys to a new sports car, she never had to ask twice," Wheaton replied.

"Where were you the night before last, Mr. Wheaton, between two and three a.m.?" I asked.

Janet, continuing to wander around the room, her hands clasped behind her back, lingering at each picture, seemingly studying everything, didn't see the change in Wheaton's expression.

"That's an easy one," he said. "I was... shall we say... visiting with a lady friend. I stayed the night at her place."

He smiled, tilted his head slightly to one side, and his eyes twinkled devilishly as he turned and looked at Janet. There was no mistaking it: he was interested in her.

"I'll need to talk to her, your friend," I said. "Would you mind giving me her name and phone number?"

"Of course not. No problem. I'm sure she'll be happy to tell you all about our evening together, but I must ask you to be discrete. She has her reputation to uphold."

"I'm sure she does," I said, dryly. "Does she know the Chestertons?"

"Who in Tennessee doesn't?" Wheaton replied, looking again at Janet.

"That's not what I meant, Mr. Wheaton. I meant does she *know* them, on a personal level."

"Yes, she knows Regina Mae quite well, and her

husband, which is one of the reasons I asked you to be discreet."

"Right," I said. "So, the name and phone number, please?"

He gave them to me, somewhat reluctantly, I thought. I made a note of them and continued.

"You have something of a reputation yourself," I said. "Is that not so, Mr. Wheaton?"

"I'm... not sure what you mean, Detective."

"Oh, I think you do. Let me ask you this: why did Mr. Chesterton cover up the sexual harassment complaints against you? They were, I believe, settled without publicity. How, exactly did you pull that off?" I watched the smile drop from his face. Behind me, I heard Janet's sharp intake of breath.

I didn't really want to know, but I was getting tired of his holier-than-thou attitude, so I figured I'd drop the bomb and watch his reaction.

He looked at me without speaking for what seemed a long moment, obviously taken aback, and then scoffed, "That was a long time ago, Detective. I was young and stupid, stepped over the line. I was already working for Edward and I... He... Well, it's all ancient history now and has nothing to do with Genevieve, so please, let's move on." He licked his lips.

"You stepped over the line?" I asked, skeptically. "That, I think, is sugarcoating it a little. Isn't it also true that the old man settled several paternity suits for you?'

"Two, there were two. Both children were adopted, went to very good families... Where the hell are you going with this, Detective? So I screwed up a couple of times when I was a kid. Who the hell doesn't? It was not a big deal."

"For you," I said with an attitude. "I'm sure it wasn't. For the women... well."

I looked him in the eye and continued, "Where am I going with it? Old habits die hard, Mr. Wheaton, so they say and..." I paused, then dropped another one on him. "Did you know that Genevieve was pregnant?"

He looked like I'd punched him in the gut.

He swallowed hard, then barely whispered, "No. No, I didn't."

Don't let up, Kate. Hit him again.

"Were you having an affair with Genevieve, Mr. Wheaton? Did you get her pregnant and then turn again to your best friend and confidant Edward Chesterton to help you one more time? It would, after all, be"—I made air quotes—"'no big deal,' would it, especially if everyone in the family, including the old man, thought Genevieve was a slut? Did... he... have her killed, Mr. Wheaton?"

It was at that point that Janet jumped in.

"I think that's a little out of line, Captain—"

I smiled inwardly as I interrupted her. "Excuse me, Sergeant? What did you say?"

She shrugged, then said, "I'm sorry, it's just that... well, I'm sorry."

Wheaton looked at her like she was dipped in chocolate. When he looked back at me his expression had hardened, his eyes narrowed, lips drawn tight. Yep, he was pissed. I decided to give him a pass.

I nodded and said, "Mr. Wheaton, I think she was killed by someone she knew, so I'll ask you again, can you think of anyone in the Chesterton family who might want to hurt Genevieve?"

I changed my tone, softened it to one bordering on sympathy. "Look, that baby is, I think, pivotal to my investigation. Edward Chesterton, either one of them, second, or third, would not have been happy about the possibility of her giving birth to a black grandchild, now would they?"

"Are you out of your mind, Captain?" he snapped. "Edward Chesterton is a saint, a great man. I wouldn't be where I am today if it wasn't for him."

"No, you'd probably be in jail or broke and up to your ears in child support. He saved you from yourself more than once. Why wouldn't he do it again?"

This time, I'd gotten to him. He was barely keeping his rage under control.

"Captain," Janet said, very quietly. "I think we've bothered Mr. Wheaton enough. It's time we left, I think."

She was standing with her back to the mantelpiece. I looked up at her. So did Wheaton. She looked back at me, defiantly, and again I had to smile to myself.

"Maybe you're right," I said, and nodded as if I was tired, trying to look defeated.

"Mr. Wheaton," I said, standing up. "Thank you for your time. We'll be in touch." And, without another word I walked out of the room, leaving Janet there to make apologies and excuses for me.

Just as I got to the front door and was about to open it, I heard her let out a quick laugh and then silence. I let myself out and waited for her on the front porch; she appeared a few minutes later.

"Okay," I muttered as we walked back to the car, our heads down. We had to keep the act going in case he was watching us from the window. "Spill it, Janet. I am dying to know what he said to you."

"Oh, that guy is a pussy cat," she said. "When you left the room, I handed him one of my business cards and told him that if he thought of anything else, he could give me a call. Then I told him that if he ever felt he needed someone to talk to, I'd be happy to listen."

"That's all it took?" I said, smiling.

"Yup! 'Oh, I'd like that,' he said. 'I'd like to talk. And then maybe we could have dinner or something.' I had to laugh. You heard me, right?"

"Yes, I heard you. Wow. He doesn't waste any time, does he?"

I put the car in drive and headed back toward Amnicola Highway and the PD. The sky was an ominous dull gray blanket so low it shrouded the peak of Lookout Mountain and offered a promise of imminent rain.

"I bet I hear from him before the end of the day," Janet said.

"Okay, but just be careful if you decide to meet with him. Make sure it's in a public place and don't let your guard down. We'll check his alibi, but I don't get the feeling he's a murderer," I said.

"You don't?" Janet said, her eyes wide.

"No... No, I don't. Do you?"

"I don't know... maybe. He reminds me of a guy I busted back when I was in uniform. He was a real smooth talker, dressed nice, smelled good. At first glance he could be a suit right out of the nearest bank, harmless, right?" She shook her head slowly. "Turned out the guy was a serial date rapist. I believe that he actually thought, even as I was putting the cuffs on him, that he could sweet-talk his way out of it. I get the same kind of vibe from Samuel Wheaton. I believe he could be... I dunno, overpowering? Yes, that's it, overpowering, literally."

"Before you go to meet him anywhere," I said, "you let me know where you are going and when. I'll have an off-duty officer keep an eye on you."

"You don't think I can take care of myself?" Janet looked hurt.

I grinned at her as I pulled the car into my designated space at the rear of the PD.

"What do you think?" I asked.

Janet simply smiled, took her right foot off the dashboard, unfolded her arms, and opened the car door.

"Never mind what I think, Cap. It's what you think that matters, right?"

"Damn right!" I said as we walked together into the PD.

11

W e walked into the PD and Janet promptly disappeared, said she had to follow-up on her leads and would get back with me as soon as she had something to report. That was fine with me. There was a lot of chatter and a lot of information to digest, and it was barely eleven o'clock in the morning. We weren't scheduled to meet again until two-thirty that afternoon, so I figured I had at least a couple of hours to myself to think things through. That being so, I headed across the road to get a decent cup of coffee, and fifteen minutes later, I was back in my office ready to begin, but it was not to be.

No sooner had I sat down at my desk when Janet burst into my office, followed by Lenny Miller. She was wild-eyed, flustered, excited, all at the same time, waving her yellow notebook like she'd just discovered a cure for cancer.

I leaned back in my chair and stared up at her. "Okay, tell me. What did you find?" I asked, waving for her to shut the door.

"You aren't going to believe this, Kate," she said excitedly.

Only rarely did she ever call me that, so I knew immediately that she'd discovered something significant.

"I'm going to let Lenny tell you. He found it. It was shock enough that Genevieve was black, but... Go on, Lenny, tell her."

"Sit down, both of you," I said, and they did.

"Now," I said, "Lenny?"

"Well, I did as you asked. I did a little digging into Genevieve's past. It turns out that not only was she black, but she also has a family."

He flipped through several screens on his iPad and then began to read from his notes.

"Her real name is Naomi Washington, not Genevieve, nor Bluford. And her parents, Benjamin and Alisha Washington are alive and well in Baton Rouge, Louisiana. She also has a brother, Nathan Watkins."

Janet smiled at me and said, "You see what I mean? I've read several news and magazine articles that quoted Genevieve directly, saying that she had no family and was a 'pull-yourself-up-by-your-bootstraps' story of survival. She fell in love with a literal heir to the throne and they were supposed to live happily ever after. And then she was murdered. I'm sorry, Cap, but the suspect pool just got a little deeper."

Did it ever. I looked at the two of them, then shook my head. Now, not only was this case not going to be closed quickly, but I was going to have to ask for permission to go down to Baton Rouge to question the family. Chief Johnston was not going to be happy. He didn't part with department funds easily.

The case was beginning to frustrate me. I'd already interviewed three people, all of whom, to put it mildly, had an issue with Genevieve for one reason or another, but in common all three couldn't forgive that she was from "the wrong side of the tracks." I had a prime suspect, maybe two —Eddie and Wheaton—but without any direct evidence they were, both of them, tenuous at best.

Lenny continued to fill me in on the life and times of Naomi Washington AKA Genevieve Bluford-Chesterton, and it turned out she really did come from the wrong side of the tracks, street actually. She'd attended predominantly black schools from kindergarten through high school graduation. She'd briefly attended BRCC—Baton Rouge Community College—on a Pell grant and a small student loan but had dropped out after only fifteen months.

She'd worked as a waitress during her time in college, and then as a salesclerk at one of the mall department stores. Her financial creditworthiness, though, was never in doubt. From the day she began work, while she was still in college, she'd saved her money. Other than the student loan, which she paid off in six months, she'd never been in debt. At the time of her move from Louisiana, she was not quite twenty-four years old and had a little over twenty thousand dollars in savings and twenty-four hundred in checking.

She and Eddie were married a year later. She was two months past her twenty-sixth birthday when Cole Meredith found her body on the Riverwalk.

It was a sad, sad story of a promising young life snuffed out on a whim. Some evil son of a bitch had decided —and I had no doubt about it—that because of her color and her infiltration into one of the most influential families in Tennessee, she no longer deserved to live. And, when I thought about it like that, I became angry, very angry. So angry I could see nothing but that poor girl fighting for her life on the dark walkway, knowing all the time that it was futile.

Lenny stopped talking. Janet said nothing. I was temporarily out of it. I was leaned back in my chair, my eyes closed, a silent observer of the events that night on the banks of the Tennessee. All I could see was Genevieve, bent half over backward, clawing at the garrote as the indistinguishable shadow twisted his fists against her neck, pulling it tighter, tighter, tighter...

"Cap?" Janet's voice jerked me violently back into the present.

"Yeah... yeah, what?"

"What now?" she asked.

"What now, indeed?" I said, trying to pull myself together. What had just happened to me was a first. Never had I been transported into... Even now, I don't even know what to call it. A window to the past? A stupid vision? I don't know.

"I'm going to Baton Rouge," I said. "I need to interview the family. I'll need to talk to the chief first. I know he's not going to like it. Still, I don't see how he has a choice, not considering who the victim is."

I stood up and walked around my desk. "Lenny, thank you. Great job. Now go see what else you can dig up." And he left the room.

"Janet," I said. "Bring your notes and come on."

Chief Johnston was in an unusually good mood that morning. Cathy, his secretary, ushered us straight into his inner sanctum. He rose from behind his desk to greet us with a thin, though somewhat intimidating smile on his lips.

He came around his desk and extended a hand to Janet. "How is Captain Gazzara treating you, Detective?" he asked.

"Oh, terrific, sir. We're working on a humdinger right now," Janet said enthusiastically.

"So I understand," he said, turning to me, his hand extended.

I shook it.

"Please, sit, both of you," he said. "You have an update for me, Catherine?" he asked, returning to his chair.

I brought him up to date with the investigation, told him about the victim, my interviews with the Chesterton family, and the revelations concerning Genevieve's hitherto unknown family.

"So," I said finally, "I need to go to Baton Rouge and interview her family."

Wait for it, Kate, I thought, expecting him to argue about budgetary nonsense, but he didn't.

"Well, you'd better get going then," he said. "It goes without saying that this is a high-profile case, and we need to wrap it up quickly and discreetly. This is no time to argue over a couple of dollars the budget isn't going to miss." He looked hard at me. "You'll go on your own, though, and I don't have to tell you: no expensive dinners or visits to the spa."

"I'll be sure to cross those off my to-do list, Chief." I smiled at him, nodded and continued, "I'll leave this afternoon and be back as soon as possible, a couple of days at most."

"You'll keep in touch; daily updates," Johnston said. "You have my cell phone number. If there's anything you need, don't hesitate to call."

"Of course, sir," I replied.

"That will be all, Captain, and good luck."

"Thank you, sir," I said.

I stood quickly and left his office. Janet followed behind me excitedly.

"Anything special you want me to do while you're gone, Cap?" she asked.

"Just keep your phone on. Take your lead from Hawk; he has a world of experience and you can learn from him. And don't forget what I said about Sam Wheaton. If he calls and wants to meet... Never mind, I'll talk to Hawk myself. If he does call, you bring Hawk in, understood?"

She didn't look at all happy about what I'd said.

"I don't think that's necess—"

"It's not up for discussion, Janet," I snapped, interrupting her. "The man is a prime suspect in a murder investigation, and he has a history of sexual abuse; he's a predator. You will *not* disobey my order. Understood?"

She heaved a huge sigh, looked up at me, her eyes wide, and said, quietly, "Understood, Captain."

I could tell she was disappointed, but it was for her own good. She had just enough experience, and more than enough self-confidence to get herself into a world of trouble.

I booked a seat on the afternoon flight out of Lovell Field to Nashville, spent an hour debriefing Hawk, Anne, and Lenny, then I took Hawk aside and briefed him about my upcoming trip and the admittedly half-assed plan for Janet to get inside Sam Wheaton's head. He didn't like the idea at all. In fact, he argued strenuously against it. In the end, however, he reluctantly agreed to keep an eye on my enthusiastic but potentially wayward sergeant.

Finally, not feeling at all confident that Janet would play by the rules, I left Hawk in charge, headed home, packed an overnight bag, and drove to the airport. Two hours later, I was on a Southwest Airlines plane out of Nashville heading to Baton Rouge, Louisiana.

12

The plane landed in Baton Rouge right on time, and I was able to get to my rental car without a hitch. The sun was already setting by the time I got to my hotel, a bare-bones place, but it had room service and a minibar.

I showered, dressed in my PJ's, ordered a burger with fries, cracked open an overpriced bottle of red wine, spread my files out on the bed, pulled up a chair and began to read.

Naomi Washington AKA Genevieve Bluford Chesterton came from a lower-class neighborhood of Baton Rouge, not a ghetto, but not Nob Hill either.

According to the information Lenny had provided, Genevieve had barely squeaked by in high school and not at all in college. She didn't have a criminal record, but she was known to associate with some individuals who did.

"Same old story," I said to myself as I continued to read through the profile. *How many of these kids go astray simply because of where they live, or the school they attend?* I wondered.

Actually, living as I did in Chattanooga, I had a pretty

good idea: you only have to drive around the projects, any time of day or night, to find out. They're out there for all to see: pushers, addicts, pimps, prostitutes, gangbangers, most of them barely old enough to drive, much less drink a beer.

It seemed, though, that our girl had managed to rise above the temptations of the simple life. She'd worked hard, saved her money, and gotten out of town.

According to Lenny's research, the last time Genevieve had lived at her parent's address was in January 2017. Her mother and father seemed to be good folks. Both were gainfully employed and, apart from a mortgage and a small car payment, were debt free. There was nothing in the file about the son, Genevieve's brother, Nathan, and I wondered why.

Damn it. Tim wouldn't have left a gap like that.

It was then that another horrible thought struck me. *Holy crap! I bet they don't even know what's happened to their daughter.*

"Why would they?" I said to my empty room.

No one in Chattanooga knew who the hell Genevieve really was, so the family wouldn't have—couldn't have— been notified. And I guarantee no one in Baton Rouge has any knowledge of her other life.

I suddenly felt weary beyond words. If there's one job a cop, any cop, hates, it's having to give the parents the news their child is dead, and now I was going to have to do it for the... oh hell, I lost count so long ago I've no idea how many times. Why didn't I think of it before?

Well okay then, I thought, sadly. *That's just how it has to be.*

I closed the file. It was slim, and I'd read it through from cover to cover. There was nothing in it that would make my job any easier, or less painful for them or for me... and I wished I'd handed Naomi Washington's family over to Janet to interview... Nah, not really.

I lay the folder on the nightstand next to the bed just as my food arrived, but somehow, I just wasn't that hungry anymore.

I set my iPhone alarm for five-thirty, crawled into bed, turned off the light, and closed my eyes, the burger and fries uneaten.

13

I woke up with a headache at three-thirty that morning not knowing where the hell I was, and no, it wasn't because of the wine. That twelve-dollar bottle held only a single glass. So I tossed and turned the rest of the night, lost in a half-world between dreams and reality populated with visions of me telling the Washingtons their daughter was dead.

I lay there sweating. The air conditioner wasn't working worth a damn, so it must have been eighty degrees or more in that hotel room.

Why I was having so much trouble with the idea of telling them was a mystery to me. I'd done it before, hundreds of times and it never got any easier, but this time it was different... And then it dawned on me.

Oh geez! It's the baby.

You see, I just couldn't imagine receiving another response like the one I'd gotten from Regina Mae when I gave her the news. If it happened again, I'd probably slap one or both of them. With that thought and a smile on my lips, I closed my eyes again and fell into a deep sleep only to be awakened some thirty minutes later by the strident voice of Bobby McFerrin urging me, "Don't Worry, Be Happy." It was five-thirty and I felt like sh—

Fortunately, I didn't feel like that for long. I took a long hot shower, washed my hair, and dried it with a piece of blue and white electric junk I found in one of the bathroom cupboards. Then I dressed in my second-best pair of jeans and a clean white blouse, hitched my Glock and badge to my belt, slipped into my signature tan leather jacket, and headed out across the road to the Waffle House. There I blew a week's calories on a heart-attack breakfast, but oh how good it was; and oh how guilty I felt.

Then, feeling ready to face the day, I entered the Washington's address into the GPS app on my iPhone and drove my rental car to the address in the Garden District.

The neighborhood was much as I expected it to be, quiet, older homes but, for the most part, the streets were clean and tidy as were the white frame houses. The lawns were neatly trimmed and the paint on the homes fresh and bright. The only indication that all was not quite as safe in the neighborhood as it might be were the black bars on the front doors and basement windows of many of the homes.

I found the house I was looking for, just one small, single-story home on a long street of 1930-something look-alikes. I pulled into the driveway and noticed the curtains of the next-door neighbor's house twitch and then part just enough to reveal a pair of dark, curious eyes. The curtains closed as soon as the owner of the eyes realized he or she had been spotted, and I smiled to myself as I turned off the engine and put the car in park.

"Here we go," I muttered, as I slammed the car door and walked to the steps and up to the front porch.

While the little home was nice enough, it was a far cry

from what Genevieve must have gotten used to, a world of difference from Eddie's and Regina Mae's homes.

The windows were tightly closed, the drapes too, and I could hear the air-conditioning unit at the left side of the house running. I took my creds from my jacket pocket and knocked on the front door.

"Who's that outside this early in the morning?" a male voice said.

I looked at my watch. It wasn't quite eight-thirty.

"How should I know? Go see," a female voice said.

"Not me. I gotta finish gettin' ready to go to work. You go."

I heaved a sigh and knocked again. I already had a headache coming on behind my right eyeball.

The door opened a crack.

"Can I help you?"

I flashed my credentials and introduced myself.

"Are you Alisha Washington?" I asked.

The door opened wide enough to reveal a once-lovely white woman, an older version of Genevieve except she had a front tooth missing.

She must have been something back in the day.

"Yes." She had an attitude and didn't look happy that the police, any police, let alone police from Chattanooga were knocking on her door. "Chattanooga? You far from home, lady. What you want?"

"Mrs. Washington, I have some news about your daughter. May I come in?"

Alisha Washington looked at me suspiciously. Then she looked up and down the street, nodded, snapped open two deadbolts on the barred screen door, pushed it open, leaned out and looked up and down the street again before stepping back into the house and holding the door open for me.

"Listen to me, woman," she said as she led the way into the darkened living room. "I don't care what that girl has done. She's over eighteen, and she ain't my responsibility no more."

There was a faint smell of marijuana in the living room, but it wasn't that strong. The place was tidy with mismatched furniture and a huge flat-screen television in the center of the wall facing the heavily draped window.

It was at that moment that a huge man in a suit and tie with coffee-colored skin appeared from the hallway. He stood stock-still, staring at me intensely.

"You must be Mr. Washington," I said. "If you have a minute, what I have to tell you concerns you both."

He just nodded, said nothing.

"Yes. What is it, then?" Alisha said.

I took a deep breath and said, "I think you'd both better sit down."

She looked at me curiously; he continued to stare at me. They sat down together on an obviously quite new sofa opposite the TV and stared up at me.

"May I sit down too?" I asked.

They both nodded as one.

"Mr. and Mrs. Washington, I'm afraid I have bad news: your daughter, Naomi, is dead. She was murdered four nights ago."

For a moment, the news seemed to just hang in the air as they both stared at me. I had the strangest feeling Alisha was waiting for me to continue.

"Mrs. Washington, are you all right?" I asked.

Very slowly, she began to shake her head.

"No... How, where?" she whispered, now holding her husband's hand in both of hers.

"In Chattanooga," I said, quietly. "She was... We think

she must have been to a party. She"—I didn't want to say *her body* or the word *strangled*—"was discovered beside the river by a dog-walker." I waited. "I'm sorry to have to tell you that she was seven weeks pregnant."

Mrs. Washington nodded as tears filled her eyes. But they didn't spill over. She sniffled a little, jerked her head back, turned her head to look at the man sitting beside her, let out a deep breath, and licked her lips. The man still hadn't said a word, but I could tell that the news had hit him hard, harder than his wife, perhaps. His eyes were glistening, and his lips were trembling.

She laid her head on his massive shoulder, still holding his hand in both of hers, only now his other hand was on top of hers.

"Have you caught him, the man who killed her?" His deep voice reminded me of James Earl Jones.

"No, not yet, but we will."

He nodded, looked up at the ceiling, and whispered, "Yes, I bet you will."

I didn't know if he meant it or if he was being sarcastic. My bet was on the latter.

Sheesh, I need to move this along.

"I know this is a really bad time but, if you could... I have some questions that only you can answer."

He sighed, nodded and said, "I'm Benjamin Washington." The attitude seeped out of him like air from a punctured tire.

"I'm supposed to be at work," he said. "I'll call and tell them I won't be in today. They'll understand. I'll do it in a minute."

He squeezed his wife's hands, then let her go and put both arms around her and pulled her to him; she sobbed silently into his shoulder.

"Please," he said. "Ask your questions."

I nodded, opened my iPad, and asked their permission to record the interview. They gave it readily.

"How long have you been married?" I asked, looking at the man—her face was still buried in his shoulder; her shoulders shaking. She was obviously crying.

"We're not actually married," he said softly. "Didn't see no need to."

I nodded.

"We've been together for almost thirty years." He stroked the back of Alisha's head, gently smoothing her graying hair.

"How old was Naomi when she left home?" I asked.

"She left in 2017. She was twenty-four."

"Did she visit often?" I asked.

"No," he said. "Just at Christmas, usually to flaunt her new things. She'd drop off her bags, then run off to visit her friends... Some friends... She didn't even spend the night with us. Then, when she'd had enough, she'd kiss us goodbye and head off back to Chattanooga."

"We saw her one Easter," Alisha said. "Ain't that right, Ben?"

She looked up at him; he slowly nodded his head.

"Did you know she'd changed her name, and that she was married?" I asked.

"No," Alisha said, sitting up and wiping her eyes. She pressed her lips together, then shook her head. "But that don't surprise me. That girl!"

"We ain't rich, Detective, but we're honest," Benjamin Washington said, "and I'll tell you, I had some wild days in my youth, but I show up at work every day. And Alisha, she works at the church, has for almost ten years. But that girl, she something else."

I looked at Alisha, but she didn't offer any further information.

"What was she like?" I asked.

"Like? She was like..." Mrs. Washington shook her head. "Detective, Naomi... she beautiful outside, ugly inside; broke my heart, but I loved her. My daughter... she hated it here, was ashamed of where she come from. I don't know why, considering she ran with every local punk in town. I took her to church with me. I tried to get her to have a little God in her life. It wasn't no use. A mother should never say this, but I was ashamed of how she turned out. I didn't raise her to be like that."

"What do you mean?" I asked.

"What do you think I mean? She was a hood rat if ever there was one. She liked them bad boys who wear their colors and flash their hand signals, making themselves look like they having some kind of palsy fit."

Alisha had obviously spent a lot of time in the hood herself. Her accent was thick and seemed to me to clash with her lily-white skin.

"When was the last time she visited?" I asked.

"Last time she was here?" Alisha said. "Christmas, five months ago."

"And she didn't tell you she was married?"

"Lord, no she didn't tell me she was married," Alisha said. She said it like it was the last thing on earth her daughter would tell her. "I can only imagine the kind of man she told 'I do' to. Was it him what killed her? Who she marry anyway?"

"His name is Edward Chesterton. She married him under the name of Genevieve Bluford, which is why we had such a hard time finding you folks. I don't know if he killed her. The investigation is ongoing, so I can't tell you very much. What I can tell you is that he's very well-off, and he comes from a long line of old money. I'm not sure how much he knew about Naomi; probably not much, since she'd changed her identity. None of his family knew she was black. Did you know she was passing herself off as white?"

"No, but it don't surprise me none," she said, shaking her head. "We had some terrible fights about her color. She hated her father because he was black." She turned her head to look up at him fondly. "He isn't perfect, not by a long way, but he was a good daddy to her and Nathan. When she told us she was leaving, he gave her two hundred dollars so she could buy some clothes as soon as she got to Chattanooga." She chuckled bitterly.

Me? I didn't have the heart to tell her about Genevieve's bank account.

"He was good enough for her to take his money, but he wasn't good enough to keep her daddy's name, take pride in her family. Wasn't good enough to accept that she was black."

I nodded, thinking how Genevieve and Eddie were slowly being revealed as a match made in hell. He knew what to do and how to do it, to upset his family and, in her own way, she was no different.

I scribbled my thoughts in my pocket notebook then looked up. Alisha had taken Benjamin's hand in hers. It was also an unusual fact that Benjamin and Alisha Washington had been together for both of their children—a rarity in the black community. Studies have proven that children who grow up with both parents tend to succeed in life. Naomi certainly did; she married a millionaire. But someone—*hell, everyone*—wasn't happy about it.

Hmm, I wonder if Nathan did as well as she did. I doubt it.

"Can I offer you something to drink, Detective, tea or water?" Benjamin asked.

I shook my head and said, "No, but thank you."

"We haven't heard from Nathan either," Alisha said.

She must have been reading my thoughts.

"He ain't nothing like Naomi. He's a good boy. We thought that if he went to Chattanooga with Naomi, he might be able to keep an eye on her," Alisha said.

She let go of her husband's hands, looked down at her own hands, and worried a hangnail as she spoke.

"Nathan is your son?" I asked.

"He's Naomi's half-brother. I had him just a year before I met Benjamin. That boy was a joy from the minute he come into the world."

She chewed her lip thoughtfully. The thin lines that were her eyebrows pinched together in the middle as she continued.

"He and Naomi grew up best friends, but then she got a taste for hoodlums and her brother didn't like that. She tried to balance the two, but those thugs don't like family. They didn't like Nathan, who just wanted to go to work and come home and play his video games."

"He loved his video games." Benjamin chuckled.

"He sure did," Alisha said. "Nathan Watkins. That's his real daddy's last name. Although he grew up with Benjamin as his daddy. That's why he turned out so good." A tear rolled down her cheek.

"Do you have Nathan's address, Mrs. Washington? I'd like to talk to him. If he was keeping an eye on his sister, maybe he'll have some idea of what happened to her." This was a promising lead.

"Yes. Ben, get that card on the fridge with Nate's address on it."

He squeezed her shoulder, rose, and walked into the kitchen.

"Detective Gazzara, can I ask you a question?" Alisha continued to worry the hangnail on her finger.

"Of course."

"Did she suffer, my Naomi? Was she in a lot of pain when she died?" she asked, holding her breath as she waited for me to answer.

"No," I lied.

Naomi/Genevieve knew what was happening to her. I was sure of that. I was also sure that the pain must have been excruciating... I thought about those two thin ligature marks around her neck and the bruises where the killer's knuckles had dug into her flesh as he pulled and... I could only imagine the terror she must have experienced as she clawed at the ligature as the life was slowly squeezed from her body. Oh yes, I knew, but I couldn't tell her mother, not then.

"Thank God," she whispered, and I felt like shit for lying to her. "My poor baby... And I would have been a grandma." Her bottom lip quivered.

Benjamin reappeared with a small card. He must have heard because his eyes were filled with tears.

"Here you go," he said, handing it to me.

I took the card, made a note of the information in my pad, and handed it back to him.

"I have one more question to ask," I said. "Do you know of anyone in Naomi's past that might have wanted to hurt her? You said that she was involved with some bad people. Did she break up with one of those thugs... or maybe knew something that could have cost her her life?"

Alisha looked me in the eye and said, "Yes, ma'am. Could be all that, and then some. I don't know none of their names. They a raggedy-ass bunch, all dress alike with their bandanas and do-rags and pants hanging below the cracks of their asses. I don't know if she crossed one of them bangers. If she did, I don't know about it. Best it stay that way too. We still gotta live here."

I'd heard that before, so many times, and it made me furious. I knew theirs was a difficult situation, but not unusual.

"I understand," I said and took out a business card and handed it to Benjamin. "If you think of anything, even if you think it is unimportant, please, give me a call anytime day or night. And... if you need help, I'll do my best for you."

"Can we see her, Naomi? Can we come to her funeral?" Alisha asked.

"Yes, of course," I said, wondering how the Chesterton family would react when they met their in-laws.

Sheesh, I'd like to be there for that one.

"It may be a while before we can release the... release her to the family for a funeral, but you're welcome to come and see her whenever you like."

She looked at her husband. He said nothing, just nodded, as if to say, "whatever you think is best."

"Can I think about it for a few days and then call you?" she asked.

"Of course, anytime."

"And if you find our boy," she said, her eyes wide, plead-ing, "tell him to call home. I just want to make sure he's okay, too."

"I'll do that. I promise. By the way, do you have a recent photo of him I could borrow?"

"Not recent, no. Just an old school photo. He doesn't like having his photo taken." She went to the sideboard, opened one of the drawers, and then handed me a five-by-seven photo of a grinning kid. "He'd just turned sixteen when that was taken," she said.

I stood and extended my hand. Alisha took it in both of hers and squeezed it hard. Benjamin did the same, and I left them. I stepped out into the warm air, felt the small hairs on the back of my neck begin to rise. I stood on the porch, my back to the door and looked across the street, then to my left then my right. All was quiet... no, all seemed eerily still. Suddenly, I had the feeling I was being watched.

Faintly, even through the closed door, I could hear Alisha sobbing and Benjamin's deep voice.

"Let us pray for her, Alisha. Let us pray that she's in a better place."

"My baby. My poor baby," Alisha cried quietly.

There was a moment of silence, and then he began, "Dear Lord, we pray that you have taken our beloved daughter into your keeping and..."

That was a first for me, and I could listen no more.

I went quickly to my car and drove back to the hotel, stopping only to pick up a large coffee.

Once again I needed to think, to focus. One thing I knew for sure was that I needed to call Janet and have Lenny do a full background check on Nathan Watkins. And that was where I was stuck. It was not yet ten-thirty and I was exhausted, my stomach was growling. I was hungry and needing a break to eat, think, and regroup.

I'd just parked the car outside the hotel and was about to get out, when I changed my mind. Instead, I reversed back out and then swung out onto the highway, looking for a "nice" restaurant where I could eat a second breakfast. I felt... I dunno, washed up, drained... whatever. Anyway, I didn't call Janet until I left for the airport a couple of hours later.

I'd felt like that before. It was all to do with the duty I'd just performed. It always left me feeling a little less than human and, as I drove, I recalled the last time I'd done such duty. Less than a month ago, I'd had to inform a mother her son was dead. He died from an overdose of heroin. Oh yeah, he was just a junkie, and we cops all knew him well. "Just a junkie?" How's that for inhumane?

How many times had I or someone else told him, "that shit will kill you"? Too many to count, but it didn't stop him. Some other kid found him lying in a front yard, dead. The kid's mother called 911, and I caught the case. All suspicious deaths are treated as homicides until proven different, but I knew what it was. I didn't have to, but I took it upon myself to tell his folks... his single-parent mother. The kid had just had his nineteenth birthday.

I felt like shit then, too. Who wouldn't?

And now I had the same kind of feelings, the kind of hangover effect I was experiencing as I drove. It was as if... Well, it was like I'd stayed up all night staring at the television: my eyes hurt and I was all-over tired.

I pulled into what looked like a halfway decent diner, stepped up to the counter, and took a seat next to a kindly looking black guy wearing a red baseball cap.

"Morning," he said as I sat down.

"Good morning." I looked sideways at him and smiled.

I ordered a cup of coffee, two scrambled eggs, and a well-done T-bone steak. *So much for Chief Johnston's warning,* I thought. *Actually, if I remember correctly, he said steak dinners.* This was breakfast so, as far as I was concerned, I was still obeying orders, even though I knew it was all a matter of semantics.

By the time I finished my food it was almost time to leave for the airport. I rushed back to the hotel, grabbed my overnight bag, and checked out.

The drive to the airport was easy enough, but I don't remember it. I was awash in thought. Over and over, in my mind, I watched as the killer strangled Genevieve. Not once did I manage to get a glance at his shadowy face. I checked my rental in and took the shuttle to the terminal. By the time I was inside and at the gate, I was a dithering mess, my mind, churning. All I wanted was to get back home and to my apartment and go to sleep.

It was just after seven o'clock that evening when I walked through the door and, of course, my phone was ringing inside my purse. I didn't recognize the number, so I let it go to voicemail, went to the kitchen, poured myself a large glass of red, and headed for the shower.

The hot shower did me a world of good. The wine was cold and wet, my sofa was waiting for me like an abandoned lover and, as luck would have it, *Pretty Woman* was playing on television: exactly the kind of brain-numbing, no-thinking kind of movie I needed. I did make it to the end of my glass of wine, but not the movie.

When I awoke, still on the sofa, the sun was already high in the eastern sky and shining in through my open drapes, and I felt better, so much better I decided to forgo my morning run. Instead, I drank a cup of coffee as I listened to the news, then I slipped into a pair of jeans, a simple white shirt and my sneakers. I tied my hair back in a ponytail and, with the exception of a little lip gloss, I decided not to wear any makeup... let my skin breathe for a change. I checked myself in the mirror and was quite pleased with what I saw.

I'd driven all the way to the station on Amnicola before I remembered the phone call of the night before. I parked my car in my designated space and checked to see if the caller had left a message. He had. Edward Eaton Chesterton the Second had indeed left a message, a message that was to be the beginning of a very strange relationship.

14

"How did it go?" Janet asked.

She placed a large cup of coffee on my desk in front of me. I looked at it dubiously, then at her.

"Where'd this come from?"

"Starbucks. I got it on my way in this morning."

I looked at my watch. It was just after eight-thirty.

"And at what time was that?"

"Just after seven, but I warmed it in the microwave. It should be okay... shouldn't it?"

I picked it up, sniffed it, sipped, sipped some more, and some more, then put it down. "Yes, it's good, and thank you," I said. "Janet, you don't have to live here, you know. Your shift starts at eight, like mine." Yeah, that's right, though mine was more than a little flexible...

Hah, that's a freakin' joke if ever I heard one.

"My trip to Baton Rouge? I love how they say that name. It went well, considering I had to inform them of their daughter's death, and that she was pregnant. None of that went well; it never does... I think I'll let you do that duty from now on." I knew I wouldn't, but to see her expression when I said it was... enlightening: the color all but drained from her face.

"Sorry, Janet," I said, "but you're going to have to do it sometime... Oh, forget it. What about Genevieve's half-brother, Nathan?"

Janet grimaced. "I haven't seen Lenny yet. I'll go and see—"

"According to the mother they were close," I said, interrupting her, "and that he came to Chattanooga, ostensibly to keep an eye on her." I took a sip.

"He didn't do a very good job then, did he?" Janet replied.

"From what I heard from the parents, he didn't have a lot of choice. She was... independent," I said, "which didn't leave him with too many options."

I took out my notebook and wrote his address on the back of one of my business cards and handed it to her.

"Here's his info. That's his last known address. I don't think it's any good, so I need you to find him. He might know who Genevieve was hanging out with, other than her husband."

"Got it." Janet was up and almost out the door when I stopped her.

"Whoa, hold on there, young lady. What about Wheaton? Did he contact you? Did you meet? Did Hawk go with you?"

I could tell by the look on her face that she had indeed met with him. I pointed to the chair for her to sit back down. She pursed her lips like Daffy Duck and rolled her eyes.

"I did meet with Sam Wheaton, or Uncle Sam as he asked me to call him. And yes, Hawk went with me, but I made him sit outside in the car... Oh, don't look at me like that. I met him for lunch, at Chantelle's. Hawk watched through the window." At that, she giggled. "He wasn't too happy, but I needed to talk to Wheaton alone, loosen him up. It didn't work. I tried to finesse my way onto the topic of the Chestertons, but he was much more interested in party-ing." Janet clicked her tongue. "It was all rather embar-rassing."

"He didn't give you any information?"

"About the Chestertons? No. He's too smart for that. I think he knew what I was after. All I could squeeze out of him was that he'd"—she did the air quote thing— "'never say a bad word about Edward Eaton Chesterton the Second.' Not because Granddad was a good guy but because he was the Golden Goose, the cash cow that just kept on giving." She paused, gave me a shifty look, then said, quietly, "He offered to take me to his summer home in Barbados."

"*Shut... Up!*" I said. "And you're telling me you're not interested? I'm shocked," I teased, then said, seriously, "Well, that's good to know. He's a predator and might just be the weak link. Have Lenny dig deeper, see if he can find any of Wheaton's victims. I want to know where he goes and who he goes with, if he has any regular girlfriends... or boyfriends. That, Janet, would be the *chef-d'oeuvre*."

"The chef dee what?" she asked, screwing up her face.

"Oh, dear," I said in mock frustration. "It's another way of saying 'the icing on the cake,' or 'the crowning glory.'"

"Oh, yeah." She half-closed her eyes, primped the back of her hair, then smiled sweetly at me and said, "He also said that I have the face of an angel and the body of a devil." She polished her nails, both hands, on the lapels of her jacket.

"No-he-didn't," I ran the words together, mocking her, grimacing.

"Oh-yes-he-did," she mimicked me, "and then he teared up. I thought he was going to cry. He told me he was lonely, and that he hadn't felt such a close connection with anyone like me... ever." She tilted her head to the side, lifted her chin, turned down the corners of her mouth, and then burst out laughing.

"You know what my father, God rest his soul, would say about that?" I chuckled. "When you got it... you got it."

"I don't got it." She laughed. "But Wheaton sure wanted to give it to me... Truthfully, though he was quite harmless. I never felt in any danger. I just felt embarrassed for the guy."

"Right?" I said. "He looked so... well put together, and he's not ugly," I added.

"He's ugly when he cries." Janet continued to chuckle as she wrinkled up her face like she was crying.

I laughed too, and I was still laughing when Chief Johnston appeared in the doorway. He was not laughing.

"I'm pleased to see you ladies are having a good time, Captain. Is there any chance you might tell me about your trip? I can only imagine what that last-minute flight to Baton Rouge must have cost."

Janet saw her cue to leave. "I'll get that information for you ASAP," she said, waving the piece of paper with Nathan Watkins's name and last known address on it.

"I haven't had a chance to type up my notes, but I did get a promising lead. The victim has a half-brother and, according to her parents, she liked to hang out with a rough crowd. It might just be gang-related; retaliation, perhaps. I just don't know yet. I'll have everything typed up for you as soon as possible, by this afternoon, sir?"

He nodded, then said, "We have to solve this one quickly, Kate. Number Two has called me twice already."

"Number Two... Oh, yes, you mean old man Chesterton," I said, smiling. "I wonder what kind of man Number One was?"

"From what I hear," he said, "this one is a chip off the old block... This afternoon then, I'll expect an update."

"Yes, sir. As soon as I can type it up."

"Don't bother with that. Takes too much time away from the job. A verbal report will do nicely." And he turned and left me sitting there, my mouth wide open.

Geez... Oh joy! I think I'm in love. What a freakin' difference to Finkle.

And then I remembered the phone call I'd ignored the night before. I flipped the screen on my phone and listened to the message.

"Detective Gazzara, this is Edward Chesterton. I've been informed that you're investigating the death of my grand-daughter-in-law. I'm ready to talk to you. Call me."

I had to chuckle at the man's self-importance.

How nice of him to clear a space on his calendar for me, I thought. *I bet he'd have a fit if I were to call and tell him I didn't need to speak to him at all.*

But I did need to speak to him, so I made the call.

"Yes?" It was the same grouchy voice that had left me a message.

"Mr. Chesterton?"

"It is. Detective Gazzara, I have time to talk to you now. I'll have my car pick you up. Where are you?"

"Excuse me, sir," I said, mildly. "That's not the way it works. I have several cases I'm working on that also need my attention. I can't just drop what I'm doing to come to you," I lied.

"Like hell you can't!" he snapped.

"Second," I said. "I don't get in cars with strangers, Mr. Chesterton. Mrs. Gazzara didn't raise no fool, so I will drive myself, thank you."

I waited for him to speak, but he didn't, so I continued, "Now that we've laid down some boundaries, I would like to talk to you, if you are available, this afternoon, say between three and four."

I smirked. The guy had probably never waited for anyone, ever, so maybe my tactic was a bit over-the-top, but I didn't care.

He'll send his car to pick me up? What an ass.

"I'm a busy man, Detective. I don't have time to wait around and—"

"Mr. Chesterton," I interrupted him—something else he wasn't used to, "you're welcome to come to the police department and speak with me here, at your convenience. I don't see any members of the press around here right now, but those guys do have a way of finding things out. There could be a mob of reporters here when you arrive. Reports of Genevieve's death are all over the media." I swear I could hear him gnashing his dentures.

"Fine, between three and four, then. My secretary will give you directions."

There was a click and a buzz, and then a pleasant-sounding woman picked up and politely gave me directions to the main Chesterton Estate on Elder Mountain. It would take me about thirty minutes to get there, depending upon the traffic.

I hung up, put my hands behind my neck, closed my eyes, leaned back in my extra comfy leather chair, and was soon lost in thought. I could see my day was already shaping up to be an interesting one.

15

I picked up my desk phone and buzzed Janet and asked her to bring in the troops. I needed to find out what had been happening while I was gone, and I needed to know about Nathan Watkins.

I wonder if Tim would like to be a cop? I sure as hell could use him... Nah, Harry would never let him go... besides, he has too much freedom where he is. Oh well, it's a nice thought. It wasn't the only nice thought I had. *Thanks for the memories, Harry.*

They wandered in, coffee in hand, iPads under their arms, one after the other, Janet first. I waited until they were seated and then I began.

"Okay people, we're in trouble. We're now into the sixth day and you know what that means: the first forty-eight hours and all that good stuff have expired and, according to the theory, we're looking at a potential unsolved case. That is unacceptable. So what do we have? I'll tell you. As far as I know, we have *nothing*, nothing but a bunch of half-assed theories and a couple of suspects but no evidence that ties any of them to the crime scene."

I looked around the group. Janet shifted uncomfortably in her seat. Anne was looking at her fingernails, turning her hand up, then down, spreading her fingers. Lenny stared at his still closed laptop. Hawk stared stoically back at me.

Geez, I was better off when it was just Janet and me to worry about...

"This is a high-profile case," I said sternly. "We have to solve it, and quickly, no two ways about it. If we don't make progress, the chief will take it away from us. That's not going to happen. Understood?"

They nodded, all except Hawk, who continued to stare at me. *What's with that guy?*

"As you know," I said, "Genevieve Chesterton is... was... she was not who or what she claimed to be. And, as you also know, she had a family in Baton Rouge who I interviewed yesterday. The parents are good folk, working-class, black father, white mother. They knew nothing of their daughter's subterfuges. They did know that, at least until she left home in 2017, she was something of a wild thing, but even that could have been a subterfuge. When she arrived in Chattanooga, she had good credit and money in the bank, which means that even while she was Naomi Washington, she was cultivating her new identity, Genevieve Bluford, and must have been doing so, quietly, for at least a couple of years."

I paused, stood, stepped over to the big board, picked up my plastic ruler, and tapped Genevieve's photograph.

"Look up the word enigma in a dictionary and you'll see a photo of this young lady. Who the hell knows what she's been up to the past four years, or who with... She does have a brother, that's a half-brother, Nathan Watkins. Lenny, how about Watkins? If you have anything, I'd like to hear it."

He opened his laptop and began flipping through his files. I picked up my empty coffee cup, shook it, put it down and muttered, "Damn it!"

"There's some swill left in the break room," Janet said, sadly. "Would you like for me to go get you a cup? Bottom of the pot, I'm afraid."

"Maybe I should just start drinking tea," I muttered.

"There's plenty of that in the break room. No one drinks it. But I think it might have been here since the Reagan Era."

"Forget it. I'll go out and get myself a cup later. Come on, Lenny. Tell me what you've got." I leaned back in my chair to listen.

"Nathan Watkins travels below the radar," he began. "He's clean. No criminal record, not even a parking ticket, which is strange if what you told me is true... Oh, I'm not questioning you, Captain. Anyway, he's never had a job, that I can find, has no credit record whatsoever. Captain, the man has never owned a credit card or borrowed a dime. He does have a social security number, but he's never applied for a driver's license, never filed a tax return. It's almost as if he doesn't exist. That's it. That's all I have. Sorry."

I looked at him, my mind in a whirl. I didn't know what to say to him.

Finally, I said, "That can't be right, Lenny. He was born in Baton Rouge, went to school there. I have a photo of him."

I rummaged through my file, found the old five-by-seven Alisha had given me.

"See?" I said, "That's him, when he was sixteen." I stood and fixed the photo on the board below Genevieve's. "Janet, have copies made please." I turned again to Lenny.

"Right," Lenny said, "I hear you, but that's *all* there is. He graduated high school, but he was a mediocre student. That's it. After graduation, he dropped off the map; nothing."

"How about his address?" I asked.

He shrugged. "The one you gave me doesn't exist. No such street, no such number, and could not find him listed as owning or renting anywhere in the Tri-State area. The phone number doesn't work either: burner, purchased at Walmart in Baton Rouge two years ago."

"Well, damn!" I muttered. "Keep digging, Lenny. There must be something."

"Captain," Janet said. "I have something. While you were gone I went to Club Suave... No, wait, I think you'd better hear what Hawk and Anne have to say first."

I looked at her, she shrugged. I looked at Hawk, he shrugged. I looked at Anne, she did the same. I was rapidly becoming frustrated. Dealing with these people was like dealing with a bunch of closed-mouthed informants.

"Oh, for Pete's sake," I said finally. "Do I have to drag it out of you? Hawk, I asked you and Anne to check out the crime scene, and then do the rounds of the clubs... So? Did you figure out what she was doing down there on the River-walk by herself?" I asked.

"It's hard to tell. It was Friday night, and you know how that can be. There were several clubs close by, some of them open until one or two o'clock in the morning, four in fact. We visited them all, showed her photo to everyone who would look at it, but no one working at any of them remembered seeing her, except for just one guy at a place called Club Suave—it's on Delta—but even that one was iffy.

"One of the bartenders, a John Cooper, thought she might have been there, late, but he wasn't sure; the place was busy, noisy, full to capacity. I mentioned it to Janet, figured she might want to follow it up."

"So you don't know who she was with?" I asked.

"Nope," Hawk said. "Those people don't like cops, much less do they like to talk to them."

"Janet," I said, turning to look at her. "You mentioned Club Suave. You want to tell me about it?"

She perked up, sat up straight, opened her iPad, shuffled through several notebooks, and looked up at me.

I almost rolled my eyes but nodded instead.

"Club Suave," she began. "I went there last night, at about nine o'clock. There weren't many people there at that time of night, it being a Wednesday and all..." She caught the look on my face and changed tack.

"Club Suave is an exclusive dance club. It caters to the young and the beautiful. You know, the kind where the bouncers let you in based on your looks and the quality of your clothes... Anyway, I talked to John Cooper. He's a really nice guy and..." Again, she caught the look.

"It turns out," she continued, "that not only was Genevieve a regular there but so was her brother and his friends," Janet said.

"Wait a minute," I said. "Her brother?"

I looked at Lenny. He shrugged.

"Yes," Janet said. "He goes there often, but always with Genevieve. The bartender didn't know what Nathan's name was—not until I told him—just his street name... Boo, but he did know he was Genevieve's brother. Apparently, Nathan, or Boo, lives in a crib—his word, not mine—in an old house on Bailey Avenue. I drove by it this morning. It's not a very nice place."

Boo? I thought. *What the hell kind of name is that?*

"Club Suave!" I said it like I had eaten a raw onion.

"I've never been there, but I've heard of it. It's over on the North Side, right? It's owned by a black guy, name of... Rolland something."

I looked at Lenny. He nodded and made note.

"That's it," Janet said.

"High-end, you say? Yeah, right," I said sarcastically, "and how many times have we been called out to that place?"

"Like every weekend," Janet said. "Well, in the summertime anyway."

"So," I said, thoughtfully, "Genevieve and her brother frequented the same club, moved in the same circles... I wonder if Eddie knew about that? I find it a little hard to believe that he didn't. One more thing he isn't telling us. More to the point, I wonder if he was there last Friday night?"

"It's not a great neighborhood, where he lives, her brother," Janet replied. "I've been in worse, but I'm just letting you know. With a street name like Boo, I have a feeling he's dealing to make a living, but street level, nickel and dime sales. Well, not exactly nickel and dime, but... oh, you know what I mean."

I smiled at her and said, "Enough to get him into the clubs," I replied.

Janet nodded and said, "I guess."

"You want to go pay him a visit?" I asked.

"Oh, yeah," she said, leaping to her feet and heading for the door.

"Be careful," I shouted after her.

"Bad idea, Captain," Hawk said as the door closed behind her.

"You think?" I said. "Why?"

"She's just a kid; more moxie than experience. I know

that area, and so do you. It's not safe for her to go there alone. She'll talk herself into deep shit."

I let the words sink in, looked at Anne, then again at Hawk and nodded my agreement. I picked up my phone and called Janet's iPhone and told her I'd had second thoughts and that her project was on hold until tomorrow, that I wanted to be there to confront Nathan-slash-Boo, so we'd go together. I could tell she was pissed, and I didn't blame her. As a distraction, I told her to team up with Anne to check into Eddie's alibi.

"You heard that, Anne?"

"Uh... yeah, and thank you ma'am, but I'm not sure I can stand too much of that perky little shit. She'll drive me frickin' nuts. Can't you find her something else to do?"

I grinned at her and said, "Let her have her head, Anne. She's perky, yes, but she's also very bright. She's fun and has a nose for rooting things out."

"She's a pig, you mean?" Anne grinned at me as she said it, but I could tell she wasn't happy.

Well, she's part of the freakin' team now, so she needs to suck it up.

"Hawk," I said. "You're with me. Give me an hour and then we'll go visit Granddad. I'll buzz you when I'm ready to leave."

They left and I settled down to work on more mundane things, to clear away some of the crap that had accumulated over the past week. I answered a couple of emails and managed to plow through a half-dozen files that I could then close and, thankfully, send them to the place where closed cases go to die.

When I finally looked up from my work, it was almost three o'clock. I didn't want to get to Chesterton's place until just before four o'clock. I'd realized during that first phone conversation that if I wanted to make any headway with the old man, I first had to establish control. He'd be angry that I'd wasted most of his day, but that was the plan. He was used to having things done his way and that was what made him strong, intimidating. I had to show him from the outset that I was no pushover either. He needed to learn that I was not impressed by either his social or business status; that alone should have been enough to render him powerless.

So, at approximately three-fifteen I stepped out of my office and went to find Hawk.

"Grab your iPad and let's go," I said.

16

I t was exactly three-fifty-five when we arrived at Chesterton's beautiful, multi-million-dollar home. I'd followed his secretary's instructions to Elder Mountain and found the great house hidden from view by a couple hundred acres of trees. We drove through the open wrought iron gates to a large, ornate fountain where the driveway divided and went off in two different directions. We took the right-hand fork and drove through beautifully manicured lawns until we eventually found ourselves in front of a magnificent, natural stone three-story antebellum palace complete with the obligatory columns each of which had to be at least six feet in diameter.

Seven steps of smooth gray slate led up to a front porch big enough, I was sure, for the whole family to get together. I tried not to gawk, but I couldn't help it. It reminded me so much of Robert E. Lee's great house at Arlington.

Geez, I thought, as I slammed the car door shut, *what can't you do when you have an unlimited supply of cash?*

I parked the car at the foot of the steps and stepped out into the late afternoon sunshine. I stared, for a moment, up at the great edifice in awe, and then mounted the steps with Hawk at my side. It wasn't until we were almost at the front door that I saw him.

"It's about time!" he said loudly.

The man was sitting in a rocking chair outside a massive pair of open French doors—they had to be at least twelve feet tall. A small white table was positioned between him and three more seats. A cup of coffee and a cigarette smoldering in an ashtray along with several butts completed the picture.

"Who's that with you, your father?"

"Mr. Chesterton?" I said, waving, smiling brightly. "This is Sergeant Hawkins—"

I was interrupted when an elderly bloodhound emerged from the house, his head down, front feet wide apart, growling menacingly at me.

"Jack! Heel!"

The dog instantly laid down at his feet but didn't take its eyes off me.

"I'm sorry, Mr. Chesterton, I'm going to have to ask you to put the dog away," I said with one hand in my purse, on my mace, and the other instinctively stopping Hawk short. "It's for your safety and mine."

So, I thought, *the old man wants to play games of his own. This is going to be an interesting afternoon.*

"Jack won't hurt you, ma'am." Chesterton smirked, leaning forward to pick up his cigarette. He was indeed a handsome man, and he looked just like he did in the newspaper clippings in the file. He had a full head of gray hair and a thick mustache, cowboy style.

Damned if he doesn't look just like Sam Elliott.

He wore boots, too, but I doubt they'd ever kicked a cow patty or had been adorned by spurs. His posture was relaxed, reclined in a white wicker rocking chair that looked as if it had been plucked from a Tennessee Williams novel. The wicker was intricately woven, the jade-colored cushions thick and comfortable. The man looked totally at ease.

"I'm afraid I must insist," I said, batting my eyelashes, smiling at him, tilting my head.

He glared at me for a moment, then raised his voice and without taking his eyes off me, said loudly, "Pauline, come and get the dog."

A small woman, about five feet tall, dressed in a gray maid's uniform appeared almost instantly in the doorway, snapped her fingers, and patted her thigh. Jack rose to his feet, presented his head to his master for a pat, then circled around the old man's chair and followed the maid into the house.

We approached the table, and he motioned for us to sit.

"Jack is a good-looking dog," Hawk said, pleasantly. "Is he a purebred bloodhound?"

"She," Chesterton replied. "Jack is a she. And yes, she's got purer blood than some of the folks in my family."

He took a final drag of the cigarette then stubbed it out.

"Ah... yes," I said. "You must be talking about Genevieve." He'd opened the door and I walked right on in.

"That's right. I am," he snapped.

Okay, he surprised me with his boldness. I should have seen it coming.

"Why don't you get down to it, Detective," he said, without rancor. "I know why you're here, and I ain't got all day. So either shit or get off the pot."

"My mother used to say that," I replied, and it was true. "Mr. Chesterton," I said, taking my iPad from my purse. "I'm informing you that I'll be recording this conversation.

If you have any objection, please tell me now and we can do this another day at the police department."

He shrugged, leaned back in his chair, smiling, steepled his fingers in front of him and shook his head, and again I was taken by his good looks. Unlike so many other good-looking men, however, he had that steely glint in his gray eyes that told me he could be just as vicious as he could be charming. I wasn't sure what side of himself he was going to present, but I took him at his word and wasted no more of his time.

"Mr. Chesterton," I began, "your grandson has accused you of killing Genevieve. Do you know why he might have said that?"

He didn't flinch.

"That boy has always thought with his pecker," Chesterton said. "I'm not surprised. I told him that if he didn't get the marriage annulled within the year that I was going to cut him off, and I meant it. I had already begun proceedings to make good on my promise. He was... angry. Still is, I guess."

Damn, something else little Eddie neglected to tell me.

"Why did you want the marriage annulled?"

"Gazzara. What is that, Italian?"

He pronounced it I-talian. "Yes, sir. On my father's side."

"What's your mama?" He smirked.

"She was Danish," I replied.

"Well now, that ain't so bad. You see, Detective Gazzara, Sergeant Hawkins," he said and nodded at Hawk, "the Chesterton family traveled to this great country from England on the Mayflower, but our ancestry goes back much further than that, to the Dark Ages, in fact. We're Anglo Saxons; we invaded England in the fifth century. There are Chesterton's all the way from Maine to Florida. We built an empire here, and I'm not about to have generations of hard work watered down by the blood of inferiors."

He coughed, cleared his throat, then said, "I know what you're thinking. Why that racist SOB. Who the hell does he think he is? Ain't I right?"

"My opinion of you isn't the issue, Mr. Chesterton," I replied. "I'm trying to find out who killed Genevieve. I will say this, though, that kind of rhetoric doesn't do anything to eliminate you from the list of suspects."

I glanced sideways at Hawk. His expression was stoic as he stared unblinking at the patriarch.

Whew, he looks pissed, I thought. *I wonder what the hell he's thinking.*

"It ain't a crime to decide who gets my money and who doesn't," the old man growled. "If my grandson loved that... that piece of trash enough to marry her, then he doesn't need me to be financing him. It's my money. I can toss it in the fireplace to keep warm if I so choose."

He shook another cigarette from a pack on the table, tore a match from a book, lit it, then let it dangle for a few breaths from the corner of his mouth before coughing violently and setting it in the ashtray.

"It's quite obvious that you knew she was black," I said. "How did you know?"

There's no way he could have known about her blood type. It's impossible.

"Detective Gazzara, of all people, you should know that you can take the girl out of the ghetto, but you can't take the ghetto out of the girl." He smirked.

"You mean that somehow you just knew, that you have some kind of sixth sense that can identify racial traits that are invisible to the rest of us? Is that what you are saying? I don't believe you." I shook my head, frowning.

"Ha, that sure would save me a fortune in private investigators. You never heard the girl talk. She'd mastered the accent but, every once in a while, she made a slip, just a small one to be sure, but I knew... As soon as Eddie told me he was going to marry that slut, I had my people do a thorough background check on her. I know her daddy is black and her momma white, and that they live in a five-room shack in the worst part of town." He picked up his cigarette, took a drag, and began to cough as if he was about to lose his lungs.

"Most of what you say isn't true," I said. "It's a fairly nice home in an older neighborhood. I know, I was there only yesterday."

He ignored my comment and continued as if I hadn't spoken, "I knew where she went to eat, sleep, screw, who she ran with. I had her followed every minute she was awake."

"If that's true," Hawk said, "somebody really screwed up, didn't they? Or did they?"

"Screwed up?" The old man glared at him.

"They weren't watching her the night she died, or whoever you had following her, killed her."

"That's bullshit," he snapped. "You're fishing."

"So what the hell happened then?" Hawk persisted. "Your people just stood by and watched as some asshole strangled the life out of the poor kid? People like you, old man, sicken me. You represent the worst of your kind, a past you can't let go. You're a sad—"

"You... you... you arrogant son of a bitch," Chesterton snarled, interrupting him, sitting upright in his chair. "You watch your damn mouth or get the hell off my property."

"Screw you, you overprivileged, self-righteous—"

"That's enough, Sergeant," I snapped, more for effect than out of outrage at my partner's outburst. Truth be told, I wish I could have said those things myself, but with rank comes responsibility.

I turned back to Chesterton. He was once again reclining in his chair. He crossed his legs, took a huge drag on the cigarette, lifted his head and blew a perfect smoke ring, watched it rise, then lowered his eyes, looked at me and said quietly, "You should teach your half-wit sergeant some manners, Captain, before someone does it for you."

Hawk opened his mouth to speak, but before he could, I held up my hand, silencing him.

"I think you both need to calm down," I said. "How did your grandson and Genevieve meet?" I asked, changing the subject in the hope I might drag the interview back on track.

The old man stared at me for a moment, two thin tendrils of smoke drifting out of his nostrils. He looked like a sleeping dragon.

"I don't know," he said finally. "He never would tell me. All I know is, he met her... somewhere, then put her to work at my company," he said. "Three months later the idiot asked her to marry him. The rest, as they say, is history."

"So," I said, "you found out her real name and that her parents were still alive, but you never told him, and you allowed him to marry her anyway? I don't get that."

"Detective, I'm going to school you on people... and life. Listen to me. It might do you some good. It is better to know a little dirt about someone than to know all the good deeds they may have done because, in the end, no one cares about the good deeds." He stared at me, quietly for a short moment, then continued, "But they will burn you at the stake for even the smallest indiscretion. You see, I was able to keep Genevieve in line with that little bit of information."

He was obviously very pleased with himself.

"And don't kid yourself," he said. "Eddie might not have known who she was, but he sure as hell knew exactly what she was. Sure, when he was growing up he did his duty, dated the local bluebloods, but they weren't his flavor, not at all. I lost count of the number of times his daddy caught him sampling the local color, if you get my meaning."

Holy cow! Really?

"What did Genevieve do when you confronted her, told her that you'd found out about her?" I was intrigued. This whole scenario was better than *Gone With The Wind*. Hawk seemed to be as engrossed as I was.

"What do you think?" he snapped. "She lost it, became hysterical. She begged me not to tell anyone. She said that she was more ashamed of her heritage than I was. Can you believe that?" He chuckled.

"But she wouldn't leave?" I asked.

"No. She promised to treat Eddie well and said she'd be quiet and not cause any trouble with the rest of the family, especially Regina Mae. Not that I gave a shit if she made trouble with her, the loopy bitch. So I gave her a chance."

He frowned, shook his head, then said, more to himself than to us, "I should have known better. Those people can't keep their mouths shut. It's only a matter of time before they expose themselves, and she did, which is why I told Eddie to get rid of her, or else." He launched another smoke ring and watched it rise.

I waited, but he just continued to stare at the smoke, so I said, "So, what did she do... to expose herself?"

"She must have had... she liked goin' to the clubs where her kind... you know, those places. The clubs where her kind get together. Places where we can't go. Those people see my grandson there and the next thing I know he's the one who's dead..." He paused, then, almost as an afterthought, said, "He went with her, one time that I know of, and some big goon literally handed his ass to him."

He shook his head, obviously exasperated, or maybe it was disappointment he was feeling.

"My grandson isn't a fighter. He isn't good with numbers, either. Ha, and he sure as hell's not good with women. Damned if I didn't get stuck with the runt of the litter. I need some great-grandsons and quick."

I got the impression that he was thinking out loud.

"Did you know Genevieve was pregnant when she died?"

That was the only time I saw Granddad Chesterton pause.

He looked at me and squinted, took one last deep drag on his cigarette and stubbed it out. He blew two more tiny smoke rings into the air tilting his chin up but never taking his eyes from mine.

"No, Captain, I didn't." He shook his head, slowly, then looked me in the eye and said, "I *am* sorry that the child had to die, as I am that Genevieve did, but it's probably for the best. You see, dollars to donuts the child wasn't Eddie's anyway. And even if it was—oh yes, I'd have had a DNA test done—and even if it was, I wouldn't have accepted it. Call me what you want, but I'm telling you the truth."

I looked down at my iPad, then at Hawk—he was staring at the old man with something akin to hate in his eyes. And then Chesterton, the old bastard, was smiling at me.

"Don't you dare judge me, Captain. You think I just woke up one morning feeling the way I do about these people? Well, I didn't. I grew up here, worked hard to keep what my father handed to me, not like that idiot grandson of mine." He swallowed and the smugness left his face. "Let me tell you a story, a true story... my story."

He didn't wait for an answer.

"My best friend all through grade school was a boy by the name of Reginald Hobbs, Reggie. Black as the ace of spades, he was. A good kid who came from a good, hard-working family. But all that changed when we went to high school. I went to a private school, Reggie to a public school. It didn't bother me, not one bit, that he went to the black high school and I went to the white one. This was back when kids of color weren't supposed to mix with whites.

"Anyway... one Saturday afternoon, it was, I saw him walking with four other boys, all about the same age, all black like Reggie. I went running up to him to, I don't know, maybe to play some ball or go swimming; it was what we'd always done. Those boys, including Reggie, said yeah, sounds like fun, said we'd take a shortcut to the ball field down a dirt path. I didn't think anything of it. We were all laughing and talking and the next thing I know, when we were away from the road and no one could see or hear us, those five boys jumped me.

"Back then I could take a punch as well as any other kid, but you see, Detective Gazzara, what I couldn't take was that Reggie had turned on me: he was in it just as deep as those boys who didn't know me. He didn't even hesitate. It was like all those years of friendship between us were just pretend. And I'm supposed to forgive and forget? Hell no! I'm supposed to not judge a book by its cover? Hell no! Those five little bastards beat me up because I was white; no other reason. He's dead now, Reggie. Shot in the head by one of his own kind. Go figure."

He looked... sad, yes, that's it sad.

"So you had Genevieve killed as payback?" Hawk said, quietly.

"No! I didn't. I had them arrested, Reggie along with them, crying and bawling for his mama the entire time! That day I learned that the only thing people, any people, respect is someone bigger and more powerful than they are, and I made my mind up right there and then that I was going to make damn sure that anyone who had any thoughts of taking me down would think long and hard before they made a move. I made up my mind I would be twice as big, twice as powerful as anyone on the planet, and I am, Captain. You know it and so does everyone else. Why do you think you were able to roll right onto my property without having to pass through some sort of security?"

I took a deep breath but said nothing.

Chesterton leaned forward and looked me square in the eyes. "I'll tell you why. It's because everyone within five hundred miles of this place knows I'll shoot them dead if they try anything on my land, and that I've got the money to get away with it."

"Genevieve wasn't shot. She was strangled," I said.

"That's right. She was. But not by me. Like I told you, I was going to make good on my threat to take away Eddie's allowance, his inheritance, all of it. I didn't need to kill anyone. It was my money to take back. She wasn't standing in the way. She was the cause of it. Maybe you should take another look at my grandson. He's the one with reason to kill her." He pointed at me then leaned back in his chair.

"So you think your grandson killed Genevieve? Her husband?" I asked.

I have to admit I was more than a little flabbergasted, unsure of what to say next. I arrived at the party thinking I was so smart to make the man wait and throw him off his game and well, he'd aced me.

"Isn't that usually who the guilty party is, the husband?" Chesterton smirked, then called for Pauline.

She came bustling out to the porch. Without uttering a word, she picked up the ashtray, took it back inside, and returned a moment later with a clean one.

"It has been known to turn out that way," I replied. "Mr. Chesterton, where were you the night Genevieve was murdered?" I knew he'd have an alibi; of course he would and it would be airtight, but so what? He could have paid someone to do it for him.

However, as I sat there watching him, looking for tells, and as much as I hated to admit it, my gut was telling me he wasn't my man. It was telling me not only that he didn't kill Genevieve, but he also didn't pay anybody to do it for him. He just wanted her gone, and he was using his money to force his grandson to get rid of her.

"I was having dinner with one of the board members of my company at St. John's," he said lightly. "I know the owners so you can verify it with them. I also ran into one of our State Representatives and his lovely wife, who will also verify my whereabouts." He seemed to be enjoying himself.

"I do appreciate your time, Mr. Chesterton," I said as I stood up.

I turned off my iPad and took a business card from my pocket and handed it to him.

"If you think of anything that might shed some light on what happened to Genevieve, I really would appreciate a call."

"Will do, Detective. You and Sergeant Hawkins have a lovely evening, both of you, you hear?"

He remained seated, took another cigarette from the

pack, lit it, and blew the smoke up in the air with all the satisfaction of a sailor on shore leave.

I turned as if to leave, then made as if I'd changed my mind, turned back to him and said, "By the way, Mr. Chesterton. Who's the Frenchman?"

He didn't even flinch. If there was a tell, I didn't catch it.

"Frenchman?" he said. "What Frenchman?"

"Your grandson suggested I ask you about the Frenchman," I said.

He shook his head and said, "The lad's mind must be wandering. Maybe he's talking about someone who works for me. There were more than six thousand, worldwide, at the last count. I can't keep track of them all."

I nodded, and we left him blowing smoke rings.

I let Hawk drive us back to the PD. I was exhausted, dumbfounded, my head whirling. I'd planned to take control of the interview, but it hadn't worked out that way. I felt like I'd just gone twelve rounds with a heavyweight... and, on thinking about it, that's exactly what I'd done. It dawned on me then, that Chesterton probably had more experience dealing with law enforcement than I'd given him credit for. Oh yeah, where there was money there was scandal, corruption and crime, and there I was treating him like he'd never dealt with the law before, and the guy probably reveled in my naiveté.

Oh well, there's no point beating myself up. The man played me, and I let him. But, as Scarlet said, tomorrow is another day, and he won't catch me lacking next time. I'll take his advice: bigger is better, and the police department is bigger than he is, and it's all mine.

"So? What are your thoughts?" I finally asked Hawk.

"Where the hell do I begin?"

"Well," I said, "he might be repugnant and crude, but a guy that honest about his feelings is a guy who knows who he is."

"He's a son of a bitch, is what he is," Hawk said.

"Yeah, that," I said. "That's what I was thinking too, but a forthright son of a bitch, and a racist, but I don't think he killed her, or had her killed, and he has an alibi that can easily be verified."

I looked at my watch. It was almost six. It had been a long afternoon.

"I don't know about you," I said, "but I'm beat, in more ways than one. He's a tough old bird, is Chesterton. I think we need to call it a day... Be sure to check his alibi. I'm sure it will be solid, but you never know and if we don't... well. Hey, you see how he looked like Sam Elliott?"

Hawk cut me a dirty look but said nothing.

17

The following morning, Friday, I made good on my promise to go with Janet to interview Nathan Watkins—or Boo as he was known on the street. But first I needed to bring the rest of the team up to speed and see what they had found out the previous afternoon. Thus, we assembled in my office at eight o'clock that morning.

"So, what have we got?" I asked when everyone was settled. "Anne, what about Eddie's alibi? You checked it out, right?" I asked. Eddie, I already knew from my own interview, was a narcissistic kid with a drinking problem and a severe case of affluenza.

"We did, and he doesn't have one, not for the hours between twelve-thirty and two, but I doubt that it matters. His relationship with the truth is strained, to say the least... Okay, so we went to the Sorbonne and spoke with Laura. She said Eddie and two friends entered the bar at around ten-thirty and all three were already drunk out of their minds. She said it was just after twelve when they left, staggered out of the bar, all three of them. We talked to both of the friends, Alex Pruitt and George Martinez. They both said they left the Sorbonne around one-thirty, which was either a lie or they were too drunk to know. Either way, none of them have an alibi."

"Well," I said, "if anyone's to be believed, it's Laura. Did you ask him about Club Suave?"

"We did," Janet said. "Well, I did. He said they didn't go there. He said they ate barbeque at Rusty's—Rusty doesn't remember them, I checked—and then they went to the Mellow Mushroom—I couldn't find anyone there that remembered them either—and from there they went to the Sorbonne..." and then she ran out of steam, glanced at Anne and shrugged.

"So that means the suspect pool just grew by two," I said. "They could have gone from the Sorbonne to Club Suave, all three of them, and all three could have been involved in the murder. Hawk, you and Anne go talk to the people working in that arcade under Eddie's apartment. Maybe that coffee shop is an all-nighter and somebody saw them come home. Maybe you can provide them with an alibi."

I turned to Lenny. "What've you got for me, Lenny?"

"Well, I did some digging into Sam Wheaton's background, like you asked."

"Okay," I said. "Let's hear it."

"Well, yeah, okay," he said as he flipped through the screens on his iPad, and then put it down on his lap.

"I have it all written up for you," he said, handed me three pieces of paper clipped together, and like sets to each of the others in the room, then picked up his iPad and began.

"So Sam Wheaton got his start on Wall Street right after he graduated from NYU—New York University—with a degree in Risk Assessment, but in 1988 he was fired for an unspecified Regulation D infraction... My guess is that he was manipulating funds, but what do I know? He was unemployed for almost six months until he founded a business and financial consulting company, STW Risk Management Company.

"STW Risk is unique in that it was formed, according to Wheaton's blurb, to manage the assets of small loan companies—à la some of the more substantial payday loan vendors—and clients with assets of more than twenty-five million dollars. But there's one notable exception, CDE International Finance Corporation, Chesterton's company, whose assets are estimated, though I couldn't confirm it, to be in excess of three-billion dollars."

Holy Cow, I thought. *Three billion. That really is motive, and not just for Eddie.*

"Any word on how well Eddie and Wheaton get along?" I asked, interrupting Lenny's flow.

Lenny shook his head and said, "No, not really. I found nothing to suggest any differences between them. Eddie works for CDE so they must interact... when Eddie bothers to show up, I guess."

"How about Number Three, Eddie's father?" I said.

"Same. Wheaton, so it seems, is everybody's friend."

I looked at Janet. She smiled self-consciously. Fortunately, no one else caught it. I nodded for Lenny to continue.

"Okay, so Wheaton met Edward Chesterton the Second, the chairman and CEO of CDE international in 1986 through a mutual acquaintance, Robert Marks, an insurance executive, and his wife, in Naples, Florida, and the two of them hit it off. A year later, Wheaton became Chesterton's financial adviser and right-hand man. In less than a year, Wheaton had sorted out Chesterton's somewhat expansive enterprises and was given power of attorney that allowed him to hire people, sign checks, buy and sell properties, borrow money, and do pretty much anything else of a legally binding nature on Chesterton's behalf.

"If ever there was an arrangement that offered an opportunity for abuse, this one has to be it," he continued. "I was, however, unable to find anything that would indicate that Wheaton has ever abused the privilege. True, he lives extremely well, but his company is successful and Chesterton pays him an 'exorbitant amount,' said to be one percent of CDE's net profit."

He paused, flipped through several screens on his iPad, and then continued, "In 1996, Wheaton relocated STW Risk to the island of St. Thomas in the US Virgin Islands. By relocating to the US Virgin Islands, he was able to legally reduce his clients'—and his own—federal income taxes by 90 percent. The US Virgin Islands are, in fact, a US Government, officially sanctioned offshore tax haven, which makes it one heck of a good deal considering that the USVI offers all of the advantages of being part of the United States banking system, but with a three-and-a-half percent income tax rate. I read somewhere, in Newsweek, I think it was, that the USVI is a slice of paradise that some experts consider the nation's one and only, officially sanctioned, full-blown offshore tax shelter."

"No dirt?" Anne asked skeptically.

"No. That's it. I have nothing else for you. As far as I can tell, except for the two sexual harassment suits and his paternity problems, he's clean."

"So what does all this mean, then?" Anne asked, flipping through her hard copy.

I was wondering the same thing myself.

"It means," Hawk said, "that this man Wheaton knows all of the family's dirty little secrets, which makes him a very powerful man; and a very dangerous man, a man to be wary of. Did he know the girl was black, I wonder, and that she was pregnant?"

"He says he didn't," I said, "and I understand what you're saying, Hawk, but does any of it give Wheaton a motive to kill the girl, other than a possible rejection of his sexual advances?"

"Sexual advances?" Anne asked. "That's a bit of a stretch, isn't it? How old is he?" She looked up at Wheaton's photograph and smiled. "Good looking dude, though."

I looked at her, then at Janet, who blushed and looked away, but not before Anne caught it.

"Ahhh," Anne said, "I see. Are you going to tell us about it?"

Janet opened her mouth to speak, but before she could, I interrupted her.

"There's nothing to tell yet," I said. "We offered the bait, and he's nibbling but we have yet to set the hook. You'll know, all of you, when we have something... or nothing."

I looked up at the board, shook my head, and wondered how the hell I was going to sort it all out. I stared at the blank square that represented the Frenchman for a couple of seconds, and at the big black question mark I'd drawn beside it and then, still looking up at it, I said, "Lenny, Hawk, see what you can find out about this Frenchman that Eddie dropped on us. There could be something to it, or it could simply be a red herring." I shook my head and sighed and checked my watch. It was already after ten.

I need a break, I thought. *I need to get out of here.*

"So we all know what to do right?" I asked, then looked at each of them in turn. "So let's go to it. Janet, grab your stuff. Let's go find Nathan Watkins, or Boo, or whatever the hell his name is."

18

It took us little time to find the address where Nathan Watkins was supposed to live. It was actually off Bailey on Caxton in the Highland Park area where the homes were not that much different from the Washington home in Baton Rouge: older homes, most of them, simple, ranch-style frame houses with security bars on the windows and doors.

When we found the address I wasn't too surprised by its appearance. A two-story, wood-sided house built around the turn of the century. It wasn't unique. I could think of dozens just like it, most of them turned either into apartments or offices. This one appeared to be unchanged, though it was obvious that more than one family was living there.

Nor did it appear to be the home—headquarters—of a drug lord. There were no members of a "crew" watching from the front and back porch, no suspicious looking expensive cars with custom rims or tinted windows parked either in front, at the rear, or even nearby. It was, to all intents and purposes, just another old house in a depressed section of the city. It was, I hoped, where the kid we needed to talk to lived. He wasn't going to like it; of that I was certain. Highland Park is where an unofficial neighborhood watch keeps a wary eye out for unwelcome visitors, and once word got out that we were here, Nathan would have some explaining to do.

We parked on the street one house down from Nathan's and walked the short distance to the front porch. The front door was closed, but as we mounted the steps we could hear raised voices coming from inside.

"I don't care!" a female voice shouted. "I want it out of this house! I live here, too and I don't want nothin' to do with you or your honky friends!"

"That's not happenin'," a male voice replied. "If you don't like it you can get the hell out!"

We stood for a moment on the porch, listening.

"You in too deep," the female voice pleaded. "You gonna take everyone else with you and that means me. I can't leave my baby just cause you done somethin' stupid. My brother in jail. My cousin in jail. Now my baby-daddy gonna be in jail. What am I supposed to... Who the hell is that?"

"That's our cue," I said to Janet. "You take the back. I'll go this way."

She nodded, drew her weapon, ran down the porch steps, and headed to the back of the house. I drew my Glock, held it down by my leg and knocked on the door. There was a sudden rush of feet on hardwood floors somewhere inside.

"Police!" I shouted. "Come on out with your hands up."

The occupants, already in an elevated state, would, I hoped, calm themselves down and comply. That was what usually happened when the police arrived. Domestic situations of any kind are extremely dangerous. You never quite know what to expect: an irate husband or boyfriend armed with an AR15, or worse.

And, of course, these two didn't open the door, but I knew they were in what I supposed was a living room off to the right.

"Miss, sir, please open the door," I said, my Glock still at my side. "My name is Detective Gazzara. I just want to talk to Nathan Watkins. Is he here?"

Before either of them could answer I heard Janet shouting from the backyard. "Show me your hands! Get down on the ground and show me your hands!"

Oh crap, what the hell has she done?

I ran down the steps and around the back of the house to find my partner, all one-hundred-fifteen pounds of her, straddling a young man twice her size and face down on the floor as she yanked one arm behind him, slapped a cuff on his wrist, and then did the same to the other.

The back door flew open and a young woman stepped outside, her face streaked with tears.

"Get your hands up!" I shouted, pointing the Glock at her.

She did as she was told, slowly sat down on the concrete step, and said not a single word.

She looked to be about twenty years old and at least seven months pregnant if not more.

"Keep your hands up where I can see them," I said. "Is there anyone else inside the house?"

She shook her head.

"Stand up. Do you have any weapons on you? Any needles or anything that might stick me?" I asked as I patted her down.

"No, ma'am." The voice was subdued, shaky, nothing

like the strident voice I'd heard from the front porch. She sounded scared, and that was good.

"Sit down," I said to her, "and keep your hands where I can see them."

"Nathan Watkins?" Janet leaned down and shouted in the man's ear. "Is that you?"

"I don't know no Nathan Watkins," he muttered defiantly.

"You don't know who you are?" Janet said, smiling widely at me. "Well, that's okay. I guess we'll all find out who you are together. Come on, get up and have a seat next to your sweetheart."

She helped him up by pulling on his handcuffed arms. He grimaced and grunted and let out a couple of gasps.

"I'm not hurting you, am I?" she said. "A big tough guy like you, diving through a window just to get away from little old me, and I'm hurting you? Boy, are you ever going to have a fine time in the tank with the other bangers. They'll eat your lunch."

"Keep an eye on them both while I clear the house," I said as I brushed past the woman and went inside.

The girl was right; there was no one else inside, though it was obvious that the place was occupied by at least a half dozen people besides our two. I also found a small amount of weed on the kitchen table. Not enough to charge them with possession for resale, but enough for an excuse to take them both in if they didn't play ball.

When I stepped outside again, Janet had them both seated together on the back stoop. The man looked at me defiantly, his eyebrows pinched together in the middle. Inwardly, I smiled. *And here we have yet another one,* I thought. How many just like him I'd run into over the past fifteen years or so, I'd lost count. They're all the same, so predictable. I was sure we weren't going to get very far with this one.

"Nathan Watkins?" I said as I stepped around him so that my back was toward the sun and he had to look up at me. "That is you, right?"

He didn't reply. He just continued staring up at me, his eyes narrowed to mere slits, his forehead one huge frown.

I glanced at the girl. The tears were gone. Her face had hardened. She said nothing.

I didn't care about the woman at all, but if the guy was indeed Nathan then I wanted to talk to him, and if he wasn't going to cooperate... well, I was just going to have to persuade him that it was in his best interest to do so. But first, I had to find out if he was... Nathan.

I stared down at the woman, thought for a moment, then said, "Well, it seems that you have a problem, ma'am. Stand up please." I helped her to her feet and then led her to the far end of the stoop, just out of earshot of the man I figured was Nathan Watkins.

I held the baggie up in front of her and said, "I found this on your kitchen table and we both know what it is, don't we? It's not a whole lot but, DCS takes a dim view of expectant mothers using illegal substances, but you knew that, right? This," I said, wagging the baggie in front of her nose, "is enough reason for them to take your child away from you. Is that what you want?"

Her eyes filled with tears again.

"Look, this ain't my house. I just live here with Nathan," she said quietly. "That his weed, not mine."

"So, he is Nathan Watkins?" I asked.

The girl nodded her head.

"And what's your name?"

"Sheila Teverson," she muttered.

I nodded, making a mental note of her name, then said, "Why did he take off running when we arrived?"

I watched her face. She shrugged and shook her head.

I continued, "You're sure? He didn't tell you he was in some kind of trouble?"

"No," she said. "Boo don't do nothin'. I mean, he ain't no thug."

Sheila Teverson's definition of a thug was probably a lot different from mine, and I wasn't about to take her word for it that Nathan wasn't one. He'd tried to run, so he was obviously up to something illegal, or he had something else to hide. I was sure that she knew what it was, but she was putting on the innocent act, hoping I'd fall for it. As if!

"You're sure?" I asked.

She nodded enthusiastically. I turned and looked at Janet. She was talking quietly to Nathan. He wasn't looking at her. His replies were mumbled and he barely moved his lips. And then I looked toward the sidewalk. Several neighbors were approaching.

Uh oh! I thought. *Time to get out of here.*

"Sergeant," I said, "please escort Mr. Watkins to the car."

"But I told you," Sheila pouted. "He ain't no thug. He didn't do nothin'."

"Just keep your mouth shut, Sheila!" Nathan yelled.

"This ain't right. He didn't do nothin'," Sheila continued to protest. She glared at me. "You said you'd let him go."

"I said no such thing! I told you what would happen to you if I decided to turn you both in. He was coming with me no matter what. Now you can go back inside and maybe you'll get to keep your baby."

Sheila was pissed, I could tell. She'd figured she had me

when she confirmed his identity, and now she was taking it personally.

"You lied to me," she screamed. "You made me think you was trying to help. Better watch your back, bitch."

By then the small group of neighbors had gathered on the sidewalk. Several were mumbling angrily, and I had a feeling things were about to get nasty. If the group grew any bigger... I knew things could deteriorate fast. Sheila knew it too, and she kept shouting about how bad her man was being treated, how she'd been lied to.

It wasn't an unusual situation, and it's why we all hate having to deal with domestic calls. A woman calls 911 claiming she's being abused. We respond, arrest the boyfriend, and the abused female complainant pitches a fit and starts screaming at the officers. Inevitably, the cops are the bad guys. It never made any sense to me.

I left her to it, joined Janet at the car, and loaded Nathan into the back seat before the situation escalated further, and we headed back to the police department.

"You know, Nathan," I said, glancing at him in the rearview mirror, "if you'd just given us a minute of your time you wouldn't be in this mess. Tell me, why the hell did you run?"

He said nothing, just stared truculently up at the mirror.

"We just wanted to talk to you about your sister, Naomi, to tell you that... to tell you that she's dead."

I watched for his reaction in the rearview mirror. There wasn't one. Either he already knew, or he didn't care.

"I see," I said. "Think about it, Nathan."

19

Unlike his sister, Nathan looked black. His skin was the color of lightly creamed coffee, his hair straighter than you might expect, but also black. He was tall, well-built... ripped, some would say. He did have his sister's eyes though; the eyes that glared at me when I pulled him from the back seat of my car were the same as those I'd seen on Doc's examining table, staring up into nothingness.

"What the hell's the matter with you?" I asked him as I paraded him past the duty sergeant's desk to the nearest interrogation room. "You could still be home right now. But no, you had to do it the hard way. You happy now?"

I pulled out a seat for my guest at the plain steel table in the center of the room. He flopped down onto it, all attitude and screw you. And don't they all? From high school kids trying to act tough in the principal's office knowing that their parents weren't going to do anything about their shenanigans to the idiots like Nathan with street cred to protect and expand. Except this wasn't the principal's office.

It was a murder investigation, his sister's murder, and the way he was acting was suspicious to say the least.

"You want anything to drink? Some water? A Coke?" Janet asked loudly making Nathan jump slightly.

He shook his head no.

I tapped Janet on the shoulder and beckoned for her to follow me out into the observation room. She did and shut the door behind her.

"Go see if any of the others are in the building," I said. "If they are, I want them to watch this interview, okay?"

She nodded. "I'll go check. Back in a few."

She returned a few minutes later followed by Hawk and Anne. I explained what I was about to do and then I reentered the interrogation room alone, leaving the three of them to observe. And so it began.

"Now, Nathan. This can be as easy as you want to make it," I started. "But let me warn you: I don't have all day, so don't waste my time. Let's get on with it, shall we?"

He didn't answer. He just stared harshly at me.

"Tell me about your sister, Nathan. You already knew she was dead, right?"

I thought for a minute he wasn't going to answer, then he looked up at me, his face had softened a little, and he looked down at his cuffed wrists.

"Yeah," he said. "I got the word, on the street. Look, I didn't have nothin' to do with Naomi. I ain't seen her in weeks, more'n that."

"But your parents sent you here with her to keep an eye on her. What did you tell them when you found out she was dead?" I asked.

He took a deep breath, shook his head and said, "I didn't tell them."

"Why not? Don't you think they have a right to know? They're her parents. She was their only daughter," I said, trying to get him to open up.

"They didn't need to know."

He leaned back in his chair. "She broke their hearts, forgot all about them when she married that white boy. She forgot where she came from and who her people was."

"How about you, Nathan? Did she forget about you too?"

He shrugged. "Yeah, mostly... but I was here; they wasn't. I tried to stay in touch, but... I saw her now an' then, when she was out partyin', sometimes. How'd she die anyway? Can I see her?"

"Do you want to see her?"

He nodded his head, slowly.

"I can arrange that, but first I need you to cooperate."

"I'm cooperatin', ain't I?" he said, his voice two octaves higher.

"Nathan," I said, "to all intents and purposes, you don't exist. You haven't filed a tax return in years; you haven't applied for a driver's license since you arrived here. Your girlfriend said you owned the house where we found you, but there's no record of you owning property anywhere. Can you explain that?"

"Yeah," he grinned at me, "I can. I like to stay under the... like the radar. That way I stay clean."

"Stay clean?"

"Yeah, do what I want, whenever, whatever, see?"

"So how do you earn money, make a living, provide for your family?"

"Odd jobs; this an' that, for cash, you know."

"No, I don't know. I do know you don't leech off the

welfare system so I imagine you do a little dealing, right? Sell a little weed, some coke, a little meth? Is that why you like to stay 'under the radar'?"

"You the smart one, Detective. You figure it out."

I nodded, stared hard at him. He didn't flinch; he just grinned up at me, totally in control of himself.

"Nathan, did it bother you that your sister married into big money and then... how shall I put it... disowned you and the rest of her family, cut you all off?"

"Hell, yeah. I mean, I covered her ass, right? Kept her out of trouble, saved her ass more than once. If not for me, she be in serious trouble."

"It doesn't come any more serious than dead, Nathan. Where were you that night... when she needed you most?"

He looked sour, like he was about to sneeze, then looked up at me and said, "I told ya, I ain't seen her in weeks. I didn't know she was inta that kinda shit. Look," he said, seriously, "early on, when we was not long come to town, I saved her from getting into serious trouble with some bad dudes, a couple of times, before she hooked up with her sugar-daddy. She liked her dope, but she didn't like payin' for it, not even when she had money. She partied all the time an' she didn't care who with."

Nathan folded his arms across his chest. "She hooked up with her man, and then she didn't bother with her brother no more. So I don't bother with her; simple as that."

"Nathan, were you jealous of your sister?" I asked softly.

"Naw. It's just that I knew where she came from, what she was. I could have blown the whistle on her any time, but I didn't. You'd think that count for somethin' right? Well it didn't. She cut my ass off. Don't want to know me no more." He looked down at his cuffed hands, then looked up at me and continued. "Look, Naomi could pass. She used it. She wanted to be white, and this is what it got her. Serve her right," he mumbled.

I sensed a heavy dose of sibling rivalry in his tone whether he wanted to admit it or not.

"So where were you?"

"When? When she got killed? I don't know... When exactly was that?"

"Sometime between midnight and two in the morning, Saturday morning."

He shrugged. "Hangin' out, prob'ly, at Sheppy's, like most nights: play a little pool, smoke a little dope, just chill, you know?"

"Can anyone corroborate that for you?"

"Corrob'rate? You mean say I was with 'em. Sure, a half-dozen dudes, at least."

Oh yeah, and if you'll believe any one of them, I have a hundred acres of swampland in Florida I'll sell you.

"Names?" I asked.

He rattled off a half-dozen. I made note of them, and we'd check his alibi, but it would mean little to nothing. The street looks after its own.

I thought for a minute and then changed tack.

"Did you go to her wedding?" I asked.

"What? Me? Are you kiddin'?" He gave me a weird look then said, "Wasn't invited."

"So when you moved here from Baton Rouge, despite your promise to your parents, you went your separate ways?" I asked.

"No, not right away. She made 'friends' in the neighborhood; me too." He made air quotes with his fingers when he said the word friends.

"What do you mean?" I asked.

"She wanted to be high society, but she couldn't give up the hood." Nathan smirked. "She liked to get dirty. Be seen at the club. Get high. You know. You find any white friends she had? Nope. You didn't, did you? Just that honky she married."

It was true. We'd found no friends, white or black. She was almost as much of an enigma as was Nathan. The only one who really knew anything about her was Chesterton Two, a bigot who put a private investigator on her tail.

"I heard when she got married it was all white women in the bridal party. Like a regular Klan rally. That musta been some booty call." Nathan snickered.

"Spare me the Malcolm X speech, Nathan," I said. "So you're saying you didn't know any of her new friends?"

"No, I ain't sayin' 'at. I knew the black ones. The hoes didn't like her, but the bros... she fine with them. She had a couple of boys she'd hook up with regular at the clubs. She liked that black—"

"Did you see your sister with these men?" I said, interrupting him before he could finish the thought.

Nathan nodded. "Yeah, I did."

"Give me their names, please."

"Nope."

"What do you mean, no?" I snapped.

"Lady, you know better'n to ask me shit like 'at. I mean, you want me to end up dead, like Naomi?"

I should have seen that coming.

"I ain't saying another word, sister." He held up his cuffed wrists, and said, "An' if I ain't under arrest, then you need to take these cop locks off."

I sighed, shook my head and said, "Come on, Nathan, this is your sister we're talking about. We need to find her killer."

He shrugged, looked down at the table, then back up at me and said, "Look, I'm sorry what happened to Naomi, but there ain't nothin' I can do. Lady, she asked for it. She a bitch; she lie, an' manipulate anyone to get what she want. Hell, she manipulating you now, from the grave."

"Why do you say that?" I asked.

"She wanted to be something she's not. She played white and got inta y'all's world, but she wanted to play bad girl too. She wanted the best o' both worlds; she did that. Now she's dead and playing the victim. And I'll tell you right now she ain't no victim. She deserved whatever she got."

"That's cold, Nathan. You think the baby deserved what she got too?"

"Baby? What baby?"

"She was pregnant, Nathan."

His mouth dropped open, his eyes widened, and his head moved slowly from side to side.

"Aw, man. You shittin' me, right?"

I shook my head.

"Oh, man, that's so messed up." He looked up at me, his eyes glistening.

So he does care.

"Anything you want to say, Nathan?" I asked.

He looked at me, then slowly held his hands up again and said, "Come on, Lady. Lemme go, huh?"

I removed the cuffs and said, "I need those names, Nathan. How about it?"

He just looked at me and shook his head.

I handed him my business card with instructions to call me if he changed his mind. It was a forlorn hope, but you never know.

"Nathan, your mom asked me to pass on a message. She

wants you to call home. She just wants to know you are all right," I said, fulfilling my promise to Alisha Washington.

His eyes watered and he nodded his head once. Whether he'd call or not I didn't know.

I stood behind him and pointed at the one-way glass and then beckoned. Janet entered the room almost immediately.

"Show him out, Sergeant," I said, and she did.

"I don't know what's with him," I said when we all reassembled in my office. "His sister's dead, and he doesn't seem to care, although the news about the baby seemed to upset him, some. It's not natural."

"Maybe they didn't like each other," Hawk said, his voice dripping with sarcasm.

"He knows a lot more than he's telling," Anne said. "Her sex life, drug use, he's playing us. He was tight with her, had to be. If they weren't on friendly terms, he wouldn't know those intimate details. He said he hadn't seen her in weeks; I don't believe it. He's the key, right?"

"Could be," I said. "Hawk, any comments?"

"Yeah, the guy's a rat. Why don't you let me talk to him, alone?"

I smiled and said, "How long until you retire? You do want to hang onto your pension, right?"

He shrugged, then said, "All we need is names. Shouldn't be too difficult to get them from him. Just give me the word."

I stared at him. *Geez, he's cold!*

"Did you and Anne check out Eddie's alibi?" I asked him. "Did anyone at the coffee shop see what time he and his friends arrived home?"

It was Anne that answered. "Unfortunately, the café closes at eleven, so no."

"Okay," I said. "So, Hawk, you take Anne with you and go check out Nathan's alibi. You made a note of the people he said he was with, right?"

"I did," Janet said, handing a piece of paper to Anne.

"He also said Genevieve liked to visit the clubs," I said. "I want to know which ones, who she went with, who she met, who she left with. I also want to know if Nathan went with her. I want to know who she was screwing. Go talk to people. Start with Club Suave. It's where she was the night she died so it's as good a place as any."

Hawk nodded and rose to his feet; so did Anne, and they left.

"Janet," I said, after the door closed behind them, "Anything you want to add?"

"I think he's hiding something. I just can't figure out how to find out what it is."

"Maybe he's clean... well, as far as his sister's death is concerned," I replied. "But you're right, and so's Anne. I think he's the key."

"It didn't bother you that he didn't seem upset that his sister was dead, murdered?" Janet asked. "I wanted to come in there and slap him silly."

I smiled at the thought of Janet slapping big bad Boo.

"No," I said, "because I think he actually was upset about it, very upset, and he was hiding it. I'm thinking we need to find out exactly what Nathan is into. You up for a late night?"

"Always." Janet rubbed her hands together.

"Great. Go home and get something to eat and put on some comfortable clothes. It might be a long night. We'll meet back here at eight." Little did I know how long a night it would be.

She left, and I set aside the Genevieve Chesterton file

and set about catching up on some paperwork. It never seemed to end. By six o'clock that evening, I was done, and I headed home to shower, change clothes, and get ready for... a night I'll not easily forget.

20

"To say that the freaks come out at night would be an understatement in his part of town," Janet said as we sat in the car parked under a tree two blocks from Nathan's house.

"Yeah," I said, "and it's not even that late... His house is kind of quiet, though; the lights are on in the living room, but... Maybe he decided to stay home. If nothing happens by one o'clock, we'll get out of here."

I was watching Nathan's home through a powerful pair of binoculars, watching the windows for signs of life, moving shadows on the blinds. I'd been at it for almost two hours, seen nothing, and my arms were aching. Janet was right though: it was only fifteen minutes after ten o'clock, still a little early for a Friday night street party, but the neighborhood was already coming to life.

People were out on their stoops, doors wide open, music playing loudly. Any other night I would have been worried about sitting there in the dark; it was asking for trouble. Thankfully, though, there was a party going around the corner and cars were parked on both sides of the street for a half-block in each direction. Even so we still had to duck down out of sight when someone drove by. Let's face it, two white women in a parked, unmarked white Dodge Charger screamed cops. If we were exposed, well... these days, who knows what might happen.

So, we'd been sitting there for a while; the twenty-two-ounce coffee Janet had brought was just about done and what little was left was cold. I put the binoculars down and finished it off; cold coffee is good, especially when there's nothing else.

"How come you've never married, Cap?" Janet asked.

"What?"

"Well, I don't get it. You never date, not that I know of, and you're hot when you... well, I've seen you. You can't be short on offers... to go out, I mean."

"Getting a little personal, aren't we, Sergeant?" It wasn't the first time I'd been asked the question, so I supposed I shouldn't have been surprised.

"Well, yeah, but I'm your partner, right? It's kind of... Okay, I'm being nosey. Just askin'," she said, taking some kind of granola thing from her pocket and offering it to me.

I shook my head. If it had been a cheeseburger I'd have snatched her hand off, but I wasn't in the mood for healthy.

"Oh, I don't know," I said, a little reluctantly. I wasn't comfortable talking about my personal life. "It's a cop thing, I guess. None of the guys I know could make marriage work, so how the hell am I, a woman, to make a go of it? I've been a cop so long now I can't remember being anything else." I chuckled.

After pondering her question, I continued, "Yes, I get asked out, now and then, but I don't often go. Maybe I should? I dunno. It's a whole lot of hassle for... nothing?"

"But don't you, you know, miss it?"

"Miss what? And before you answer, if you're asking about what I think you are, that's way too personal. Change the subject, okay?"

"Oh come on, Kate. It's me, little old Janet. I know you must have needs. I sure as hell do."

"*Enough*," I snapped.

"You still haven't answered my first question," she persisted, undaunted.

I turned in my seat and stared at her. The little b... didn't flinch, stared right back at me, smiling sweetly.

"Look," I said, giving in a little. "I don't know why. Maybe I haven't met 'Mr. Right' yet," I said, sarcastically, making air quotes with my fingers.

And then she really stepped over the line.

"Tell me about Harry Starke," she said, no longer smiling. "How come you let him get away?"

Suddenly, I felt flushed, angry. "That's enough, Janet! How the hell did you know about him anyway?"

"I'm sorry," she said. "I didn't mean to upset you. I was just asking to help pass the time."

Upset me? Hell, I thought I was beyond that after all this time... guess not. Damn!

"I'm not upset. Just change the subject."

She sat quietly for a long moment, staring out through the windshield, then said, "You said you'd been a cop so long you can't remember anything else. So can I ask, why did you become a cop?"

I heaved a sigh, turned my head to look at her. She raised her eyebrows and shrugged.

"I don't really know. I got the idea in high school, I guess. Who knows? After I graduated high school I went on to UTK and got a BS in forensic psychology... and then I applied for a job at the PD. It seemed like the right thing to do. How about you?"

"Retaliation. This redhead didn't make any friends in school, just the opposite, in fact. I was bullied... by the girls and the boys. So I decided I wouldn't take any more crap... not from anyone. What was it Al Capone said? 'You only get so far with a kind word. But you get a lot further with a kind word and a gun.' Maybe I didn't get that quite right, but you get the idea."

"Yeah," I said. "I heard that one too, but I'm not sure old Al is the best role model to quote. But I do understand... and I hate that you were bullied."

She shook her head, stared out through the windshield and said, "Thank you. There wasn't a whole lot I could do about it... not then, anyway. I mean, I'm barely five foot five. Some people think it's fun to push people like me around. I think it's the red hair that makes them do it. Well, I decided to do something about it. I took karate and became a cop."

The way she said it was deadly serious, but it came across as kind of funny.

"Karate?" I smiled. "Are you serious?"

"Oh, I am. Really. I have a black belt, first level, shodan." She turned to look at me and said, "I'm going to tell you a secret. If you repeat it, I'll have to kill you."

"And I believe you," I joked.

"My first day as a rookie cop, when I put on my uniform to go to work that day, when I first put on my weapon and my badge, I stood in front of the mirror in my bedroom and just stared at myself. I don't know how long for. It could have been just a few minutes or twenty minutes before I left and went to work. Isn't that weird?"

"No, not really. And I get it," I said. "I do it myself,

usually before I go out on a date which, as I said, isn't very often."

"And then, they paired me with Keith Manners," she said and shook her head, chuckling.

"Keith Manners? He's huge... like almost seven feet tall."

"I know, right?" she said. "We looked like a freaking circus sideshow, but he's such a treasure and I learned a lot from him. I'm not sure if they put me with him to make sure I didn't get hurt or if it was a joke, but he sure kicked this baby bird out of the nest. It was a case of fly or the cat will get you. The key to being a good cop, Keith always said, is doing the unexpected, and that's what I try to do. That's why I was able to take Nathan down. He wasn't expecting it."

Janet looked wistfully out of the side window, then said, "I miss Keith. I was only with him for a few months before he retired what, three years ago? Then the chief kind of took me under his wing."

"Did you let him know you made detective?"

"Hell yeah. He was the third phone call I made after my mom and my boyfriend," she said, raising her own binoculars. "Uh-oh."

"What, what do you see?"

"Looks like our boy is on the move." Janet pointed.

I put my binoculars to my eyes and watched as Nathan descended the front steps and strutted along the sidewalk toward us, then made a right turn just before reaching the block where we were parked.

"I'll follow him," Janet said.

Before I could stop her, she'd hopped out of the car. She may as well have been holding up a neon sign that read

"COPS." Her red hair and pale skin were a beacon in the darkness.

I scanned the street and saw that I wasn't the only one who thought she looked out of place. An old woman in a jogging suit sitting on a porch swing at a house across the street tapped her companion, a female in her early twenties, on the shoulder and pointed at Janet. The younger girl was wearing a tank top and short shorts, both of which left very little to the imagination. The younger woman stood, craned her neck to look, then took out her phone, punched in a number, and began talking.

Janet stood at the corner for a few seconds, looking this way and that, as if she was lost, then bent down, tied her shoe, looked around again and then checked her watch. She stood up, put her hands on her hips, shaking her head, then walked back to the car.

Not bad, Janet, I thought, *but beyond stupid.*

I'll admit she did look lost, like some dumb ass looking to score some weed, or maybe find her boyfriend who told her to meet him at some house party. It was plausible. But what she did wasn't how it should have been done. I had my own rules of surveillance—safety being the priority—and jumping out of the car in a dangerous neighborhood, at any hour, even to shadow a murder suspect, was not one of them.

When she got back in the car, I laid into her.

"That was damn stupid," I said angrily. "Do it again and you'll find yourself back in records as a filing clerk. That pair on the porch spotted you before you got across the road. We're blown now, damn it."

"I'm sorry."

She didn't sound at all sorry.

"I just didn't want to lose him. He went into a convenience store on the corner of the next block. That way," she said as she pointed.

"I mean it, Janet. I don't need for you to get yourself killed. Do it again, and you're gone."

I didn't look at her as I started the car, but I could feel her discomfort.

Too damn bad. Maybe it'll teach her a lesson.

Ever conscious of the pair of women on the porch, I turned on the lights, eased the car forward, made a left, and parked the car a half-block away from the convenience store.

I raised my glasses and took a peek. There were three guys out front, two seated on the floor with their backs against the front wall of the store, and one standing in front of them smoking a cigarette. And so we waited, watching.

We didn't have to wait long. Just a couple minutes later, Nathan appeared through the open door, tapping a pack of cigarettes against his palm, then shaking hands and doing that complicated high five thing with the smoker.

All four were dressed similarly: jeans at half-mast, baggy T-shirts and tennis shoes that probably cost more than a set of tires for the Charger.

A car turned the corner behind us. Bright lights lit up the interior of the Charger. I could actually feel the thud of the bass as the vehicle slowly approached. My heart started to race.

"Get down," I hissed to Janet. When she looked at me like I was crazy, I added, "Do it."

The huge, black SUV rolled slowly by and I suddenly had a horrible feeling that we were about to receive a hailstorm of bullets, but of course that didn't happen. Oh yeah, I reached for my weapon, just in case, but I didn't need it. The huge car cruised on by without incident. I peeked out through the side window, but their tinted windows blocked my view, but not theirs, I was sure.

It was a Cadillac Escalade, one of those huge luxury monstrosities, and it slowly made its way down the street, the rims on the wheels glittered in the light from the street-lamps. The behemoth came to a stop outside the convenience store, and Nathan hopped in through the rear door. The smoker dropped his cigarette, ground it out under his foot, then joined Nathan inside the Caddy. The car pulled away immediately, its tires squealing softly, and turned right onto McCallie Avenue.

"Wow," Janet said, "a Cadillac like that in this neighborhood? Some people pay less in rent than the car payment for that thing. What's it doing here?"

"Hell," I muttered, more to myself than to her, "I bet my rent is less than the car payment... I think it came by specifically to pick up Nathan and his buddy. What do you say we see where that party bus is going?"

"Yes, ma'am," she said, brightly, my earlier admonishments seemingly forgotten. "I know it makes me sound racist, but come on, you don't have to be a genius to figure it out that a hundred-thousand-dollar car in this neighborhood isn't being driven by Mother Teresa."

"Really?" I asked her, dryly.

"You know it."

I didn't turn the headlights on until I saw the Cadillac's taillights disappear around the corner, then I slowly pulled away and followed the Caddy heading north on McCallie toward the Missionary Ridge Tunnel. We exited the tunnel and the Caddy drove on for maybe a mile then made a right onto Germantown Road and headed for I-24.

"Ok, let's see who owns that puppy," Janet said as she radioed in the license plate number.

21

We didn't speak as I followed the Cadillac onto the interstate. I was focused on the cars around me, trying to keep a safe distance while making sure I didn't lose the Caddy. They were driving fast; speeds in excess of seventy-five. The speeds didn't bother me: the Charger Interceptor could handle speeds far in excess of a hundred. It was the speed limit—fifty-five—that did.

"Do you think they know they are being followed?" Janet asked, clicking off her mike.

"No. I think it's just the way they like to drive," I muttered.

The adventure on the expressway lasted only a few minutes until the Caddy swung right at Exit 178 onto Highway 27 toward downtown. We crossed the river heading north and then took the Manufacturer's Road exit at a sedate forty-miles-an-hour... And I knew right then where we were headed.

"Club Suave. I should have known," I muttered. "Hell, we could have saved ourselves the aggravation and just staked the place out. We certainly would have blended in a little better... and why didn't they just take McCallie to the Market Street Bridge? Would have saved them time and a ton of gas money."

Just as we pulled in behind the suspect, dispatch came back with the name of the owner of the car, one Reverend Talbot Montgomery.

Club Suave was located just off a busy street on the North Side. The parking lot was nearly packed so it was much easier for us to blend in.

"Whoa. Did dispatch say the Caddy is registered to a Reverend?" Janet asked, as we watched the car doors open and a half dozen boys from the hood pile out.

"Confirm that," I ordered.

She radioed in and received an immediate confirmative from dispatch.

"I don't care who owns it," she said, setting the mike back in its holder. "I don't believe any of those boys are reverends. You think it's stolen?"

"Stolen?" I said. "Maybe, check with dispatch and see if it's been reported." She did, and it hadn't.

From a row farther back we watched as the driver, a tall skinny kid, Nathan, and the smoker hopped out of the car followed by three other similarly dressed dudes. They looked like a bunch of guys who were out to meet girls, drink some booze and party.

A group of five young women were also heading toward the club entrance. Our six heroes stepped up behind them and the catcalling started.

"Nathan's not acting like a guy who just found out his sister's been murdered," I said. "We've got nothing we can bust them on, other than speeding, and I don't think it would be wise for us to follow them into that club. As I recall, the owners are not big fans of the badge. No matter, let's just sit and watch for a minute." And we did.

I watched as our group approached the entrance. The bouncer looked happy to see them and quickly unhooked the rope allowing them to enter without having to stand in line.

"Looks like they're well known," I said, as handshakes were exchanged. I'd learned early on in my career that it's not what you know that opens doors in this town, it's who you know. And whoever that driver was, the bouncer knew him and the rest of the group well.

Like the Cadillac, Club Suave pulsed with the sound of thudding bass oozing out through the walls. A line of maybe thirty people waited in front of the crimson rope, hoping to be allowed to enter. Young women, most of them black, fidgeted, shifted from one high heel to another, tugging at their short skirts, adjusting and readjusting ample bosoms that were, in most cases, barely confined to the outfits they were wearing.

There were men too, though not so many as the women. Those that weren't with a woman smoked nonchalantly, arrogantly, constantly hitching up their jeans and rubber-necking along the line.

The bouncer, a mountain of a man, was the sole judge, jury, and executioner at the head of the line making sure that no one crossed the velvet rope without his permission.

I checked my watch. It was almost ten-thirty. I shook my head. I'd had enough. I decided Nathan either just didn't give a damn about his dead sister, or he was somehow involved in her death, and so would join my growing list of suspects.

"So what do we do now?" Janet asked as I started the engine.

"We sleep on it," I said. "I'm beat. All tonight has done for us is to confirm Nathan as a suspect and provide us with yet another group of possible suspects: that group that just went into the club with him. We need to find out who was driving the Cadillac. Nathan wouldn't say who his sister's friends from the hood were; maybe we just caught ourselves a break and that's them, though they probably won't be as polite as her new family."

"Some of her new family weren't all that polite either," Janet said, dourly, making me chuckle as we pulled out of the parking lot.

"Ain't that the truth?" I said. "Maybe in the morning we might have a better grasp on things. Right now, I'm bushed."

Janet yawned, nodding, and said, "Yes, ma'am."

And I drove back to the PD to get her car.

"I thought you were tired," she said as I parked and climbed out of the car.

"I am, but after all that coffee..." I shrugged. "A quick bathroom break and then I'm heading home."

"Are you sure you don't need me for anything?"

"No, Janet. Go on home. I'll see you bright and early Monday morning."

She nodded, walked to her car, started the motor, revved it, honked the horn at me, waved and peeled out of the parking lot. I shook my head as I watched her go.

Good thing the chief didn't see that, I thought, smiling to myself as I walked to the rear entrance of the building.

I did need to use the bathroom, but I also wanted to be alone for a while, to mull over what we'd seen that night. I was having a tough time relating Nathan to the owner of that Cadillac Escalade. He didn't belong in it any more than Genevieve belonged in the Chesterton family.

The idea that the Caddy was registered to a Reverend

Montgomery was stuck in my head. There was something about that name that was familiar. I'd never been to one of his services, but I knew I'd never get to sleep if I didn't do a little digging. I looked at my watch. It was ten-forty-five.

I need to get on with it or I won't get any sleep anyway. Not that it would matter. I had almost a whole weekend to chill out and rest... and I was ready for it.

You may not believe this, but when I walked into the PD that night, the place was jumping. Janet's words were never truer: the freaks do indeed come out at night, especially on a Friday night. From what I could tell every last one of them was in the police station.

I elbowed my way past the front desk and through a sea of blue uniforms to my office. It was noisy but invigorating. Yeah, that's right. There's something about a police station full of cops and their suspects: drunks, hookers, youngsters with attitudes—male and female, rednecks and the homeless. The noise was louder than it usually was during the daytime. The smell of bad cologne, body odor, and cigarette smoke on the perps mingled with the scent of burnt coffee. The conversation, if you can call it that, was loud and often profane. Shakespeare, I'm sure, would have learned a thing or two had he been present that night.

I grabbed a mug of the crappy coffee, did my thing in the restroom, then went to my office and slammed the door shut, leaned my back against it, laid the back of my head against the wood, closed my eyes, and breathed deeply, the cup of coffee still clenched tightly in my fingers. The quiet inside the room was deafening; my head was throbbing, but only for a minute. I opened my eyes and stared across the room at the storyboard, my back still against the door, and I sipped the scalding hot liquid in the cup... Nope, can't call it coffee; it had to have been made at least a couple of hours ago.

Where the hell do they buy these crappy grounds? I wondered.

Slowly, I began to feel my second wind kick in and I went to work.

I dove into Reverend Talbot Montgomery's background, and it didn't take but a couple of minutes for me to find a very interesting, and perhaps coincidental, link to the Chesterton family. I typed his name into People Search and found that the Reverend "Monty" Montgomery lived... Come on, guess. Where do you think? Yeah... He lived in the same exclusive building as Regina Mae Cottonwell-Chesterton.

Now, maybe I was being a bit ageist, if there is such a thing, and maybe my thinking was getting a little jaded, but I didn't think any of the men that piled out of that Cadillac at Club Suave looked like they were men of the cloth.

Hmm, I thought skeptically as I checked my watch. *It's not quite eleven... I'm thinking it might be worth me paying the Reverend a late-night visit. I wonder if he knows where his Cadillac is? I think he should know, and I think I should be the one to tell him; it's the right thing to do.* I smiled to myself at the thought.

22

"How can I help you, Detective?"

The night doorman at Regina Mae Cottonwell-Chesterton's apartment building looked like he'd stepped out of a beautiful dream. He was tall, with a broad chest, blue eyes and a five o'clock shadow the likes of which you see only in the movies. The sleeves of his jacket stretched tightly as his muscles moved beneath them. His hair, a gorgeous golden color, but close-cropped, suggested he might have done some time in the military.

A marine, maybe? I wondered. *Whatever, he's a fine-looking...*

"I need to talk to one of the tenants... Daniel," I said as I glanced at his shiny brass name tag. "The Reverend Talbot Montgomery."

As much as I wanted to stay and chit-chat with this amazing specimen of the male species I didn't, nor did I ask him for his phone number; nor, unfortunately, did he ask for mine, not that I'd have given it to him... I think. Mixing business and pleasure was never a good idea.

He reached for the phone, but I stopped him.

"I'd prefer that you not notify him. If it won't get you in trouble."

"Would I be placed under arrest for obstructing a police officer?" His blue eyes twinkled.

"You might be," I replied, unable to stop myself from smiling at him.

"Well, that might not be so bad, right?"

His eyes never left mine, but I suddenly had a horrible feeling he knew exactly what I looked like naked.

He swept his hand in the direction of the elevators, indicating I was being allowed to pass, and said, "Second floor, number one."

I thanked him and walked across the hall knowing damn well he was checking me out. It was all I could do to stop myself from doing a runway walk. I pushed the elevator button—it opened immediately—stepped inside and turned around. He smiled and waved playfully. I did the same, and then I felt like an idiot.

"Focus, Kate. This isn't the Dating Game," I scolded myself.

The elevator door opened and I stepped out into a lobby, similar to Regina Mae's, but smaller. The reverend's door was to the left. A small, gold cross hung next to a small brass plate upon which the legend, Rev. Talbot (Monty) Montgomery and Family, was engraved.

And Family? Hmm.

I stepped up to the door and pushed the button. It was one of those video doorbell things. I put my hand over the lens, wondering if the man was already sound asleep.

"Who is it?" a deep voice echoed tinnily through my fingers.

I removed my hand, held up my badge, and identified myself.

The sound of locks opening echoed across the hallway. The door opened to reveal a... let's say, a robust man whose stomach made its appearance before his face.

"Reverend Montgomery?' I asked, holding up my badge.

He nodded. "Yes," he said, frowning. "It's very late, Captain. What can I do for you?"

"It is," I said, "and I'm sorry..."

"It's my son, isn't it? Is he all right? Please tell me he's all right." The man's eyes bugged with worry.

"Is your son driving your Cadillac tonight?" I asked.

"Oh, dear God, don't tell me. Was he in an accident?"

"No, sir," I said firmly. "Your son is fine. May I come in?"

The reverend took a step back, wrapping his maroon silk robe tightly across his flannel pajamas, then stepped aside for me to enter.

Oh... m'God. Are you serious? I thought as I looked around the apartment.

It was all glass, brass—gold paint and plate, I was sure— and mirrors. I felt like I was walking into the Presidential Suite at the Flamingo Hotel in Las Vegas. There was no southern charm about the reverend's residence... more a rather tacky display of the wealth he'd siphoned from the pockets of "the faithful," his congregation.

"What's this all about, Detective? Has my son been arrested?" he said as he led me to a gray leather sofa in the living room. "Please, sit down."

"Arrested?" I asked as I sat down. "That's a strange question. Why would you ask that?"

"Well, you... you're here; it's late and—"

"No, he's not been arrested," I said, interrupting him, "not yet anyway, but I do have a couple questions for you,

Reverend. Do you mind if I record our conversation?" I asked as I took my iPad from my bag.

He nodded and sat down opposite me, his back to the wall of windows that overlooked the city.

"Please call me Monty."

"Thank you," I said, uncomfortable with the idea. "I'm investigating the murder of Mrs. Genevieve Chesterton. Her body was found last Saturday morning on the River-walk, and I'd also like to talk to your son. Is he here, or is he out driving your Cadillac?"

I watched the color drain from his face.

"Oh, dear Lord. That poor, poor woman," he muttered. "No, Treyshawn, my son, isn't here, and yes, he has my car, with my permission, of course. He went out with some of his friends. He's a popular boy. It comes with the territory when you have a rather well-known family name. I'm sure you understand."

"Yes, sir, I do understand. Who is he with, do you know?"

"No, ma'am. He's basically a good boy, and I trust him. Well, you have to, don't you?" He shrugged, and his belly shook. "I know that it may not be the right thing to do, but his mama, God rest her soul, kept a tight rein on the boy... too tight, I think. Now that she's gone... he's making up for lost time, enjoying life, with his friends, on the streets, unfortunately. I don't like it, but he's an adult and can do pretty much as he wishes, and he has to learn."

He paused, thought for a minute, then continued, "And I feel that if he's to enjoy the Lord's salvation, he must be allowed the freedom... the opportunity to expel the gangster within. To do that he must learn that material things and a life of crime have nothing to offer but pain and damnation. And he *will* learn. I have faith in him."

As I sat there listening to his diatribe, I looked around the room, and it was all I could do not to roll my eyes. I had to bite my tongue. Seated in his luxurious apartment, surrounded by expensive baubles and "material things," the man was the very definition of the word hypocrite, and I dearly wanted to call him out, but I didn't. I wanted him to talk to me, and I already knew that was something he loved to do, so I figured I'd give him plenty of rope, as they say.

"You mentioned his friends," I said. "Would you mind giving me their names?"

"Umm," he wriggled uncomfortably in his seat, as if he was sitting on something sharp. "Well, I don't really know who they are. I know there's Dewayne... and Jamar... but I don't know their last names."

Of course you don't, I thought. *You're full of it. You don't know crap about your son, nor do you want to: out of sight, out of mind.*

"How about Nathan Watkins?" I asked. "Is he one of Treyshawn's friends?"

Monty nodded. His eyebrows lifted. He looked pleased, like a kid about to give a tough schoolteacher the right answer.

This should be interesting.

"Yes, I think so. I met Nathan once. It was maybe three months ago. He came to one of my fundraisers as Treyshawn's guest. They didn't stay long. My son is not interested in my political affiliations. He doesn't understand how the squeaky wheel gets the grease."

I nodded. *So Monty thinks of himself as a politician, does he? Why am I not surprised? Okay, so let's try this...*

"Did your son know Genevieve Chesterton? Did he ever mention the name?" I asked, watching his face, looking for a tell. I was disappointed. He didn't even blink.

"No," he said. "Not that I recall. But then, he doesn't talk much about his lady friends." Monty replied, smiling bashfully. "Boys always think they know more than their father's when it comes to women. Don't you agree?"

"I wouldn't know, Reverend," I replied, dryly. "I am a woman."

"But you're also a police officer, and I would have thought you'd have known about such things."

He was right. I have a degree in forensic psychology, so I did know, and I believed him when he said his son didn't talk about his girlfriends, but there was something about Monty that was rubbing me the wrong way. I pressed on.

"What does your son do for a living, Reverend?"

He hesitated, then said, "He's unemployed at the moment, but helps me out whenever I have a need; I give him a small allowance."

"Indeed, and how small is small?"

Again, he hesitated, then seemed to give in to the inevitable and said softly, "One thousand dollars a week."

Holy cow. Are you serious? That's almost what I make.

I stared at him, disbelieving, then finally, I asked, "How about Genevieve's mother-in-law, Mrs. Regina Mae Cottonwell-Chesterton? You must know her; she lives in this building. Have you ever spoken to her?" I watched his reaction.

"I've only seen her. I have never spoken to her other than to say good morning or good evening. She's usually escorted by her son. A tall fellow, rather skinny, and like Treyshawn, a bit of a mama's boy, from his appearance. But, there are worse things to be, I suppose." He chuckled.

"Does Treyshawn know Mrs. Cottonwell-Chesterton's son? His name's Eddie, by the way."

"I mean no offense, Detective, but my boy doesn't

associate much with his white brothers. I like to think it's because it reminds him too much of his mama."

"His mother was white?" I asked.

He ran his hand over his short salt-and-peppered hair, smiled sadly, then nodded and said, "We met at church, oh, it would have been almost thirty years ago now. I knew she was to be my wife the second I laid eyes on her..." he paused, looked to be deep in thought, then continued, "She was a very Godly woman, my rock, you might say. And she had a way with people; she was not afraid to ask the local politicians to dig deep in return for our support... I do miss her so."

"What happened to her?" *Not that I care, but keep on talking, my friend.*

"Cancer. It runs in her family," he replied sadly.

"That's too bad," I said. "I'm truly sorry... Monty."

I looked at my watch. It was a quarter to midnight.

"Please don't be offended," I said, "but I need to ask you: does your son date white women?"

"I... er... I don't know. I don't think so. If he does, he hasn't met any worth bringing home."

"Has your son ever been arrested?"

"No, ma'am. Not that boy." He sighed and shook his head. "He's a good boy. He *is* a good boy. Not the brightest, I'll admit, but he stays out of trouble." He looked at me, must have seen something in my expression, because he said, softly, "I can assure you he had nothing to do with this girl's death."

"Your son was seen, earlier this evening, with Nathan Watkins. Did you know he was Genevieve Chesterton's brother?"

"I did not... no!"

"They were seen entering Club Suave, together. That's

not the kind of place 'good boys' frequent. Genevieve also used to frequent Club Suave. Treyshawn, being Nathan's friend, must have known her. Therefore, you can understand why I am asking these questions." I watched his eyes, his face: nothing. He didn't seem to be too bothered that his son was patronizing a place like Club Suave.

"Yes, Detective. I totally understand," he said, looking down at his hands. "But Treyshawn is young, younger than his years. He's twenty-six years old and still thinks like a teenager, and not necessarily with his brain."

That's something to consider, I thought, as I watched his face. *I need to talk to this man-boy.*

"I'm sorry for Mrs. Cottonwell-Chesterton's loss, and her son's. I'll be sure to offer my condolences the next time I see her. And I'll say prayers for them and Genevieve. She attends a different church, but I believe God listens to all our prayers." He took another deep breath and stared at me.

"Do you know where Treyshawn was last Friday night?" I asked softly.

The Reverend Monty might have been a snake-oil salesman in the world of religion, but I didn't get the feeling he was trying to hide anything about his son. But I did get the impression they weren't close.

He thought about it before he answered, and then said, "He was out, with his friends, I suppose. I know, because I was up late myself, watching Mel Gibson's movie, *The Passion of the Christ.* I've watched it many times... Many, many times."

"What time did he come home?"

He shrugged, thought for a minute, then said, "I'm not sure. I do know it must have been very late because I was very late going to bed, and he wasn't home..." He didn't finish what he was saying.

"And what time did you go to bed?" I asked, keeping up the pressure.

He shook his head, then said, "A little after midnight, I think."

"Do you know where he was, where he went?"

He shook his head, then clasped his hands together in his lap and hung his head but said nothing more. He was thinking deeply about something. What, I didn't know. Maybe it was the movie. Maybe it was something else, something he didn't want me to know.

There was no point in trying to grill him further. The Reverend Talbot "Monty" Montgomery was, I think, being as honest as he could be, but I was pretty sure he knew he wasn't in possession of all the facts, and it was bothering him.

It was time for me to go. I tapped the button on my iPad to stop the recording, rose to my feet, and slipped the tablet into my bag.

"Thank you for your time and patience, Reverend," I said. "I really do appreciate it, and your cooperation. If you can think of anything that might help me with my investigation, please give me a call."

I handed him a business card.

"I will have to talk to your son. He isn't planning any long trips, I hope?"

"No, ma'am," he replied. "Treyshawn will be available to speak to you whenever you call. I'll make sure of it. And if you need me for anything further, please don't hesitate to ask."

I offered him my hand and thanked him, and I left him standing at the open door.

The elevator descended, the door opened, and I stepped

out and looked around for the gorgeous doorman, but the lobby was empty.

Feeling a little let down, I made my way to the revolving exit door and was just about to step inside when I heard a noise behind me. Automatically, I turned and looked to see what it was, and got the shock of my life.

A door behind the front desk, just a few yards to the right, had opened and two people had stepped out of what appeared to be a maintenance room and suddenly I was staring, eye-to-eye, at Regina Mae Cottonwell-Chesterton dressed in her robe. Behind her was a somewhat disheveled doorman.

23

*O*h yeah, I thought, as I stepped back out of the revolving door. *Now that I need to investigate.*

Regina Mae Cottonwell-Chesterton said something I couldn't hear to the dreamboat who was now back behind the front desk, and then she sprinted to her private elevator.

"Mrs. Chesterton!" I shouted.

But Regina Mae took no notice. She tugged at her silk robe, strutted into the elevator, turned around, pressed the button, and then her eyes locked on mine and held them for a split second before the doors slid shut.

I saw panic in those eyes, or was it defiance? I whirled around and stepped over to the front desk where Mr. Muscles was fumbling with his shirt buttons and trying to tuck in his shirttails at the same time.

"Well," I said. "Just look at you. You should zip up while you're at it. So, Regina Mae? One of the perks of working the night shift?"

"It's not what you think," he said, jerking up on the zipper.

"You should be careful doing it like that," I said. "You could lose your... Well, you could hurt yourself. So, what is it you think I think?"

"Regina and I have known each other a long time. I've been a doorman here for almost six years and—"

"And you know when her husband's out of town," I said, cutting him off. "Just as you know the nightly routines of most if not all of the tenants. Tell me what else do you know and who else are you servicing, Mister..."

"Racine. Daniel Racine." His cheeks were flushed, and he was sweating profusely.

The result of getting caught or his wild interlude with Regina Mae? I wondered.

"Look," he said, smiling at me, "you've got it all wrong. I—"

"Of course I have," I said sarcastically, interrupting him. "So tell me, how often does Regina Mae visit you?" I asked as I took a small notepad from my bag.

"Am I going to lose my job?"

"That depends on how honest you are with me, Mr. Racine. Now tell me, how often does she come down here and what exactly is going on?"

Daniel Racine was as dumb as he was beautiful. He spilled the beans on poor Regina Mae as if he was trying to save himself from the electric chair. They'd been carrying on for almost eighteen months. It had started out as harmless flirting but quickly intensified when Regina Mae turned up at the front desk one night wearing nothing but a silk robe.

"It wasn't my fault," he said, self-consciously trying to tidy his hair with his fingers. "She, she initiated it," he stammered.

"Oh really?" I asked, with real interest. "And how, exactly, did that work?"

"I'm not lying. Look, women... they like me," he said, without a hint of modesty. "They do. I saw the way you looked at me when you came in, so I flirted with you. You didn't seem to mind. After all, you flirted back. It's in my nature to—"

"To sleep with the lonely females in the building?" I interrupted him.

"*No*. Not at all."

"Tell me something," I said. "How many women in this building are you sleeping with, Mr. Racine?"

He took a deep breath and ran his fingers through his hair. "Three, including Regina Mae... Are you going to have me fired?"

"On the contrary. I'm going to use you, Daniel. Not unlike the horny housewives in this, this Peyton Place are using you... Oh, now don't get the wrong idea," I said when I saw him begin to grin. "You'll be keeping your pants on. Understand?" I smirked.

"Yes, ma'am."

"Good, now listen up. When Regina Mae asks what we talked about, and she will, you're going to tell her that you didn't say anything to me about your affair with her. Understand?"

"Yes, ma'am." Daniel nodded, his eyes bulging like he suddenly understood a difficult math problem.

"I want you to convince her she has nothing to worry about," I said. "And I want you to call me when Treyshawn Montgomery comes home."

"Yes... *What?*" he asked, frowning. "Why?"

"Just be a good boy, Daniel, and do as you're told, and don't ask questions. You're in enough trouble with Regina Mae. You wouldn't want to add me to the mix as well, now would you?"

He shook his head, somewhat enthusiastically, so I thought, and I had to smile at him as I slid my business card across the top of the desk toward him.

He let out a deep breath, looked at the card, picked it up, then locked eyes with me and said, "So you're not going to rat me out?"

"Not tonight," I replied and turned and walked toward the front door.

"Wait," he called after me.

I stopped, turned around, and stared at him. "Yes?"

"I don't suppose you'd let me take you to dinner... No, of course you wouldn't."

I shook my head, smiling at his audacity, and then I left him. He truly was a lovely man.

What a shame, I thought as I walked to my car.

It didn't matter to me that he wasn't too bright. I could have easily overlooked that character flaw for two, maybe even three months. But I can't tolerate a cheater. The sad thing about it was, though, that I knew he didn't think he was cheating. No, he would argue that it was Regina Mae who was the cheater. He was just enjoying the ride... Sorry, no pun intended. He wasn't married, so he wasn't doing anything wrong. Yeah, I'd heard it before from a man even better looking and certainly smarter than Daniel Racine.

"But still not smart enough," I muttered to the night as I pushed the memory of my lost love out of my mind.

I got in my car and drove toward home. The streets were pleasantly quiet, just a few cars traveling along with me. I wondered how many of them were heading home after an illicit encounter. *Bastards!*

"That's a very negative way of looking at things, Kate," I said to myself as I spotted a twenty-four-hour liquor store. I pulled in and a few minutes later pulled out again with a couple of bottles of what I thought would be a nice red wine —it was on sale for six dollars, regular price fifteen—and two bags of pork rinds. Had they sold ice cream I would have snagged a pint of chocolate-chip—it would complement the red wine admirably. But they didn't so I figured I'd make do with what I had, and then go to bed.

Oh, dear Lord. What a way to live. I really do need to get out more.

Once inside the privacy of my own apartment, I decided to forgo the shower, pour myself a glass of wine and just flop. So I did. I unscrewed the cap on the bottle—now if that doesn't tell you something, I don't know what will— filled the glass, took a long slow sip, my eyes closed, and savored the taste of decadence... It crossed my mind to really pamper myself and drink and eat in a tub full of hot, scented bubbles, but I was too exhausted to make the effort. Instead, I sat down at my coffee table, my legs stretched out in front of me and, with an old episode of Star Trek playing on the television in the background, I wrote down my thoughts about what had transpired that evening.

It had indeed been quite an evening, what with our stakeout, the wild ride on Interstate 24, my interview with the Reverend Monty and finally my run-in with Gorgeous George... Daniel.

As I perused what I'd written, I realized my list of suspects was growing, almost exponentially, but I was still no closer to finding Genevieve's killer. And I didn't see that changing anytime soon.

I picked up the now empty bottle of red, looked at it, shook my head, felt my eyes click first to one side then the other, trying to catch up with my face. *Wow, that's some powerful stuff,* I thought as I walked a little unsteadily to the kitchen and dropped the bottle into the garbage can.

"So what if I'm buzzed?" I argued with the image of Captain Kirk. "I think I'm more honest, more forthright when I'm buzzed. Let's face it, the only people who are ever truly honest are drunks and children. Right? Hmm, maybe I should try plying my suspects with booze before I question them." *That's a great idea,* I thought, blearily. "I'll run it by the chief. Maybe he'll increase my budget to cover the cost," I giggled.

Oh, yeah? I thought. *And maybe he'll just kick your silly ass out.*

The sheer stupidity of the idea made me laugh out loud and say to Kirk, "I'd love to talk to Edward Eaton Chesterton the Second while he's under the 'fluence of a little extra sauce."

That was the last thing I remembered until I woke up in bed the next morning with a blinding headache.

24

The weekend passed uneventfully for a change: no call-outs, no late-night phone calls, not even one from Janet. I ran six miles early on Saturday morning, and again on Sunday. The rest of the time I spent relaxing, but always on the alert for the dreaded phone call; it never came, and I couldn't remember the last time that had happened. So, I should have been bright and perky when I arrived at my office early that Monday in May, but I wasn't.

Yes, I'd been able to relax. I ate sensibly, didn't drink a single drop of wine, or any other alcoholic beverage, and I slept well, but when I got out of bed that Monday morning, I was blessed with a headache that bordered on a migraine, so what was wrong? I couldn't figure it out. I took three aspirin, washed them down with black coffee, hit the shower, and then dressed for work: blue jeans, light blue blouse, lightweight tan blazer.

I stopped on the way to the office to grab a large coffee to go, then parked the car in my spot, and pushed my way through the rear door into the building.

"Hey, Captain," Randy Lewis called as I walked out of the elevator. "What's with the sunglasses? Paparazzi following you?" Randy was one of my favorite uniformed cops.

"Very funny," I snapped as I slowly made my way through the crowded room toward my office, trying to hang onto my bag and iPhone and to not slop the overfull, extra-large cup of steaming hot coffee. It had a lid on it, but you know how reliable those are, right? And it was so hot I didn't dare sip it for fear of losing all sensation in my taste buds.

"Rough night, Captain?" some wag at the far side of the room shouted.

"Who's the lucky guy?" another yelled. "I'd hate to see what he looks like this morning."

"No guy, asshole. I have a headache, so shut the hell up and find something useful to do." I rolled my eyes behind my sunglasses, then realized they couldn't see the move.

"Geez, you guys are hilarious," I muttered to the group of grinning uniforms hanging around the water cooler, waiting for their shift to start.

Finally, I made it into my office, my refuge, but wouldn't you know it, little miss perky was already there waiting for me.

"Don't start," I said, testily, before Janet could speak. "I have a headache, so sit quietly for a minute or go someplace else."

"Yes, ma'am," she whispered.

I immediately felt sorry for being so snarky.

"Sorry, Janet. Just give me a few minutes to drink a little coffee, okay?"

And so we sat there; me with my eyes closed sipping on

the still scalding coffee, and Janet thumbing through Pinterest on her iPhone.

Finally, I opened my eyes, set the coffee on my desk, and looked at her. I closed my eyes again, rolled them under the lids so she couldn't see it, sighed inwardly and said, "Okay, Janet. I can see you're dying to tell me something. What is it?"

"So, I did some digging on Reverend Talbot 'Monty' Montgomery. He has a son named—"

"Treyshawn. I know."

I told her about my late night on Friday. I did, of course, leave out the part where I flirted with the doorman. I did tell her how I caught Regina Mae making a late-night booty call to avail herself of the amenities, the hunky doorman.

"*NO WAY!*" she shrieked, and pain speared through my brain. "You're lying," she gasped.

"What?" I asked, my eyes barely open. "I don't lie... well, only when I need to, but why in the world would I lie about something like that?"

"That kind of stuff only happens in movies," Janet squeaked. "So, are you going to use it to squeeze her for more information? No wait! I can do it... Can I do it, Kate, please, please? I could wear a wire or something?"

"Janet, I love your enthusiasm, but you need to calm down, take it easy. I need to—"

"I'll try," she said, interrupting me. I know she heard me, but she didn't hear me, if you understand what I mean. "This isn't nearly as juicy," she said, "but I ran the Montgomerys through the databa—"

"Please, Janet, stop," I said, putting my hands over my ears. "You're killing me. Go get the others. There's no point in going over everything twice."

She jumped to her feet and left and then returned ten

minutes later, followed by the rest of the team: Hawk, Anne, and Lenny. I waited until they were seated and looking at me expectantly, and I told them to take notes. Then I related the events of the previous Friday: our stakeout at Nathan Watkins' home, the Cadillac, Treyshawn and my interview with Monty Montgomery... and I glossed over my encounter with Dirty Dan and Regina Mae.

While I talked, I stood and brought the storyboard up to date. I added the names of Nathan Watkins, the Reverend Monty, and Treyshawn.

"So," I said, stepping away from the board and staring at it, "this is what we have: six people of interest including our prime suspect, Eddie Chesterton and the mysterious Frenchman he so obligingly dropped on us, but let's not forget that the murder could just have been a random act of violence... although the method would tend to negate that. And I think there's still something we're missing. The questions we have to answer are twofold. First one: who benefits from Genevieve's death?"

I looked around the room. Janet was nibbling on the eraser at the end of her pencil; Lenny stared at me over the screen of his laptop; Anne had her legs crossed and her arms folded; Hawk was leaning back in his chair, his eyes half-closed and I wondered for a minute if he was asleep. He wasn't.

"Well?" I prodded.

"I... don't think anyone does," Janet said hesitantly. "She had no money or property of her own. There was a small life insurance policy... well, small for that family, two-hundred-and-fifty thousand. That's a drop in the ocean for them, even for Eddie. Not a motive, I shouldn't think. It's less than his annual allowance. No one gains, in my opinion."

"That's true," I said, "so then the question becomes: Why did she have to die, and why did she have to die in such a gruesome way? Was the act premeditated, an act of opportunity, or a random act by a mugger? It wouldn't be the first time, would it? So, what could be the motive? Not money. Revenge, maybe? Hate? Love? Or just plain old rejection?"

I paused, waited to see if anyone would jump in. One did.

"You left one out," Hawk said.

Everyone turned to look at him.

"Oh?" I said. "Do tell."

"I think it was a professional hit."

"And why's that?" I asked.

"Look at the marks on her neck," he said, pointing at one of the autopsy photos.

"Okay, I'm looking, so?"

"Looks like it was done with a garrote to me, a short loop of thin twine, like this." He took a piece of black twine from his pocket and tied the ends together to make it a loop, then he threaded it around the fingers of both hands, and continued, "Also, see how the ligature marks are slightly angled upward from front to back, and notice the position of the bruises where his knuckles bit into her neck. He was tall, taller than her, and she was... how tall was she?"

I looked at the autopsy report and said, "five-ten."

Hawk nodded and said, "And she was wearing four-inch heels, as I recall. That puts her at six-two... Stand up a minute, Anne."

She gave him a funny look, but she did as she was asked. Hawk stood, left his seat and went to stand behind her.

"How tall are you, Anne?" he asked.

"Five-nine, why?"

"Five-nine," he said, nodding, and you're wearing..." he looked down at her feet, "flats. I'm five-eleven, so we're of comparable heights to the vic and her killer. Now look..."

He stood behind her, clenched his fists, the loop of twine still wrapped around his fingers, slipped the garrote over her head and pulled it tight, placing his fists on either side of her neck, his elbows down, his forearms against her back.

"See what I mean?" he said. "He would have used his forearms against her back and his fists against her neck for leverage. We're looking for a guy at least six-two, maybe even a little taller."

He removed the loop from around Anne's neck, and they both sat down again.

"That could be both Eddie and Nathan," I said.

"And Treyshawn," Janet piped up.

"Or the Frenchman," Hawk said, returning to his seat. "He could have been hired by either Wheaton or the old man. If Eddie knew about him, Wheaton would certainly have known too."

"We don't know how tall he is," I said, "or if he even exists. Janet's right, Treyshawn is tall enough, so are Nathan and Eddie."

"But you've just said, they don't have motive," Anne said. "Why would her brother want to kill her? Why would her husband, or some friend of her brother's? It makes no sense. A professional hit, though..."

"I told you," I said. "Love, hate, lust, revenge. We still don't know what's in any of their heads. We already know Wheaton's a predator, so he could have lusted after her, been rejected, and wanted revenge. So could Treyshawn, for that matter, or his two friends."

You'll be believing your own BS next, Kate, I thought, grimly.

I stared at Hawk, mulling it over. He was right, why would they want to kill her, and so horribly? But I still wasn't buying it.

"Okay," I said. "Let's suppose you're right. Who would want to hire a professional killer?" I already knew the answer, but I wanted to see what Hawk would say.

"Old man Chesterton, of course," Hawk said.

Oh yeah, I was right. I shook my head.

"I don't see it, Hawk. Why, what would be his motive?"

"You interviewed the bigoted, racist old bastard, so you tell me. You think he wanted a black grandson or grand-daughter inheriting his stash? Hell no. My money's on him and his Frenchman."

I stared at him, as did the others. I hesitated, then said, "Okay, Hawk. I'll buy in. You and Anne find the French-man, and quickly."

He nodded but said nothing.

"How about Wheaton's alibi?" I asked him.

It was Anne that answered. She flipped through the screens on her iPad and then said, "He was with a Lucy Weston. She lives in a gated community off Highway 8. According to her, the subject arrived at her home around eight-thirty on Friday evening May third and didn't leave until after nine the following morning, Saturday. So, he's in the clear."

"Is she credible?" I asked, looking at one and then the other.

Neither of them answered, though Hawk shrugged.

"Oh come on, people. Either she is or she isn't. If she isn't, then—"

"I wouldn't trust her with my dirty laundry," Hawk said. "She's twenty years younger than he is and in it for his money. Sure, she's going to protect him; as in protecting her investment, if you can call selling your body an investment."

"Sheesh," Janet said. "Why don't you tell us what you really think."

"So," I said to Hawk, "was she lying or not?"

He lowered his head, closed his eyes and slowly shook his head, then he looked up at me and said, helplessly, "I don't know, Kate. Unless we can prove she's lying, we have to take her word for it and rule him out as the actual killer. But let's not forget, he could have hired it done."

I nodded. "I'm not ruling him out, not yet anyway. Lenny." I turned to look at him. "Any luck finding those two girls Wheaton supposedly assaulted?"

"Working on it," he said.

I stared at him, "Any idea when you might know something?"

"As soon as I can, Captain."

"I want you to dig into old man Chesterton's company. I want backgrounds on all his senior staff, especially any with French-sounding names."

"You got it."

Geez, I thought inwardly. I heaved a huge sigh. *This guy is tough to deal with... I wonder if it's me? Maybe he doesn't like me. Okay, tough; he's going to have to suck it up and deal with it.*

I sat down, swiveled my chair so I could see the story-board, stared at it making mental notes, then I turned again to face my team.

"Okay," I said, making notes on a yellow pad. "Hawk,

Anne, finding the Frenchman is your number one priority, but I also want you to check Nathan Watkins' alibi. He claims he was with friends at a place called Sheppy's. Do you know it?"

"Yup!" Hawk said, nodding.

"Good, and while you're at it, see if you can find Treyshawn's two friends..." I checked my notes, "Dewayne and Jamar and interview them both, separately. Find out what they were doing that night, who they were with. I want to know specifically what Treyshawn was doing that night. Janet and I will deal with Treyshawn himself. That doorman should have called me by now. If he... well, never mind." I didn't want to get into all the details right then.

"Janet," I continued and she looked up at me, expectantly. "What did you find out about the Montgomerys?"

"Well," Janet said, "as I started to say earlier, I ran the Montgomerys through the database. Neither one has priors. There are a lot of political affiliations, but—"

She was interrupted by my phone ringing.

"Maybe this is my doorman," I said, looking at the 'unknown number' flag on the iPhone screen. "I told Daniel to call the minute Treyshawn got home, but I have a feeling he's one slippery—"

I answered the call, "Captain Gazzara."

"*Captain Gazzara*, what in the hell do you think you are doing?"

Well, it certainly wasn't the doorman.

"Excuse me?" I snapped, sending spears of pain around the back of my eyes.

"I received a phone call from my daughter-in-law. She said that you were skulking around her apartment at all hours of the night spying on her. We're not talking surveillance here, Captain. We're talking downright harassment."

Geez, it's the old man!

"Mr. Chesterton?" I asked.

"Of course it's Mr. Chesterton! Who the hell else would it be? Now unless you have cause to be slinking around her apartment building, and I'm confident that you don't, you will leave me with no choice but to report you to your superiors."

"Mr. Chesterton, I go wherever the trail leads me. It just so happens that—"

"It just so happens, Miss Gazzara, that your trail crossed the path of the biggest man-whore in all of Tennessee, Daniel Racine. That doorman has been through more women than the revolving door in the lobby." Chesterton stopped talking, took a deep breath, cleared his throat, and then continued, "If you think you can pump that shit-for-brains for information by sleeping with him, I'll have both your jobs."

"What?"

"My daughter-in-law may not be running on all cylinders, but I won't tolerate my kin being harassed. Now, I know you've become quite comfortable working with the neighborhood darkies and that you're reluctant to arrest any of them. You're one of those "woke" cops I'm always hearing about, I'm sure, but I'm telling you now that I show no preference for men or women when it comes to throwing the hammer down."

"Are you threatening me, Mr. Chesterton?" I asked.

"It ain't a threat to tell an incompetent to do their damn job," he snarled. "If I find out you've been skulking around my daughter-in-law's apartment without probable cause, I'll have that shiny badge of yours and you'll be lucky to get a job as a security guard at Roscoe's Coat Factory." Then the line went dead.

I looked around the room. As far as I could tell, only Janet had heard the diatribe.

"Okay, people," I said, "go get 'em. I'll check in with you later."

I waited until the door closed and then looked at Janet and laughed out loud, suffering yet another stab of pain as a result.

"Oh... My... God," Janet said, her eyes wide. "What was that all about? He threatened you. We can arrest him for that. I'll go get him, right now. Just gimme the word, Kate."

I shook my head, then said, "Nope, that was just too funny. I needed a good laugh, and anyway I have a better idea."

"We're going to visit Regina Mae, right?" Janet asked. I swear she was almost salivating at the idea.

"No. Granddad Chesterton said to leave the poor delicate peach alone. We're going to go and talk to his grandson."

I stood, grabbed my iPad, adjusted my badge on my belt, and took a deep breath. Oh yes, I was pissed off that Chesterton had the temerity to make such a call, but I wasn't the least bit threatened by the old man. He didn't know why I was at the apartment building that night, and that was good. I intended to let it stay that way, at least for now.

Every once in a while, when I became angry, I'd channel my inner Dirty Harry. This was one of those times. Maybe it was my elevated state of emotion that finally rid me of the headache, but suddenly it was gone, and I was ready to take on the world.

But, like all good plans, this one went awry when the chief showed up in my office.

"Detective Toliver, I need to talk to Captain Gazzara in private, if you'd give us a moment, please."

My first thought was that Granddad Chesterton had indeed put in a call to the chief and threatened to file charges against me and the entire department if the chief didn't put a muzzle on me.

"I received a call from Mrs. Evelyn Karl yesterday. You remember her, of course. It seems she's nominated you for the Chattanooga Police Officer of the Year award."

"Evelyn Karl?" I said, just a little stunned at the news. "Yes, I remember her... What on earth?" *Officer of the year? Yay,* I thought sarcastically, *that's a first and one I can do without.*

"Oh, good lord, Chief. Do I have to?"

He smiled. "Of course you do. Why wouldn't you?"

I simply shrugged and basically accepted my fate.

Evelyn Karl's granddaughter, Molly, was a runaway. We, that is I, found her in a crack house and returned her to her grandmother. She went to rehab, I think. Quite frankly I was sure I'd be hearing from Evelyn Karl again, but only to tell me the girl ran away again. Molly was your typical problem child.

It was a sad story. The girl was a product of a broken family, a black family. The father had left them just after Molly was born. The mother had questionable and an insatiable taste in men so grandma stepped in and tried to raise the child.

It was a story we cops hear many times during our careers. Evelyn reported her missing and I caught the case, one of Henry Finkle's last favors, and I say that with tongue in cheek. Anyway, I didn't have much hope of finding her. I figured she was a runaway and if she was, I was pretty well certain she was in the hands of a pimp sex trafficker who had her drugged and for sale on the streets.

I can't say I did anything differently than I have for other parents who tell me their child hasn't come home. All I can remember is that I called Evelyn Karl every other day to tell her where I was going and what I was doing. It was only blind luck that I even stumbled across Molly. I was called out to an armed robbery, and wouldn't you know it; one of the witnesses was a scrawny girl that vaguely resembled Molly's photograph.

One of the uniforms took her statement, but she was gone before I could talk to her. It wasn't hard to find her though. When I walked into that crack house that afternoon they scattered like roaches, all but the scrawny kid. She wasn't high, but she would have been if I hadn't intervened.

"Molly?" I asked, crouching down beside her.

"Yeah?"

"You ready to go home?"

She looked up at me with tears in her eyes and nodded.

"Would you like me to take you to your grandmother? She's been looking for you."

"Yeah." That was all she said.

She didn't talk in the car on the way to the station. When we arrived I asked her if she'd like some water or a Coke, but she shook her head. When her grandmother walked in, however, it was like a gate opened. Molly ran to her, crying and babbling and apologizing... and so did Evelyn. It was very touching.

So I had Evelyn sign the papers, gave her the address of a rehab facility where she could get Molly some help, and suggested she take her to the hospital for a checkup. She said she would do just that, and I let it go. I didn't really think she would, but once I handed the kid over it was out of my hands, so I went back to working on the real cases, the murders, rapes, you know, the stuff that makes the news, good for the TV stations and ratings.

I never gave Evelyn or her granddaughter a second thought. Not until now

"Well, I can't tell Mrs. Karl what to do, but I don't need this, not now, Chief."

"Of course you do. You want my job someday, don't you? You need to sign a couple of forms and confirm her statement."

"Well, okay, I guess." Was all I could think of to say. *Me Chief of Police? That's a hoot.*

"They'll be in my office tomorrow morning. I've got to sign off on them, too. Any time you have a few minutes."

He put his hand on the doorknob and I had hoped that was the end of it. But, of course, it wasn't.

"Tell me, Kate: how's the Chesterton case going? Good news, I hope?"

"If no news is good news, then yes, Chief. Good news."

"Smartass," he said, smiling. "Keep me informed. No nasty surprises, okay?"

"Yes, sir... and no, sir."

He smiled again, nodded, opened the door and stepped out into the corridor.

"Everything okay, Cap?" Janet asked, opening the door and poking her nose inside.

"Grab your badge and let's go."

A few minutes later we were in the car and headed west in the direction of Eddie Chesterton's apartment.

25

"I don't think I'd like to live in an apartment building with an arcade in the lobby," Janet said as we walked inside.

"Oh, yes? Why is that?"

"Well, think about it. You can get your dry cleaning here. Your groceries here... well some, at that convenience store. You can get a coffee here, have a drink here. Drinks lead to talking to strangers. That can lead to hookups. If everyone in your building is staying close to home, it could become one big, nasty, incestuous group," she said with her lips pulled down at the corners as she studied everyone walking around. "Gross. I'll bet fifty percent of these people have slept together. If not literally then by two degrees of separation."

Oh yeah, I had to laugh at that, especially when I thought about Regina Mae and Dirty Dan.

"You don't need an arcade for that... Wow, Janet, you have a weird way of thinking. You came up with all that just by observing the convenience store and the dry cleaner?" I asked.

"I did." She lifted her chin proudly.

I grinned and said, "You amaze me, Toliver."

"I amaze myself," she said as she stepped aside for me to enter the elevator.

I stood outside Eddie's door, put my finger to my lips and looked at Janet, then put my ear to the door and listened. I could hear the soft sounds of cool jazz, and possibly the clinking of glasses, but no voices. Well, it was a little too early for drinks, although Eddie did offer me one the first visit.

I knocked on the door and covered the peephole with my hand.

"Who is it?" Eddie Chesterton barked; he sounded frustrated.

"Eddie? It's Captain Gazzara. We need to talk."

The door opened a crack, but the chain was still on.

"Come on, Eddie. Open the door. Let us in."

The door closed and I heard the sound of the chain being removed, then it opened again, and there he was in all his glory.

"My Lord, Eddie. Don't you ever get dressed?"

He tugged at the sleeves and the belt of the same robe he'd been wearing the first time I talked to him. His hair was disheveled, his eyes bloodshot, and he needed a shave.

"What do you want this time?" he said as he turned his back on us and walked unsteadily to the kitchen.

"I need answers to some questions," I said as I tapped my iPad.

"I'm going to record the interview. You okay with that, Eddie?"

He shrugged, and told me, "yeah, whatever," then he took a coffee cup from a small cabinet. His hand shook as he poured his coffee; the man was nervous. He kept glancing toward what I assumed must be his bedroom.

I read the date, time, and those present, into the recording app, and then introduced Janet. "This is Sergeant Toliver." I jerked my thumb toward Janet. "Sergeant, this is Mr. Chesterton, Eddie, as he likes to be called."

She nodded at him and said, "I'll start the Q and A with who's in the bedroom?" Janet asked.

"No one," Eddie snapped.

Janet wasn't about to play games.

"Well let's see, shall we?"

With her hand on her weapon, she stepped over to the bedroom door and knocked loudly on it.

"Chattanooga Police!" she shouted. "Come out with your hands up... Now!"

Seconds later the door opened and a young woman emerged wearing nothing but skimpy lace underwear. Her skin was flawless, the color of creamy coffee, and her hair was weaved into a fantastic French braid that reached almost to her waist.

"So soon, Eddie?" I asked. "What's your name, honey?"

"Camille Bolton." She kept her hands up. Her nails were long, bright green daggers.

"Camille," Janet said, "put your hands down and take a seat on the couch."

"She's just a friend," Eddie shouted. "She doesn't have anything to do with anything!"

"Hush," I said. "The neighbors will hear you."

I sat down opposite the girl. She was gorgeous. I couldn't take my eyes off her. *No... nothing like that, for Pete's sake. She was lovely, and I was wondering what the hell she was doing with a jerk like Eddie.*

"Camille, how do you know Eddie?"

"We just met last night," she said. "I mean, we knew each other from the club, but we just hooked up last night. He said he'd just broke up with his girlfriend."

Her eyes bounced back and forth from me to Janet and back again, then she seemed to gain confidence and said, "Look, I don't know what he's into, but I ain't got nothing to do with it. Can I get my clothes on?"

I nodded and said, "Go ahead. Janet, go with her. Keep an eye on her."

She looked harmless enough but looks can be deceiving, and I wasn't about to take any chances. Anyway, she didn't seem to mind the company, but she scowled at Eddie like an angry cat; he visibly withered under her glare.

"What are you doing here, Detective?" he said angrily. "I told you it was my grandfather who had my wife killed. Why haven't you arrested him yet?"

"Eddie, your wife has been dead little more than a week and you've already got some poor girl in your bed? And you lied to her. You told her you'd broken up with your girl-friend. That wasn't nice of you, Eddie, now was it?" I asked like I was a disappointed mother. "You can see how I might find that suspicious, can't you?"

And then I heard laughter coming from the bedroom. It sounded like Camille. It seemed that she and Janet were getting along quite well.

"I'm lonely," he whined. "You don't know what it's like, coming home to an empty apartment, waking up in the morning and Genevieve's not here. I miss her. I needed some company that's all. No big deal. I just didn't know what else to do."

"Some people go to church, Eddie. Some people join a therapy group. Some even take a few days, weeks, months just to mourn and grieve and get their mind around the fact that their loved one is gone. I'm just spit-balling here." I smirked. "In all the times I've had to break the bad news to a loved one, never once did anyone go right out and pick up a newer model. That's pretty damn cold, Eddie."

"I know how it looks," he stammered.

"Oh yeah? How does it look, Eddie? Tell me."

"Bad?" He put his hands on the counter of his kitchen island. "It looks bad. I know. But I'm just so upset. I loved Jennifer."

"Genevieve?"

"Genevieve!" he corrected himself, then screwed up his eyes and tried to cry.

It was an embarrassing display. He couldn't; he just looked constipated. I wanted to slap the cuffs on him and take him in just for bad acting, but I let him continue.

"You see? I don't even know what I'm saying. My heart is broken and I... wanted some relief. I just wanted to forget what my grandfather did for a little while."

Just then Camille came out of the bedroom. She was wearing a hot pink, spandex top and a tight black skirt that barely covered her butt; between them they highlighted every curve, and there were plenty of them. Without paying any attention to Janet or me, she stared at Eddie. He smiled up at her, sheepishly.

"Dead wife?" she snapped. "Are you serious? What kind of creep are you? I need cab fare." Camille put her hands on her hips.

Eddie sighed. "Uhm, can't we settle this later?"

"You think I'm going to take the bus dressed like this? Boy, you crazy."

"I don't know if I have any cash on me right now and—"

"I know you didn't just say that." Camille flipped her hair. "You got cash somewhere. Find it!"

I had to smile at Eddie's distress. Camille had moxie, that was for sure.

Eddie looked first at Janet and then at me.

"Don't look at me," I said. "I'm just a cop, remember?"

He rose unsteadily to his feet, hustled around the kitchen, opened a couple of drawers, looked bewildered, then went into his office. I, of course, followed him and watched as he knelt down in front of a small safe. After a couple of clicks and snaps he opened the safe door and took out several bills.

I followed him back into the kitchen and watched as he handed them to Camille. Judging by the flash of her eyes, they were big enough to get her home and then some, maybe even big enough for her to forget about what had just happened to her. She snatched them out of his hand, spun on her four-inch heels and, without so much as a word, flounced out of the apartment slamming the door behind her so loudly it made Eddie jump.

"That was nice of you," I said. "Now, can we get back to business?"

"I'm not feeling well," Eddie said, licking his lips, trying to look sick. "I think I need to lie down."

"You can do that later. I wonder what your grandfather would do if he knew you had a woman like Camille in your apartment?"

At first he just looked at me, then sighed, lowered his head, and said, "He doesn't care what I do."

He walked over to the sofa and flopped down on it.

"Oh, I think you are wrong there," I said. "He made it very clear to me that he doesn't like people of color."

"Yeah, well, screw him," Eddie snapped back, suddenly not so woozy. "What he doesn't know won't hurt him."

"Do you think he knew that Genevieve was black?" I asked.

Eddie froze, and I mean he *froze!*

"What? What are you talking about?" He practically choked on the words. "Genevieve wasn't black." Bless him, he tried, but I could tell by the look on his face that he knew that she was.

"Yes, she was." I explained Doc's findings and told him about my visit to her biological parents. "But you did know, didn't you, Eddie?"

"Her parents?" he asked, seemingly dumbfounded. "She told me she didn't have any family."

He stood, paced, then finally sat down on one of the bar stools at his kitchen island.

"Okay," he said resignedly. "Yes, I did know. I knew she was black, but I didn't know she had a family... She was the right kind of black, didn't look it, not at all, but behind closed doors she sure as hell acted like it, in all the right ways."

"Wow," Janet muttered. "Nice way to talk about your wife. You really are a piece of work."

"I meant it as a compliment," he said. "I loved her. What did my grandfather say? Did he say anything about my money?"

"He might have mentioned your *allowance*," I said. It was a cheap dig, but I couldn't help myself. What kind of grown man gets an allowance?

"Screw my allowance. Did he say anything about my inheritance?"

"Not a word... Eddie, you mean to tell me that your wife didn't tell you that she had a family in Baton Rouge? You want to tell me how your grandfather knew and you didn't? And you are aware he also knew Genevieve was black?"

"No. How could he know that? Genevieve looked like she'd just stepped out of an Irish Spring commercial for God's sake. When I met her in Baton Rouge, she was a nobody. No, the old man didn't know." Eddie swallowed hard. "You're lying. He would have no way of knowing unless you told him. I didn't, and I know Genevieve didn't. I even arranged for her to get that job at CDE." He started to pace again.

"You met her in Baton Rouge?" I asked.

"Yeah. I was with my mother on one of her fundraisers. My father was out of town, as usual. It isn't proper for a Southern lady to travel unescorted, at least, my mother doesn't think so." Eddie winced at the thought.

"That was when I met Genevieve. She was like an angel. We talked for hours on the phone... She was perfect. Sure, she was a little rough around the edges but nothing that couldn't be fixed. No one knew she was black."

"You obviously don't know your grandfather very well, Eddie," Janet said. "He had a thorough background check done on your wife."

"He would have said something to me. He would have told me. He would have gone ballistic." Eddie sounded terrified. "Oh, my God. I made sure everything looked right. What have I—"

"Had Genevieve told you she was pregnant?" I asked, interrupting him before he freaked out.

He shook his head but wouldn't look at me. Whatever came out of his mouth next was going to be a lie.

"No. No, I didn't know until Mother shared the news with me after you told her." He put his head in his hands. "I knew she'd be good at making babies. We spent so much time—"

"Eddie," I said, interrupting him, not wanting to hear

what he was going to say next, "I need you to think for me. Do you know Treyshawn Montgomery?"

He looked at me as if I just dropped something nasty into his hand. His shoulders slumped. He took a deep breath and then released it in a long, defeated sigh and rolled his eyes.

"Yes, I know him. Everyone knows Treyshawn. He's a dealer. But he only deals to those of us who know how to keep a secret. He doesn't sell to Bubba down the street. You understand?"

"So you're telling us that you've bought illegal drugs from Treyshawn Montgomery?" Janet asked.

"Of course. Everyone I know has," Eddie said, wiping the sweat from his top lip.

"How about Genevieve?" I asked. "Did she buy from him?

"Sometimes. I think so. I don't know what she did when I wasn't with her, but everyone who's anyone likes to do a little something special... and they get it from Treyshawn. I'm just saying."

"Well here's the thing, Eddie," I said. "Treyshawn and Genevieve's brother Nathan Watkins are known to be friends, good friends... Did you know about Genevieve's brother; did she ever mention him to you?"

"Nathan? I know him too. He's her *brother?*" Eddie asked, aghast.

"You didn't know?" Janet asked without looking up from scribbling her notes.

"No, she never told me about him, or that she even had a brother. I thought she just liked slumming it a little with them, that she was playing some kind of game."

"Did you ever suspect Genevieve of having an affair?" I said, interrupting his train of thought.

He looked at me, astounded, then said, hotly, "*No*. She'd never have cheated on me. Not because she loved me, which she did, but because I had money and will someday be a billionaire. She even had my initials tattooed on her back; you know that. But see, I held the purse strings. No, she'd never have cheated on me."

"Eddie, I think we should—"

"Nathan was her brother? You've got to be shitting me. I can't believe it. Do you know how much money I paid that piece of shit for pot and... he knew I was family..." his voice trailed off as he suddenly looked at Janet and me like he was hoping we hadn't heard what he'd just said. Before I could ask any more questions, however, he slammed his hand down on the kitchen counter.

"If those people think they have a claim on my money just because I was married to Genevieve, they can think again!"

"What?" I said and looked at Janet who was staring wide-eyed at him.

"Oh, I get it. I really do get it," he snarled, alert now and angry. "Those people think they've found them a gravy train, don't they? Well, Genevieve married me under false pretenses! She lied to me. She told me she had no family, no brothers or sisters. They won't get one red cent! I'll hire the best lawyers in the state and bleed them dry before I let a bunch of cotton-pickers get their hands on the money my family earned!"

"I guess the apple doesn't fall too far from the tree," Janet muttered.

"I guess not," I said, so taken aback I was wondering what the hell to say next.

"I know what you're thinking," he snapped, "and I don't frickin' care." Eddie's eyes began to water. "Genevieve," he whispered. "My Genevieve..." He looked up at me and continued, "We had a few problems, and she obviously had some secrets, but I loved her."

"Oh yeah, sure you did. We can see that," Janet said nodding, frowning. "I'm sure Camille could, too," she finished sarcastically.

"Go ahead. Make fun. I did love her. I could have married anyone I wanted. *Anyone!* But I chose her. And I'm not ashamed to tell you the sex was amazing!" He folded his arms and smirked.

"That's enough, Eddie, way more information than we needed," I said. "Will you be seeing Treyshawn any time soon?"

Once again, the man froze, and from the look on his face, I doubted we'd get anything further from him. I was only half right.

He shrugged, wiped his eyes with a paper towel, then said thoughtfully, "I don't know. Maybe... I mean no. Are you kidding me? No, I won't be seeing Treyshawn again. Not today. Not ever. Not that stinking brother either."

His Adam's apple bobbed up and down as he swallowed hard. "I think you need to leave now."

"Eddie," Janet said brightly, as she rose to her feet and snapped her notebook closed, "this conversation was really enlightening. I think it's safe to say we all learned a little something, right?" she said with a sweet smile. "My mom always said if you can learn from your mistakes it's all worth it... and boy, have you ever made some doozies."

"Words to live by, Eddie," I added as I stood up.

"I'm asking you both to leave, now," Eddie said, and then pinched his lips together so tightly they all but disappeared. "Don't make me call security."

"All right, Eddie," I said. "We've taken up enough of

your time, and I thank you for it, but I'm afraid this isn't over. Genevieve's killer is still out there, and I'm going to find him."

He snorted, then said, "That's because you people are too timid to arrest my grandfather. I have to admit, though; he is one scary son of a bitch." And with that said, he stomped to the door, yanked it open and stood there with one hand on the knob, the other hanging limply at his side. He looked like a pitiful scarecrow wearing an expensive robe and pajama bottoms. I half expected to see a huge, black crow land on his bony shoulder. We hadn't made it two steps into the hallway when the door slammed shut behind us.

26

"I get the feeling he was happy to see us go," Janet said as she started toward the elevator.

I shook my head, put my index finger to my lips, took a tiny microphone with an earbud from my bag, put the bud in my ear and placed the tiny mike against the door and whispered, "This was not an interrogation, Janet. This was baiting the hook."

I listened for a few seconds and then heard a panicked Eddie, loud and clear, talking to his mother on the phone. Just as I'd hoped, our visit had scared the pants off him.

"The police were here," he shouted. "They were asking me all kinds of questions about... no... no, they didn't say anything about you! Why aren't they questioning Granddaddy?"

I grabbed Janet's pocket notepad from her hand, gave her the mike, signaled for her to hold it against the door, and I began taking notes. Well, I tried to, but it wasn't easy.

"Mama, I feel sick... Yes. Yes, I want you to come over. But when? When is this all going to be over with?" He sounded like a spoiled child, and I guess that's exactly what he was.

"Can we go to Miami? Yes, yes, I'd like to go again. No. No, Mama, I promise I won't go clubbing without you. We can go together, just like we did when I was on spring break."

Janet had her ear to the door, and she looked sideways at me with her jaw hanging open.

"As soon as this problem with Genevieve is resolved we can go? You promise? Yes, I feel better. Do you really mean it, Mama? Yes... Yes, I know. Yes, I'll calm down. Do you think the police will arrest Granddaddy soon?"

I wasn't sure what I was listening to, but whatever this exchange between mother and son was it was creeping me out.

"And it won't affect me, right? I mean, I won't have my inheritance cut back or anything, will I?"

And then something broke.

"You promised he wouldn't take away my money," he yelled. "How do you expect me to live? I can't believe this! No! No... No, you don't! You don't love me!"

Now it was my turn to look at Janet with a slackened jaw.

The shouting subsided and I could hear Eddie muttering, but I couldn't make out the words until...

"Just make sure it's a Ferrari—a black one! And when we go to Miami, I want the Penthouse Suite at the Setai. You had it last time and I had to take one on the floor below. No! It was horrible. No, you can't use the Jacuzzi unless I say so."

Janet mouthed the word "Wow."

I nodded my head, jerked my thumb toward the elevator, and we quickly made our way back down to the lobby.

"What's with those two?" Janet asked, shimmying her shoulders as a shiver ran over her. "I feel like I need a shower after listening to that exchange. Do you think they are... you know?"

"Well, I have to admit the conversation sounded a little incestuous. It also sounded like Granddad has cut his allowance. Can you believe she's buying him a Ferrari? I think that Eddie is a little too confident that Granddad is the one who did Genevieve in."

"Do you think he did it, killed his wife?" Janet asked.

"Me thinks little Eddie doth protest too much," I said. "When we get back to the station, I want you to have Lenny dig deep into Regina Mae... and Mr. Daniel Racine. See if there's anything there. It might be a good idea to apply a little pressure to both of them."

"Got it," Janet said. "What are you going to do?"

"I'm going to try and get a handle on some of my overdue paperwork, but while I'm doing that, I'm thinking that maybe Granddad will call me again, or worse, call the chief." I smirked. "I did, after all, ignore the old goat's specific instructions so I have a feeling I might be in for some serious scolding."

Back at the PD, Janet went her way and I went mine. I closed my office door and sat down behind my desk and looked at the clock on the wall; it was just eleven-thirty with the sun peeking through the slats of my blinds.

I wished it were a little more overcast. Gray days somehow made the work easier. Well, maybe that was just me. But, regardless of it shaping up to be a bright afternoon, I did manage to wrap up several open files and answer a half-dozen emails. *Good job, Kate!*

By three-thirty I was done with office work—not finished with it, just done for the day—and was kind of surprised that Janet hadn't returned with a status report on her findings. And I hadn't heard from any of the others either. So I went looking.

Janet was not in her cubicle. Hawk and Anne were missing too. *Strange,* I thought. *I wonder where everyone is? I could call them, I suppose... Nope, I have to give them the freedom to do their jobs, not keep looking over their shoulders, trying to micro-manage them. Okay, so it's getting close to four. I need some fresh air. A jog around the park would work wonders.*

I made up my mind to cut class and was just about to leave and go home, change, and then go to the park when my phone rang; it was Janet.

"Sorry I bailed on you, Cap," she said, "but I've dug up some great information about Regina Mae." She sounded excited.

"Well, okay, but we've had a couple of late nights and I was just about to go home. How about you give me the Cliff Notes version now, and we can discuss the details tomorrow morning when the others are present?"

"Okay, I'll start with Regina Mae's boy-toy, Daniel Racine. Oh Lordy, is he ever a ripe one. He went to UTC and majored in business administration but dropped out in the middle of his junior year to work at a gay bar, Randolph's."

"Randolph's? Okay, that doesn't surprise me as much as it should," I said, more than a little disappointed. Not that I was remotely interested in him, but boy was he ever good-looking.

"Any priors?" I asked.

"Nope. He has a clean record," she said.

"You sound sad about that," I joked.

"Not really, but you know how much easier it is to question someone if you have a little dirt on them. Well I think it is, don't you? I also saw his pictures online. Whew, I wouldn't mind fifteen minutes alone with him in an interrogation room. Meow."

"Why Janet." I smiled at the thought. "What would your boyfriend think?"

"Hey, I'm not exactly dead," Janet said, "and don't tell me you'd turn him down either. And he's not gay, now is he? Not based on the info you gave me about his late-night antics with the divine Mrs. Chesterton. From what I was able to gather from his profile, and online, he's one giant puff piece, as BI as they come; goes both ways and doesn't seem to care whether he's coming or going."

I opened my mouth to speak, but Janet being Janet, continued on at her usual rapid-fire rate.

"Crazy as it may seem, Kate, I like a guy who can think on his feet, not his back, and that's not Daniel Racine. Besides, a doorman who's also a bartender doesn't sound like a winning combination, even if I didn't know he was banging some, if not all, of the residents. I wonder how much he makes... from the residents? I wonder if he services the male residents too?" And then she finally ran out of steam and took a breath.

"Ouch. Poor Daniel." I chuckled. "So, is he still bartending?"

"According to his credit report he is. He quit Randolph's about a year ago and is now working at a place called Angelo's. It's inside the Monaco Hotel, just a hop-skip-and-jump from Regina Mae's residence. How convenient. I guess he walks to work, if you can call it that, from there."

"Okay, that's enough about Dan. Now tell me about Regina Mae."

"She's got a clean record too, and good credit. Well, she would, wouldn't she? But here's the thing: she's involved with several charitable organizations that... well, you wouldn't really expect her to be helping them. Some are out of town in Baton Rouge, Louisiana."

"Oh really?" I said. "Now that is a surprise, and a coincidence, and I don't like coincidences, and especially this one."

"Right. I hear you," Janet said. "And here's another one for you. It turns out she has family there, in Baton Rouge, a cousin. What was it I heard? Once is chance, twice is a coincidence, three times and you have a pattern." She took a breath and before I could speak, continued.

"The cousin is a Mrs. Sally Booker. She's clean too. She's on the board of directors for an organization called the Louisiana Partnership of Women in Nursing. I haven't looked into them yet... Maybe I'll get Lenny to do it in the morning. Anyway, they have quite a few fundraisers and charity events every year, and last year they donated fifty grand to a women's clinic... reproductive rights, if you know what I mean. Well, it turns out that Regina Mae gives a substantial amount of money to her cousin's charity and participates in some of their fundraisers. You know?"

"Yes," I said. "I'm following you so far."

"Okay, well, you're gonna love this. You sure you don't want to wait till morning so I can tell the others at the same time?" she teased.

"Tell me now, dammit."

"Yes, ma'am. So, Talbot Montgomery's church has a sister church and it's also located in Baton Rouge and, get this, it's the same church that Sally Booker belongs to, and where, according to her income tax returns, she donates almost a fourth of her annual income. Ain't that cozy? Coincidence number four? I can't understand why she hasn't been audited."

"Oh, yes. Now that really is something," I muttered. "How long has she been a member of that church and where, exactly, is it located?" *As if I don't already know!*

"Hold on to your panties, Cap. It's about seven blocks from where the Washingtons live. Don't you think it's kind of strange that money is going to a church from one entity that is also affiliated with encouraging women to, well, you know?" Janet asked.

"I do. But politics make strange bedfellows."

I thought for a moment. This was starting to get a little too radical for my taste. "What's the name of the church?"

"The New Light Missionary Church," Janet replied.

I felt my heart jump in my chest.

27

With Janet's virtual tsunami of new information almost drowning me, I told her to go home and get some rest—fat chance of her doing that. I was going to spend some time processing what she'd told me, and we'd discuss our next step the following day.

It was going to require some sorting out, so now the idea of going home was out of the question. I did, however, need a change of scenery, which I figured would be as good as a rest. A glass of red would go down quite nicely too; I could kill three birds with one stone. *Cool!*

So I grabbed my bag, my iPad, and my phone, slipped my jacket on to cover my gun and badge, and I headed downtown to Angelo's in the Monaco Hotel.

"What are you doing here?" Daniel said in a loud whisper when I stepped up to the bar. "Are you trying to get me fired from this job, too?"

"They fired you from your doorman job?" I froze for a second.

"Yeah. Someone told the administrator that I wasn't at

the front desk during my shift, and that I left it unattended for half the night. Did you do that?"

"I don't live there, Daniel. I don't care what you do. Did it ever cross your mind that it might have been Regina Mae that threw you under the bus?" I folded my hands and leaned against the bar. "I'd like a glass of pinot noir, please."

Angelo's was a nice little place with red and white checkered tablecloths, some obviously expensive prints of the great master Michelangelo's artwork framed on the walls along with colorful maps of Italy and some of its provinces.

There was a couple seated to the right of me at the far end of the bar—which wasn't really so far I couldn't hear them talking, and boy were they talking. They seemed to be oblivious to the idea that there was anyone else in the world but each other. She was lovely in a white dress and red shoes, sparkling bands of gold around her neck, her wrists, and her fingers. He was equally lovely, for a man, in a shirt so white it seemed to give off its own light. They spoke in whispers; bossa nova music played softly from hidden speakers.

Nice.

Daniel grabbed a bottle of pinot from behind the bar. Next he grabbed a glass from the rack, turned it right-side up with a deft flick of his fingers, held it up to the light and inspected it, a delicate piece with a needle-thin stem and a huge bowl.

He poured the wine, turning the bottle as if spilling a single drop would be a sacrilege. He pushed the glass toward me across the bar top. I picked it up, swished it a couple of times, gave it the obligatory sniff, and took a sip.

Not bad, I thought. *Almost as good as the two bottles of crap I bought at the liquor store the other night.*

"Regina would never do that," he whispered.

"Do what?" I asked, looking at the glass. "Oh, you're talking about your job. You don't think she'd turn on you? Really? She got caught, Daniel. She got caught with her hands in the cookie jar, or should I say with her panties around her ankles." I smiled. "She can't get rid of me—I'm a cop—but you?" I shrugged. "You're just another toy; plenty more where you came from."

"Do you think it really was her?"

"Daniel, she lives in the penthouse. Their names are in the papers at least once a week. You were banging the wife of Edward Chesterton the Third, and you got caught... by me. Just think about that for a minute."

I watched his face, and even though he was so very, very pretty to look at, I could tell he was having trouble putting the pieces of the puzzle together. Deep, or even light, thinking was not his strong suit.

"Okay," he said. "So maybe she did drop me in it. Now that I'm no longer the doorman, you have no reason to keep harassing me for information," he said as he wiped down the bar.

"Oh, but I do, Danny, I do... and by the way, why didn't you call me when Treyshawn Montgomery arrived home?"

"Because I wasn't there, of course."

Okay, can't argue with that, I suppose.

"Good enough," I said, "but you're not off the hook. Tell me, did Regina Mae ever mention Baton Rouge during your.... conversations together?" I clicked my tongue. "Did she ever tell you she was going away and wouldn't be able to see you for a while?"

"Oh, come on Detective, I wasn't banging her all the time. Yeah, Regina goes to Baton Rouge, quite often, in fact. Maybe once a month, and usually with her son

Edward, until he got married. After that she stopped taking him."

"Did she say why?"

He actually chuckled, then said, "She said he'd caught something nasty down there. I assumed he'd gotten himself a dose of the clap."

Now that's funny, I thought, smiling to myself. *Genevieve an STD!*

"Did she talk much about Eddie and his new wife?"

"She talked about him all the time. How he'd never grown up. How he needed someone to take care of him, but no one could do it like she could. She was constantly bragging about the trips they went on together, how close they were, like she was trying to make me jealous or something. Kinda creepy, I thought."

"Eww," I said, playing along, frowning. "You think she... they might be..."

"Hah, I don't know what they were up to. I never asked. I'm not the jealous type." He winked at me.

"Did she ever talk about her daughter-in-law, Genevieve?"

"Not that I can remember. I know the wedding was a big deal. She talked a lot about the wedding, but... hmm, how shall I put it? Okay, it was like, other than a huge social event that her son was starring in, it didn't mean a whole lot. Like nothing had changed. Not like he was sharing a new life with someone else."

"Did that seem weird to you?" I asked.

"I thought she was talking about it because we were close. We were, like, having an affair, but on thinking about it, she was pretty closemouthed where the family was concerned... or their affairs. It was, like, the less I knew about her family, the better." He shrugged then continued.

"I guess maybe she thought I'd ask for more money if I knew any real family secrets."

He leaned closer to me. He smelled really good of orange and spice.

"She was paying you?" I leaned back, away from him.

"Well, it wasn't like there was a set fee. Sometimes she'd give me cash. Other times she'd give me tickets to a ball game. It just depended on her mood."

He stood back a little, folded his arms, and said, "Hey, I know what you're thinking. I'm not a prostitute. I was getting something out of it, sure, but she was getting a whole lot more."

"She sure was, a romantic rendezvous in the broom closet with Chattanooga's version of Bradley Cooper," I jabbed.

He leaned back on his heels, his arms still folded, and gave me a dirty look.

"Did she ever invite you to go to Baton Rouge with her?" I asked.

"No. She always took her son," he said. "Look, I don't know what you think Regina did or didn't do. But I know her really well, and I can tell you she's a good person. She's smart, attractive, intelligent, and she has an amazing body for a woman her age and—"

"And she's cheating on her husband which means she's not afraid to lie, right?"

I watched Daniel's lip twitch nervously in the corner.

He shrugged. "That's different."

"You think? Maybe. Maybe it is, Daniel, but let me tell you something: during my long experience as a cop, I found that people who lie about one thing, no matter how small, will lie about everything. Regina Mae is no different. What do you think she'd tell her husband if he finds out you've been screwing her? Rape? Blackmail?"

"She wouldn't... He's not going to find out, not unless you tell him." He glared at me then said, "I can't wait for her to prove you wrong, and I know she will. She'd never rat me out, especially when we were having such a good time. You think she can do without this?" He grabbed his crotch and moved it slowly up and down. "Not hardly. She'll call me. You'll see. She always does," he bragged.

I took another sip of my wine and slid off the barstool.

"What do I owe you?"

"Oh, it's on the house."

"Sure it is," I said, throwing a twenty onto the counter. "Now ring it up and give me a receipt."

He did as I asked. I grabbed the receipt and smiled sadly at him, tilting my head a little, and said, "Thanks for the chat, and good luck hunting for a new gig. I'm sure a resourceful fellow like you will find something soon."

"Maybe I should consider being a cop?" He smirked.

"Maybe," I replied. "Goodbye, Daniel... Oh, and don't think you're off the hook. I *will* see you again soon."

I left him standing there, frowning, watching me leave. I could almost feel the power of his stare.

When I reached the door, I paused, then turned and looked at him. He was smiling. He inclined his head slightly, nodded, then raised his forefinger to the side of his nose and tapped it. I raised my right hand, made a gun of my forefinger and thumb, pointed it at him, and dropped the hammer. Then, without waiting for a reaction, I turned away and walked to the restaurant door.

The aroma of garlic, peppers, and Italian sausage cooking was tempting, but the menu on the stand next to the door had no prices, and we all know what that means. It was out of my league. So, it was going to be a greasy burger with cheddar fries from a joint on East Brainerd, which was on my way home.

When I arrived home, I poured myself a glass of sweet tea—no more wine for me—and drank deeply; I was parched. Next, I inhaled the most delicious charbroiled burger I'd eaten in a long time and washed it down with more tea. Then I stripped and headed straight for the shower. I spent maybe ten minutes under the hot water, washing away the cares of the day, then I dressed in sweats and settled down to work. I intended to do what I said I was going to do, and I did. I sorted out all the new information, assimilated it and, by the time I'd finished, I had a rough idea of what I needed to do next.

28

I awoke the next day to the early morning sunshine streaming into my bedroom and a heavy feeling in my gut.

I knew that greasy burger was a mistake, I thought. *I need to go for a run. What the hell were you thinking, Kate? Eating that crap food like you had a twenty-one-year-old's metabolism.*

I slipped back into the sweats I'd abandoned the night before, stepped out of the apartment into the fresh air, did some stretches, and then set off at a brisk jog out of the complex onto East Brainerd Road. It was still early; the morning rush had barely begun, and the air still had a chill to it. I had gone only a couple of blocks before I began to feel better.

I ran my usual route: west toward Banks Road and, by the time I'd made it to Morris Lane and made the turn, my brain was firing on all eight cylinders, but I could think about nothing but the Genevieve Chesterton case. Yes, I had other cases to worry about, including the murder of a twelve-year-old girl, but my priority, because of its high profile and the people involved, had to be Genevieve.

Things had been moving fast the past couple of days, and I had a feeling they were about to go even faster. My mind was in a whirl.

Hawk and Anne, I thought. *I wonder if they found the Frenchman. Who is he? Need them to go interview him. Alibi?* I upped the pace. I was feeling the burn, breathing hard.

And what about Wheaton? Is his alibi legit? Could his "date" have made a mistake? Is she lying to cover for him? I'll have 'em go door to door, talk to the neighbors.

Is Regina banging Treyshawn? Surely not. Although... Nah. She's got her hands full with Dirty Dan... literally, ha ha ha. It's worth digging into, though.

My thighs were beginning to ache as I pushed myself to keep up the pace. My lungs were burning as I panted in rhythm with each footfall.

What about Regina Mae's trips to Baton Rouge? I wondered.

It all kept coming back to Regina Mae's visits to, and contacts in, Baton Rouge. Something was bugging me, though, and I couldn't get a handle on it. And I couldn't get my head around her relationship with her son. Was she doing the nasty with him too? Ugh! The idea was unthinkable, but it wouldn't be the first time a mother had an unhealthy relationship with her son.

What was it really about—Baton Rouge and Regina Mae's work down there? Why did Eddie go with her, on every visit, and then suddenly stop? Was it out of respect for his marriage, or was she ashamed that her son had married a gal from the "ghetto" instead of a local debutante? *And an African American, too!*

I turned left into my apartment complex, my legs rubbery, but I felt alert and sharp and like I'd burned enough calories to rid my system of the fat and grease from last night's food fest. Now I was really able to concentrate.

"Kate, what are the chances that Alisha Washington knows about that church?" I muttered while wiping sweat from my forehead.

I slowed to a brisk walk the last hundred yards, thinking hard, and by the time I reached my front door I'd come to a decision: today I would make a bold move. It would be little more than a shot in the dark, but what did I have to lose?

I poured myself a cup of strong black coffee, took a couple of sips, then showered and dressed for action: white blouse, tailored business suit with a knee-length skirt, and black pumps with two-inch heels. I put my hair up in a high-top ponytail, and then I called Janet.

She answered immediately.

"Janet, are you on your way in yet?" I asked.

"Yes, I'll be there in five minutes."

I looked at my watch and shook my head; it was twenty-five after seven.

"Good, as soon as you get there, get hold of the others and have them in my office ASAP. I'll be there by eight."

I stopped at the bagel shop just across the road from my apartment complex, picked up a large coffee for me and a to-go travel container of dark roast coffee for the team, then slid into the heavy traffic on I-75, took Highway 153 to Amnicola and was in my office twenty minutes later.

"Wow, look at you," Janet said as I walked in.

I smiled and set the coffee container on my desk. Even Hawk looked surprised. Lenny too. Janet started filling coffee mugs.

"What's going on?" Anne asked.

"Nothing, not right now anyway," I said, taking my seat behind my desk.

It was at that moment Chief Johnston walked into the room and took a seat at the back and folded his arms.

"Carry on," he said. "Don't mind me."

I looked nervously at him but relaxed when he honored me with the beginnings of a smile. Janet hustled a coffee over to him, but he declined the offer with a shake of his head.

I nodded at the chief and said to the group, "Well, first I need you to bring me up-to-date on what you've been doing. Lenny, were you able to find the two girls that obtained judgments against Sam Wheaton?"

"I did: Lesley Cooper and Leigh Mason. I gave the names to Anne." He looked at Anne, as did I.

"Anne?" I asked.

She nodded, leaned back in her chair, folded her arms and said, "I talked to both of them. No help there. They are both bound by confidentiality agreements that were part of their settlements so they couldn't talk. Sorry." She shrugged.

"I also found the Frenchman, I think," Lenny said.

Now *that* I was interested in hearing about. "Okay," I said. "Let's hear it."

"His name, if it is him, is Gaspard Boucher, which is kind of ironic since the word boucher is French for butcher. Anyway, he's a naturalized American citizen and works out of CDE's New York office. From what little I was able to learn, he's some kind of fixer. His official title is Senior VP of Special Operations. He doesn't have a record, per se, but before immigrating to the United States he was a French police officer, an Inspector with Interpol. I was unable to access those records, but I think it's him. I turned what I had over to Hawk yesterday."

I looked at Hawk.

"I made a call to a guy I know," Hawk said. "A lieutenant in the NYPD. I met him while we were both attending a three-week course at the FBI Academy... Anyway, he said he'd check out Boucher's movements from May three through five and get back to me. He hasn't, not yet anyway, but he will."

I wasn't that excited at the news, mainly because I figured it was a red herring thrown at me by Eddie to get me off his tail and implicate his grandfather, but who knows. In our game, anything can happen—ordinary or extraordinary.

"Good," I said, nodding and flipping through the screens on my iPad. "Let me know as soon as you hear anything. If we can eliminate him, fine. If not..." I glanced at the chief, "Someone's going to have to go to New York and interview him. That would be you, Hawk." Again, I glanced at the chief. He was sitting there like a stone statue.

"In the meantime," I continued, "we also need to follow up on Wheaton's alibi. I'm thinking it's probably good, but you never know. Did it check out?"

"Hawk and I went door-to-door, yesterday afternoon," Anne said. "We talked to several of the neighbors. One old biddy I talked to put his car outside Lucy Weston's garage at around ten-thirty on the Friday, and it was still there the following morning. So he was there. Whether or not he was there all night we can't be certain. We still have only Lucy's word for that."

"So, Wheaton has an alibi," I said, "but it's questionable. Okay, keep digging. Maybe you'll find something. Hawk, maybe you should give your buddy another call... No, give him a little time. We don't want to pi— upset him."

I thought for a minute, looked at the chief, and then said, "I have a couple of ideas, but I'm not ready to share them, not yet. I have a couple of things I need to follow up on and, by the looks of it, several messages.

"Janet, I need a photo of Regina Mae Chesterton. Can you find a good one for me?"

"Of course. She's all over the Chattanooga magazine for her philanthropic work and attending all the posh parties. What are you going to do with it?"

"You'll see," I said.

"Okay, people," I said. "Go to it. We have a busy day. Stay in touch."

And they left me alone there with the chief still sitting with his arms folded staring at me enigmatically.

The door closed and he rose to his feet, approached my desk, and sat down in the seat Janet had just left.

"I want you to know, Catherine," he said, "that I have every confidence in you, but I need a result, and quickly. Old man Chesterton is all over me. He wants to file a harassment charge against you. I'm holding him off, but for how long... well, I'll do my best. Are you any closer to a solution?"

"Yes, sir, I think I am. I may even have it done by the end of the day."

At that, he brightened, not just a little but a lot.

"You want to tell me about it?" he asked.

I hesitated, then said, "If you don't mind Chief, I'd rather not. If I'm wrong... I don't think I am, but..."

He nodded, stood, walked to the door, opened it, then turned to look at me and said, "Good job, Kate. Let me know as soon as you have something. I want to be there when charges are made." And then he left, closing the door gently behind him.

29

There were a half a dozen messages for me in the system, several of them from Edward Eaton Chesterton II. I tapped the button and listened to the crusty voice.

"My tax dollars at work," the old man snapped. "Of course, when I call you don't answer the phone. Detective Gazzara, I thought I made myself clear that I wanted you out doing your job and not harassing my family."

He left a total of three messages, all stating the same thing in three different ways. If I didn't stop harassing his daughter-in-law and his good-for-nothing grandson, I was going to hear from his lawyer.

"If you feel you have to solve the murder of a good-for-nothing, lying piece of trailer trash then, by all means, have at it. But harassing members of my family because we happen to have money is unacceptable," he growled. To me it sounded like he'd said this kind of thing before. "I will have charges brought against you if you do not conclude this persecution of the Chesterton family."

The message ended and the next one began.

"Captain Gazzara, this is Sam Wheaton."

You can imagine my surprise when I heard that voice.

"I must tell you that your investigation has gone on long enough. It seems to me that you have resorted to intimidating members of the Chesterton family. I'm warning you, Captain, complaints will be filed against you stating that you have overstepped your legal boundaries," Uncle Sam continued.

I sat there, stunned at what I was hearing. The worst part of it was that these same people who claimed they wanted the case solved were stonewalling me. And now I had no choice but to inform the chief that complaints from the Chestertons might be pending. He wasn't going to like that, not one bit.

But I didn't have time for that, not then. If I was going to do what I'd planned, I was going to have to work fast.

I picked up the desk phone and buzzed Janet.

"Janet, where the hell are you?"

"Almost done, Cap."

"Well, step on it. I need to get out of here."

Two minutes later she came hurrying into my office. I stood and held out my hand.

"Do you have the picture?" I asked.

"Oh, yeah. I have a really nice one. I downloaded it onto my phone. See?"

She showed me what was indeed a lovely photograph of Regina Mae. She was at the center of a group of three women at some charity event. She looked very much at home in a designer dress and wearing a collection of jewelry that would have rivaled the Queen of England's: her wedding ring rivaled the North Star.

"Send it to my phone," I said, "and then go back to your

desk and wait for my call. There's something I need to do, then we can get out of here."

"You got it," and she was gone. It was as if illusionist David Blaine had snapped his fingers and then... poof!

The door closed and I picked up my iPhone and dialed Alisha Washington's number.

"Hello? Who is this?"

"Alisha, this is Captain Gazzara."

"Oh... Hello. Have you got news?"

I took a deep breath. I knew I didn't have the news she was hoping for, but I had a feeling I was getting closer.

"Alisha, I will have, very shortly, but right now I need your help with something. I'm going to send you a photograph, and I want you to tell me if you recognize anyone. Hold on... I'm sending it now. There. Did you get it?"

She didn't answer.

"Alisha? Mrs. Washington?" I looked at my phone expecting to see the call had disconnected, but it hadn't.

"I don't believe it," she said finally, quietly.

"Alisha, do you know any of these women?"

"Yes, the one in the middle. I only met her once, but I'll never forget it." She paused, for a long minute.

"Detective," she continued, "I don't know what your opinions are on a woman's reproductive rights—hah, they call them rights—but I have a problem with people and organizations that focus on the black community and try to force their own opinions and beliefs on us. Yes, I'm white, but I *am* part of this community, and I support my church and its teachings." She cleared her throat again. "So, it was when I joined the ladies of my church and we went to say prayers... to protest outside a clinic in Baton Rouge. Well, that was where I ran into that woman."

Oh, yeah, I thought, *now we're talking!*

"You're sure it was her?"

"I'll never forget her. Never, not as long as I live. Our church holds regular vigils there. We pray for the unborn souls and I'll admit, we try to persuade women to change their minds. Well, that particular day that woman came stomping up to me—I do believe she singled me out—and began cussing and screaming at me."

"What was she saying?" I asked quietly as I made notes.

There was a pause, then she said, "She was ranting that I was breaking up families, that I had no idea what damage I was causing. 'What the hell are you talking about?' I shouted back at her. Yes, those are the words I used. I cussed. I admit it. I've dealt with angry people before, but this woman was... Well, she was like... crazy, or something."

"Did she attack you physically?" I asked.

"No. I thought at first that she was going to, but she didn't. She was just a shrill voice shouting obscenities. I don't think she dared to hit me. She got close to me, but never too close. I may be a believer, Detective, but that don't make me a doormat. I think that woman got the message."

"Yes, ma'am." I smiled. "Go on."

"Well, she continued to scream at me, us, on the sidewalk. She told us we were all no good. Then she said something truly evil..."

I heard her take a deep breath, then say, "She said... 'I hope your children die before they can have babies.'"

"You're not serious?" I said, not sure about my own feelings. *That's a direct threat, and if Regina May was involved it would make Genevieve's murder premeditated.*

"Oh, I'm serious, Detective. That bitch is crazy, pardon my language," Alisha said, with a hint of amusement.

"Was she alone or was she part of a group?" I asked.

"She was with some people from the clinic, but there

was a car waiting for her, and there was a man in it. He didn't get out, though, and I don't blame him."

"Do you remember what he looked like? Could you describe him?"

"Not really. But he had reddish hair... Slim, for sure."

Could it be that Eddie drove his mother to this clinic so she could verbally abuse his mother-in-law? My head was spinning.

"When did this take place, Alisha?"

"If I had to guess, I'd say maybe three months ago." Now it was my turn to just sit there for a moment and let it all sink in.

"Alisha," I said, "I'm going to ask you one more question, and I want you to think very carefully before you answer it."

"Okay," she said.

"Do you think that the woman knew who you were?"

"Oh!" She sounded surprised. "I don't know. I never thought about it before, but she did make a beeline for me, and it was me she was screaming about. That part about breaking up families... What did that mean? I don't know, Detective. I really don't."

"It's fine, Alisha. You've been more help than you know. Thank you for your time. I'll be in touch real soon."

"It's all right detective. Who... who is she? Did she kill my baby?" Alisha's voice wavered. I could imagine her sitting on the edge of her couch, her eyes filled with tears.

"I'm sorry, I can't talk about an ongoing investigation, but as soon as I have something, I'll call you."

"You know," she said, "when you first came to our house, I thought it would be the last time I'd hear from anyone about Naomi's murder. We're not rich folk and, well, it's not like we don't know what some people think of us, of me being white and married to a black man. So I just want to say thank you." Her voice caught in her throat, and I heard her sniffle.

"I'm just doing my job, Alisha," I said. "I'll be in touch. I promise."

Regina Mae freakin' knew who she was. She verbally attacked the woman she knew to be Genevieve's mother. Damn! That's a whole lot more than I hoped for.

I suddenly realized how tensed up I was. My body felt more exhausted than it did after my morning run. But hell, I'd just gotten a major break in the case.

I had to relax for a minute, loosen up and think, try to figure out how everything fit together. One thing I was sure of: it was more than just a coincidence that Regina Mae had showed up at the same little clinic in Baton Rouge where her son's mother-in-law just happened to be protesting, and on the same day.

But how did she know, I wondered. *Did Granddad Chesterton lie when he said he'd kept his knowledge to himself? Did he tell Regina Mae about Genevieve's racial background and her family? Maybe he accidentally let it slip... Nah, it's more likely that as soon as she found out that little Eddie was bent on marrying Genevieve she, like old man Chesterton, did her own background checks which is how she found the Washingtons and, voila, that's how she found out that the girl was black.*

I shook my head. There was a piece missing. Somewhere in this incestuous little cell there was someone, an outsider maybe, who held the key. And then something—a dose of Harry's sixth sense, maybe?—made me circle back to the two real anomalies in the story: Nathan Watkins and Treyshawn Montgomery. One a disenfranchised brother of the victim; the other a preacher's son who was also a drug dealer to Chattanooga's elite. And Regina Mae's cousin, Sally, belonged to Reverend Monty's sister church in Baton Rouge; that was another fact that picked at me.

Okay, Kate, it's time to kick it up a notch, hit the bricks and move on.

I buzzed Janet and told her to meet me at her car, a blue-and-white police cruiser. Wouldn't you just know it, she was already there when I arrived, leaning on the hood of her car looking at her phone.

"Let's go," I said, as I got into her car on the passenger side. "Hit the gas, to Reverend Montgomery's apartment to talk with Treyshawn. I think things are about to break wide open."

30

"Can I ask what this is all about?" The Reverend Montgomery looked genuinely bewildered when he opened the door. He was dressed in a designer sweat suit and a pair of Air Jordan's that must have cost more than my monthly rent.

"We'd like to talk to your son," I said lightly. "Is he home?"

"Yes, he's home, Detective. Again, I must ask you, what is this all about?"

"We just need to ask him a couple questions," Janet said.

"Is he in trouble?"

"Not at the moment," Janet replied with a sweet smile. The briefing I gave her on the way to the apartment had her chomping at the bit to get started. I'd already decided to let her take the lead; the thought being that her youthful appearance might put Treyshawn at ease, and maybe he would open up a little more to her than he would to me.

"Just one moment. I'll go and fetch him. He's still in bed."

Involuntarily, we both looked at our watches.

"It's after eleven," Janet mouthed at me, as Reverend Monty walked along the hallway and gently knocked on a closed bedroom door.

I nodded but didn't answer. *What is it with these people?* I thought. *If the police had shown up at my house, wanting to ask me questions, my mother would have been shouting, demanding to know what the hell I'd done to bring the cops to her door. I'd have been more afraid of her than the police, that's for sure.*

The Treyshawn that finally appeared looked a lot different from the gangster who climbed jauntily out of the Cadillac in front of Club Suave. It was the same kid, I had no doubt. He was tall, muscular, abs like the proverbial washboard—that was easy to see because he was bare-chested wearing only pajama bottoms—and he had one of those haircuts where the sides and back are shaved leaving a tuft on top of his head. His eyes were half-closed, his mouth hanging open slightly. He couldn't have been a day over twenty-two, maybe twenty-four at the most. He didn't come across as the hardened thug we knew him to be.

"Please sit down, Detectives," Pastor Montgomery said, then turned to his son and continued, "Now, Trey, you tell the detectives what they want to know." Then he looked at me and said, "I'll be in my study if you need me."

We sat together on the sofa; Treyshawn sat opposite us.

Janet introduced herself, then me, then informed him I would be recording the interview, and then asked him if he had any objections.

He shook his head, said no, and waited until I had the recording app running and the details read in for the record.

Before Janet could ask the first question, he asked, "Am I going to be arrested? Do I need a lawyer?"

"We just need to ask you about your relationship with Regina Mae Chesterton and her son, Eddie," Janet said.

"Oh. Well..." He shrugged. "Okay, I guess."

"Treyshawn, does the name Genevieve Chesterton ring any bells?" Janet asked, keeping her voice soft and gentle.

"No?" he replied immediately.

"How about Nathan Watkins? Do you know him?"

"No?" He shook his head, his bottom lip still hanging loose flopped sideways, back and forth.

Janet looked at me. I said nothing.

"That's funny, Treyshawn," she said, "because..." She flipped through her notebook, more for effect than her need for information, and said, "on the night of May 10 at ten-forty-three, Captain Gazzara and I saw you pick him up in a Cadillac registered to your father in front of a convenience store. Or was someone else driving your father's car that night?"

Treyshawn shook his head.

"So you do know Nathan Watkins. Why did you lie?" she asked.

He shrugged. "Yeah, I know him. We went to the club that other night. So what?"

He looked down, focused on the cover of a BET magazine on the coffee table.

"Fine," Janet said. "No more lies, okay?"

He nodded but didn't look up.

"What about Eddie Chesterton? How well do you know him?"

"He was at the club sometimes," he said, truculently.

"Good. That's better, Trey. Now, how about his wife, a pretty white girl, did you ever see her? You would have noticed her. I don't think too many white women go to Club Suave."

"Yeah. Sure, I seen her."

"So you did know Genevieve Chesterton. Another lie?"

"Nah, I mean... I didn't know that was her name," he said, licking his lips. A thin layer of sweat had begun to form on the young man's forehead. He was also bouncing his right knee as he looked up at Janet.

"Did you ever see her anywhere else, like at other clubs?" Janet asked.

"Sometimes she was here," he said.

"Here? In this apartment?" I asked, surprised.

"No. Here in the building. She said she knew people here, but I think she was coming around just to see me." He leaned back in his chair, folded his arms and smirked.

"Why would you think that?" I asked.

"She told me she was having problems with her husband. That he wasn't paying no attention to her no more; know what I mean?"

"You mean sexually?" Janet asked, wincing as if she was embarrassed.

"Yeah, that... sexually." He smirked.

"Did you sleep with her?" I asked.

"Nah. I just sort of played the game, you know. I talked to her and stuff."

"Eddie Chesterton," Janet said, very quietly, "told my partner that you, Trey, are the connection for party favors for the rich and famous of Chattanooga. What do you have to say about that?" She asked the question as if she didn't believe it herself.

"Naw, man. I don't do dat." Treyshawn smirked, shook his head, but didn't look at either one of us. He was obviously lying.

"Why do you think Eddie Chesterton would say something like that if it wasn't true?" Janet pressed him.

The only answer she got was a shrug of the shoulders.

"Did you ever see Genevieve take drugs when she was at the club or here in the building?"

"Naw. She was just a freak," he said. It was obvious he was making it up as he went. It was the go-to response of any guy who wanted to make a woman look bad.

"She was a tease, man... She liked to tease, you know? When I seen her here in the lobby and she rode the elevator up with me, we talked about hooking up, but it never happened. She probably found some other dude." He blinked, looked to the left and licked his lips again.

"Okay, so we've established that you knew Genevieve and her brother Nathan, and that you knew Genevieve's husband, Eddie." Janet scooted to the edge of the couch. "How about Regina Mae Chesterton, Eddie's mother? Do you know her?"

"No," he snapped quickly; too quickly.

"Really?" Janet said, sounding surprised. "I don't see how that's possible. She lives in this building, in the penthouse. Are you sure you haven't seen her?"

"Oh yeah, I seen her, but I never spoke to her. We never talked." He rubbed his hands together and continued, "I've never been to the penthouse."

"I didn't ask any of that, Treyshawn." Janet chuckled. "I asked if you knew her. She said she knew you."

Oh dear, Janet. That was a lie. A big fat lie.

And so it was, but it worked. The look on Treyshawn Montgomery's face told us both that he did indeed know Regina Mae and not just in passing. Janet had pulled a rabbit out of the hat.

I could almost see the wheels in Treyshawn's mind, turning so fast they must have been making his head spin. How was he going to explain to us why Regina Mae was telling the police they knew one another when he'd been telling us they didn't? He'd backed himself into a corner and there was no way out. He'd already screwed up once when he lied about knowing Nathan, and again when he said he didn't know Genevieve.

"Treyshawn," I said, impatiently, "you seem to have a very loose relationship with the truth, either that or you're in the early stages of dementia and suffering from memory loss. Which is it?"

He looked at me, sullenly, but his face was expressionless.

"It's okay, Captain," Janet said soothingly. "Treyshawn. Let's try one more time, shall we? You do know Regina Mae Cottonwell-Chesterton, don't you? You might as well tell us because she's already told us everything. She made herself a deal." *Another fib.*

"Deal? What kind of deal?" Treyshawn clenched his fists.

"The kind of deal someone makes when they need to clear their conscience," Janet said, ambiguously.

"I didn't do nothing!" he shouted. "Whatever she's telling you is a lie!"

"Okay, Sergeant," I said. "I can see where this is headed. Treyshawn, I think we'd better continue this conversation at the police department. In fact," I said and looked at Janet, "I think we need to bring Regina Mae in, too. We'll need to clear this mess up. Right, Trey?"

He didn't answer, the wheels in his head were slowly grinding away, trying to figure a way out for himself. They were losing the battle. He was about to lose it, I was sure.

"Go ahead and get dressed, Trey," Janet said. "We'll sort it out, I promise. It shouldn't take very long." More ambiguity. Sure, we'd sort it, but she didn't tell him how.

Treyshawn chewed his lower lip, made some sort of decision, pushed himself angrily up from the chair and stomped to his room.

Janet followed him and stood near the door, listening to make sure there wasn't going to be a problem. When Treyshawn yanked his bedroom door open just a couple of minutes later, he was wearing clean jeans and a T-shirt; the jeans, however, fit him perfectly, snug around his hips; the absence of his signature droopy, cargo shorts was notable.

31

I waited with Reverend Monty until Janet had escorted Treyshawn to the elevator, then I took a few minutes to speak with him. I explained the situation and my suspicions that his son was somehow embroiled in a scheme perpetrated by Regina Mae.

"I don't believe it," he said angrily. "What has my son got to do with her?"

I thought hard before I answered that. I had to be careful because one, it was an ongoing investigation and two, I had a feeling that the reverend was about to show his true colors and start calling my superiors.

"I really can't talk about..." I began, and then I saw the pain in his eyes.

I sighed and shook my head. "He's a drug dealer, Reverend. Did you know that?"

He put a hand to his head and closed his eyes.

"I tried to keep him off the streets. I gave him every opportunity, and now look where we are." His eyes filled with tears. He put his hands together, looked up at the ceiling and said, "Dear Lord, please help me in this my hour of need."

Then he looked at me and said, "You know how it is, Captain. You can take the boy off the streets, but you can't take the streets out of the boy, or something like that."

I nodded sympathetically. How many times had I heard that, or a variation of it?

"Should I get him a lawyer?" he asked.

"I think that might not be a bad idea, Reverend."

I could have told him no, but that would have been unethical and denied the boy his constitutional right. The problem was, I needed to get Treyshawn to talk, and there was no way that would happen with a lawyer present. I needed to get a move on.

When we arrived at the PD, Janet settled Treyshawn in an interview room. As we watched him through the one-way glass, I could tell by his body language that he'd come to some sort of decision. It looked to me like he'd decided not to cooperate.

He'd folded his arms, stretched his legs out straight under the steel table, slouched down on the uncomfortable steel chair, and was sucking on his bottom lip.

"We don't have any reason to hold him," Janet said as we stood together watching him. "Not unless we can link him to Regina Mae... Are you sure about her, Kate? How did you connect the dots?"

"It's a convoluted series of events and coincidences, some of which you already know, some you don't." I paused, staring at Treyshawn, thought for a minute, then continued, "See, I think Regina Mae knew all along that Genevieve was black. I think it upset her so much that she tracked down Alisha Washington and confronted her, without letting on she knew who she was. And I think she probably met with Treyshawn, on several occasions, when he was coming home late at night, and when she'd just got done visiting Daniel... maybe even with Nathan tagging along.

"Her opinion of black people is pretty radical, we know that. So when she sees this wanna-be thug, she makes some inquiries—maybe she even questioned her son Eddie about him. So she finds out who and what he is. Then she pays him to do her dirty work: get rid of her pregnant, black daughter-in-law."

Well, it sounded good to me... And it was right at that moment when I began to wonder if maybe I was assuming too much, had it all wrong. No matter, the die was cast and I was committed to follow it through.

"But where's the smoking gun?" Janet said. She looked at me and her expression morphed from pensive to shocked.

"Wait. I'm so stupid. You're right, Kate. Treyshawn would *not* do her a solid out of the goodness of his heart, now would he?"

"What? No!"

"He's not the type to volunteer his services for free." She smiled. "In your scenario you said she probably paid him, right?"

"Yes, but I don't know that..."

"How much do you think she would have paid him to kill Genevieve?"

"I couldn't say, not without—"

"*The bank statements,*" Janet all but shouted. "That's right, and that's what I mean about me being stupid. I pulled everyone's bank statements except Regina's. I only pulled her credit report." She smacked herself in the forehead with the palm of her hand.

"I got bank statements for Eddie, Wheaton and old man

Chesterton, but she slipped through the cracks. I didn't think she was seriously a suspect because she's so—"

"How long will it take you to run the report?" I asked.

"Give me fifteen minutes."

"You have ten."

She nodded, turned on her heel, and dashed out of the room. She must have pulled in some favors to get the bank statements as quick as she did. I clocked her in at just over eight minutes when she returned, smiling from ear to ear.

"I didn't think Treyshawn would have a bank account, but he does," she said excitedly. "I pulled that one too. I think you'd better send a car to pick up Regina Mae."

Janet showed me the paperwork, explained it to me quickly, and then asked the question, "Can I do it, Kate? Let me talk to him, please."

I smiled at her and said, "You got it, Janet. Go get him. Wait, hang on while I send a car to pick up Regina Mae."

She nodded excitedly, waited while I made the call, then took a deep breath and led the way into the interrogation room where Treyshawn had decided he'd had enough.

"Look," he said, sitting up straight and unfolding his arms, "if you ain't going to charge me I'm getting out of here. This is bull—" He started to his feet.

"Sit down, Treyshawn," Janet snapped at him.

He sat down again, not quite so sure of himself.

"What did you do with the ten thousand dollars that Regina Cottonwell-Chesterton transferred into your account?" Janet asked.

"I don't know what you're talking about," Treyshawn said and rolled his eyes.

"Oh, you don't?" Janet replied sweetly. "Let me show you." She sat down across from Treyshawn, placed the bank statement on the table in front of him, and pointed to the columns.

"These here are deposits into your account, see? There was a deposit of five thousand into your account on May 1, three days before Genevieve was murdered, and another five thousand on Monday, May 6, two days after. Now where could they have come from, I wonder... Oh, I know, let's look here." She swapped statements and continued.

"Now, this is Mrs. Chesterton's account, and these are her withdrawals: there's this one for cash, five thousand on May 1... and here's another one, also for cash on May 6. That's quite a coincidence, don't you think, Treyshawn?"

He didn't answer. He just stared sullenly at the sheets of paper in front of him.

"No comment, Trey? Can't say as I blame you. Now, if you look at those two withdrawals, you'll see the stupid woman made notes... so..." She looked him in the eye and said, "I'm sure you'll correct me if I'm wrong but doesn't that say 'T. Montgomery'? Oh, but maybe I'm wrong. Could that be a reference to your father, Talbot? Hmm, maybe we should go pick him up. What do you think, Trey?"

We watched as his jaw fell open and his face turned gray.

"That money was supposed to go to my dad's church. That's all," he stuttered. "She told me she made a mistake and deposited it in the wrong account, that it was supposed to go to my dad, a donation to the church. That's what she said, honest."

"Oh, no," Janet said. "That's not what happened. People like Regina don't make that kind of mistake. I know, maybe she was going to launder the money through you, and you were supposed to give it to your dad? If so, that's too bad. I thought your dad was a stand-up guy. This isn't what we'd expect of a pastor. I think we'd better bring him in, Captain."

"No. Wait. My dad... he's not involved." Treyshawn's knee started to shake and his expression changed to one of fear.

"Do you want to talk about it, Treyshawn?" Janet asked quietly. "You can spare your father the humiliation of being dragged down here in handcuffs. She didn't make a mistake, did she, Trey? Maybe she did tell you to donate it to your father's church, but you were supposed to read between the lines, right? She was just covering her ass, but you and I, we both know what it was really for, don't we?"

He didn't answer, just stared at the tabletop.

"Your father," she said. "He's a man of God, and you know what he'd tell you."

"The truth will set me free?" he asked.

"Yeah. That's what he'd tell you," Janet said.

The boy nodded but hid his face from us.

Then, in a sweet voice that I believed was truly genuine, Janet asked him if he'd like a drink, Coke or water. He shook his head. She offered him a cigarette. Again, he shook his head. She asked if he needed to use the bathroom. This time he nodded. A uniformed officer accompanied him while she and I talked.

"Good job," I said. "Really. Well done, Janet."

"Yeah, well," she said wryly. "That was the easy part. Now we need to have Regina Mae brought in. We need to put her in the hot seat."

"Just a few minutes more," I said. "Patrol is already on the way to get her, and she's mine. I can't wait." And I couldn't.

Sometimes, when solving a case, there's a clear path to the solution: you simply follow the evidence from point A to point B, and everything falls into place. But this wasn't one of those cases. There was almost no evidence at all. Sure, we followed the leads, but then I'd made a really big leap of faith and still didn't have what I needed. All I had was a whole lot of supposition, coincidence, and intuition. You can't convict on any or all of those things. Sure, the bank statements helped, but they were circumstantial, and if they stuck to their story—that the money was supposed to go to the church—the only thing they proved was that Treyshawn had stolen it.

We, that is I, still had a hell of a lot of work to do before I could make an arrest.

32

"This is preposterous!" Regina Mae shouted, causing everyone within fifty feet to stop what they were doing and gawk at her. "I've never been treated so rudely in all my life!"

"Calm down, Mrs. Chesterton!" Randy, my favorite uniformed officer ordered. "Or I'll put you in the holding tank until you can regain your composure."

"Regina Mae," I called out and waved across the station. "Thank you for taking the time to come on in and talk to us. I can imagine what a bother it must be."

"You! I should have known," Regina Mae hissed.

"Should have known what?" I asked innocently. "Look, this is just routine, a few questions for the record. Please... come with me?"

"I want you to know that I've called Grandfather Chesterton, and he's not at all happy." She squinted as she approached me.

Oh, I bet he isn't, I thought.

"You can believe me when I tell you," she continued like some superior being, "he's already speaking to our family attorneys. You, Captain, are an unmitigated disaster."

"Can I get you some coffee or water, Mrs. Chesterton? I'm sorry I can't offer you sweet tea," I said as I led her to the interrogation room next to Treyshawn's.

As planned, Janet had left the door to his room open so Regina Mae could see him, and boy did she ever.

"What is he doing here?" she shouted.

"Who?" I asked.

"That boy," Regina Mae snarled.

"Treyshawn Montgomery?" I asked, acting surprised, closing the door behind me. "You know him? Oh, yes, of course you do. He lives in your building, with his father. Have you ever met Reverend Montgomery?" I asked, conversationally.

She hesitated, then snapped, "No! Well, just to say hello to."

"Hmm, please sit down, Mrs. Chesterton. I should tell you that our conversation is being recorded: sound and video. Have you ever attended his church?" I asked, without skipping a beat from one subject to the other.

"Absolutely not."

"Treyshawn mentioned that only last week you made a substantial donation to his father's church, ten thousand dollars, I believe. Why would he say such a thing?"

"I don't know. I'm sure the nasty creature would lie about anything. You know how those people are."

"Those people? You mean Christians?" I asked.

"You are in law enforcement, Detective. You know what kind of people I'm talking about."

She folded her hands together in her lap and sat there looking demurely at me. I had the feeling she expected me to agree with her. Her polished nails and expensive jewelry looked completely out of place in the plain, dreary room.

"How often do you go to Baton Rouge, Mrs. Chesterton?"

That took her aback.

"Quite... often," she said hesitantly. "I have kin there. I go at least once every couple of months. My cousin and her family do excellent work for the unfortunates of the inner city." She cocked her head to one side and squinted at me.

"And you attend fundraisers there?" I asked.

"Of course. They organize fundraisers for her charity, the Louisiana Partnership of Women in Nursing." Regina Mae raised her chin with pride. "I'm proud to be involved."

"Do you ever take anyone with you to Baton Rouge?"

"Yes, I do. My son, Edward, usually accompanies me. I don't like to travel alone. So many men get the wrong impression about a lady traveling on her own."

I wasn't sure if she'd forgotten I'd caught her with Daniel only a couple of nights ago, or if she was intentionally ignoring that fact. Either way, her babe-in-the-woods act was falling flat.

"That's where he first met Genevieve, isn't it?" I leaned back in my chair and crossed my arms and stared at her, watching her eyes for any sign of a tell. "He was with you at one of your charity events, wasn't he?"

Regina Mae pinched her lips together so hard they turned white.

"So," I said, lightly, "you could say it was you who brought them together. That must have made you very proud." I smiled, then hardened my voice and said, "Until it didn't."

"I am telling you, Captain, that I had nothing to do with that girl's death and—"

"You mean your daughter-in-law," I interrupted.

"I had nothing to do with my daughter-in-law's death, but I understand what you're trying to do. Well, you won't get away with it. You're a lowlife targeting the wealthy of this city, to show the world that Chattanooga isn't racist." She paused, smirking. "You hate people of privilege, like me. You're just as bad as the rest of them."

"Funny you should mention hate. When was the last time you were in Baton Rouge? I ask because I have a really funny story to tell you." I watched for a reaction. Other than a slight lowering of her head, there was none.

"As you know, Genevieve's mother and father are both alive and well and living in that city. You did know that, didn't you? That's why you went with your cousin... Sadie?"

"Sally," Regina Mae hissed.

"Sally." I snapped my fingers. "Right. You went with Sally to confront a group of peaceful protesters in front of a women's clinic. Do you remember that?"

She shrugged. "No. I've attended a lot of such events in Baton Rouge. One event is much like another."

"In fact," I said, "you verbally attacked a woman there, one of those protestors, Genevieve's mother. She positively identified you, so please don't deny it."

Regina Mae's face turned bright red, but she said nothing.

"You also threatened her children. You said, and I quote, 'I hope your children die before they can have babies.'"

I stood, walked to the wall opposite the one-way glass, leaned against it, folded my arms and stared at her. The bitch stared right back at me, unflinching.

"And then guess what?" I asked but didn't wait for an answer. "Her only daughter is horribly murdered and... she just happens to be pregnant. Wow. That's a horrible thing to say. I wouldn't want to have that on my conscience. How do you live with yourself, Mrs. Chesterton?"

She sat stone-still, glaring at me.

Before I could continue, there was a knock on the door and Janet stepped in.

"Sorry to interrupt, Captain. Oh, hello, Mrs. Chesterton," she said politely.

"What is it you want, Sergeant?" I asked.

"Well, let me tell you... and, Mrs. Chesterton, you might like to hear this too. I was just talking to Treyshawn Montgomery in the room next door and, well... what have you been saying to him, Mrs. Chesterton?"

"I haven't said anything to him. I don't speak to that kind of creature," she hissed, glaring first at Janet, then at me.

"Oh dear," Janet said. "I wish you hadn't said that. You see I believe him, so we've subpoenaed your phone records which means... well, we'll be able to confirm his statement easily enough."

"Wait, I'm lost," I said, playing the game along with Janet. "What did he tell you?"

"Treyshawn said that Regina Mae arranged for him to meet up with Genevieve," Janet said.

"Now that I find really hard to believe," I said sarcastically, "since Mrs. Chesterton is such an upstanding citizen, and Treyshawn is a known drug dealer. And she claimed that she doesn't talk to... What was it you called him? 'A creature like that,' wasn't it? You can't tell me that she would introduce her daughter-in-law to him. I don't believe it."

Now she was angry, close to exploding.

"Look, I'm not trying to embarrass you, Regina Mae," I

said as if trying to placate her, but then I paused for a moment before I dropped the hammer on her.

"When I interviewed Daniel Racine... you know him, don't you?" I said, smiling at her.

She didn't answer.

"Well," I continued, "he said that you often waited for Treyshawn, in the lobby, at all hours of the night, and that you knew him quite well." It was a bit of a stretch, but what the hell?

"That was how you and Racine became so well acquainted, wasn't it?" Janet asked. "Your affair with him helped pass the time while you were waiting for Treyshawn. Good-looking guy, Racine; not bad if you can get it, I suppose, but that was a mistake, wasn't it? Racine will look good on the witness stand." She paused.

I watched Regina. Her face was expressionless, but I could see the hate in her eyes.

"Then," Janet continued, "you somehow managed to persuade Treyshawn to kill Genevieve. You offered him ten grand; hard for a creature like him to turn down. And no one, so you thought, would ever connect the two of you. It was perfect... but it wasn't, was it?"

"You're going to take the word of a drug dealer?" Regina Mae scoffed. "I don't think so. My daughter-in-law was a liar and a whore who latched onto my son in the hopes of getting her dirty black hands on our family's money. That's what you've got? That's what you've pieced together? Pathetic! I'll have both your jobs before this day is finished."

"Oh, I don't think so," I said.

Just then Randy knocked on the door. I stepped over and opened it, and he whispered to me.

"Oh, thanks. Regina Mae, there is someone here to see

you. I'll go get him. Randy, please ask the chief to come to the observation room."

Janet stayed with Regina Mae. She told me later that the woman kept rolling her eyes and mumbled degrading comments about her, Janet's, financial status, cheap haircut, clothing, and so on. But that stopped when Edward Chesterton the Second stepped into view.

Janet and I left the two of them alone to talk, retreated to the observation room and joined the chief behind the one-way glass. I had no idea how their conversation was going to go. It was being recorded, but I didn't want to miss a second.

"Oh, Granddaddy, thank goodness you are here," Regina Mae twittered, rising to her feet and hugging his neck. "I tell you, you'll own half this city before this is all done."

"I already do," he said, pushing her away from him. "Shut your stupid mouth and sit down."

She sat down on the steel chair with a thump.

He scowled at her and said, "What in God's name have you done, Regina? It was bad enough that my son married you, but I always thought you had enough good sense to stay out of grown-up matters. I was wrong again."

"Granddaddy, this is all a huge misunderstanding," she said firmly.

"That boy in the next room said you paid him to kill Eddie's wife... And damned if you didn't do it with my money. He said you arranged it, transferred the money—from the bank I've used since I was thirteen—to your bank account, and then deposited it in *his* bank account, thinking that no one would figure out the connection."

"You said it yourself a hundred times, Granddaddy, that

those people can't be trusted. No one will believe him. He's a drug dealer and comes from—"

"His father is a pastor, you silly bitch. More God-fearing than you," Chesterton whispered as he stared at his daughter-in-law.

"I did the world a favor," she said defiantly.

And there it is, the confession. I have her.

I looked at the chief. He nodded, but held up his hand, placed a finger to his lips and nodded at the scene still unfolding before us.

"Can you imagine," Regina Mae continued, "the shame that would have come with a half-breed baby? What if the child was darker than Genevieve? Suppose some retarded gene popped up. How would we explain it? How would you have looked to all the men who look up to you? They'd see you had poisoned blood in your family tree. I had to do what needed to be done, and I did."

He sat down opposite her, shaking his head, unbelieving of what he was hearing. "I've put a call in to Edward. He's on his way home. I've also called my attorney."

She still didn't get it.

"That sounds fine, Granddaddy. The sooner I can get out of here the better. We'll make this department crawl on its belly before this is over." She pushed herself up to stand, but the old man held up his hand.

"Not so fast. Sit down. The lawyer is for Edward, not you." He clenched his teeth. "No son of mine will remain married to a murderer. The divorce papers will be ready by tomorrow morning."

"Granddaddy, you can't be serious. This lying little piece of garbage has you hoodwinked." And then it hit her what was happening to her. *"You're turning on me?"* she said incredulously. "After everything I've done for this family. I gave you your only grandson and this is the thanks I get?"

"That you did, and maybe now the boy will learn how to be a man," he growled. "You ruined him. You treated him as if he was your property. You babied him, ruled him, covered for him and, even when he did make a decision on his own, even if it was a bad decision, you went right ahead and made it worse. *You made it worse! You ruined the family name!*" He glared across the table at her.

"This all could have been dealt with," he said. "The girl's ethnicity, the child she was carrying, it all could have been handled and the Chesterton name would have remained unsullied, but not anymore. For all I care you can rot in here, or in hell where you belong."

Old man Chesterton stood, walked to the door and banged on it. Officer Randy opened it immediately and the old man, taller and meaner looking than he'd been when I first interviewed him, stormed out of the building without saying another word.

I looked at the chief. He had a grim smile on his face, made even more so by his huge mustache. He nodded to me, then turned and left the room.

I turned to Janet and told her to go and charge Treyshawn with capital murder, then I returned to the interrogation room and told Regina Mae to stand.

"Stand up, Mrs. Chesterton."

Slowly, she rose to her feet, both hands on the table.

"Regina Mae Cottonwell-Chesterton, I'm arresting you for conspiracy to murder in the death of Genevieve Chesterton and her fetus. You have the right to remain silent..." And so it went on.

When I guided her out of the small room and handed her over to Randy, Janet already had Treyshawn in handcuffs. He looked angry, probably blaming Regina Mae for the decisions he'd made. I'm sure his public defender would present him as an impressionable young man who just wanted to prove himself, and that Regina Mae was the real culprit, the real mastermind behind the plot to kill Genevieve Chesterton, as indeed she was.

I also had no doubt that Regina Mae's defense attorneys would try to cut her a deal; that wouldn't happen; not in today's racial climate. This trial was going to be as big a media circus as Genevieve's wedding was just a year ago.

"What's the matter, Cap?" Janet asked after the two suspects had been taken away to booking.

"I don't know. I'm afraid of how this is going to play out in the media. We're going to have a tough time if it turns into a big racial issue." I shook my head. "I gotta go call the Washingtons, tell them we've made an arrest."

EPILOGUE

Two weeks had gone by since I'd wrapped up the Genevieve Chesterton murder, and the case was in the hands of a passel of overpriced lawyers and sleazy reporters. I was pretty happy with the outcome: the perps were going to get what they deserved, but there were a couple of loose ends: Eddie Chesterton and Nathan Watkins. What part did they play in Genevieve's murder, if any? I'm pretty sure that Eddie knew that Regina and Treyshawn murdered Genevieve, and that would have made him an accessory, but I couldn't prove it. Eddie denied it, of course, and his mother was adamant that he didn't know. Nathan? I don't know. Maybe he knew what his friend did, maybe he didn't. He denied knowing anything, and Treyshawn wouldn't snitch. So, both Eddie and Nathan walked.

Me? As I said, two weeks had gone by and I was in my office sipping coffee when there was a gentle knock on the door.

"Yes!" I shouted.

The door opened and Randy said, "Someone to see you, Captain."

I nodded, and a nervous young woman entered.

"Can I help you?" I asked, puzzled.

"Detective Gazzara, you probably don't remember me. I looked a bit different the last time you saw me," she said. "My name is Molly. Evelyn Karl is my grandmother."

"Oh, yes," I said and smiled at her. "You're right. I wouldn't have recognized you. How are you doing, Molly? Come on in. Sit down."

I stared in disbelief at the girl sitting in front of me. Just a few months ago she was a scrawny, pale punk on her way to the junkyard, and when I say junk, I mean she was a junkie. Now, she was a healthy young lady with color in her cheeks and her hair in pretty pigtails.

"I don't want to take a lot of your time," she said, looking down at her shoes. "Grandma told me she nominated you for the policeman of the year award... but you didn't get it."

"Oh, that's okay. The cop who did get the award saved a baby from a hostage situation at a convenience store, and he got shot in the process. I was happy to see him get the honors." I smiled.

"Well, I think you should have gotten it and so does Grandma," Molly said, shaking her head. "She said that no one else worried about me running away except her and you. No one else gave a damn except you, were her exact words, and that it's cases like mine, cases that don't have any glory, that matter. That's what Grandma says."

"Well, you can tell your grandma I appreciate that. Where is she, by the way?"

"She's getting her hair done. She's at Adele's, downtown," Molly said. Then she sat there awkwardly twiddling her fingers, then said, "Why did you do it?"

"Do what?"

"Why did you go out of your way to find me?"

I didn't tell her that it was just a random stroke of luck that she just happened to be at the scene of another crime. I didn't know what to tell her, but then...

"I could tell you that I just happened to be at the right place at the right time. And so were you. But I believe there's no such thing as an accident. I believe we crossed paths at the exact moment that fate, or God, decided we should. I can't explain it, Molly. In my line of work, we take the miracles when and as they come, and we don't question them."

Molly smiled bashfully and nodded her head.

"Are you in rehab?" I asked.

"Yeah."

"And how is that going?"

"Pretty good. I'm feeling better and I've gained weight." She rolled her eyes.

"Don't worry about that. You are supposed to have some weight on you. Look at me. I'm no skinny mini. But I think I do okay." I patted my stomach. It looked a whole lot bigger than it was because of my pants, and my blouse tucked inside them. They made me look fat, but I didn't need to flaunt my runner's body, especially not to her.

"Detective, when did you decide you wanted to become a cop?"

It was the second time I'd been asked that question inside of a week.

"Tell you what," I said, "why don't you give your grandma a call and let her know where you are? I'll get us a couple of Cokes and tell you all about it." I smiled.

"Are you sure? You don't have bad guys to catch or something?" she said, her eyes bright and clear.

"I'm sure. Because that's the thing about police work. It's never done." I laughed. "There will always be bad guys."

"Okay then, that sounds great."

I got up from my desk and watched as Molly took out her phone and proceeded to text her grandmother.

"Anything I can help with, Cap?" Janet asked as I walked by her cubicle on my way to get the Cokes.

"No. Just hold my calls for half an hour or so."

The End

ACKNOWLEDGMENTS

As always, I owe a great deal of thanks to my editor, Diane, for her insight and expertise. Thank you, Diane.

Thanks also to my beta readers whose last-minute inspection picked up those small but, to the reader, annoying typos. I love you guys. Thank you.

Once again, I have to thank all of my friends in law enforcement for their help and expertise: Ron, Gene, David for firearms, on the range and off. Gene for his expertise in close combat, Laura for CSI, and finally Dr. Frank King, Hamilton County's ex-chief medical examiner, without whom there would be no Doc Sheddon. Many thanks for all you did for me, Frank.

To my wife, Jo, who suffers a lonely life while I'm writing these books: thank you for your love and patience.

Finally, a great big thank you goes to my oh so loyal fans. Without you there would be no Kate, no Harry, Tim, Doc... well, you get the idea.

9 780578 580006